NOTHING BUT TROUBLE

P. DANGELICO

MALIBU UNIVERSITY SERIES

NOTHING BUT TROUBLE *(MALIBU UNIVERSITY SERIES)*

Copyright © 2019 P. Dangelico

All rights reserved.

ISBN: 9781090723482

Published by P. Dangelico

Cover Design: Regina Wamba, MaeIDesign
Photo: Regina Wamba, Exclusive Stock
Proofreading: Judy's Proofreading
Playlist on Spotify

www.pdangelico.com

ALSO BY P. DANGELICO

Contemporary Romance (Single POV)

Wrecking Ball
Sledgehammer
Bulldozer

Contemporary Romance (Dual POV)

Baby Maker
Tiebreaker
Risk Taker (coming soon)

Erotic Romance

A Million Different Ways (The Horn Duet Book 1)
A Million Different Ways To Lose You (Book 2)

New Adult Romance

Nothing But Trouble (Malibu University Series)
Nothing But Wild (2019)
Nothing But Good (2019)
Nothing But Heart (2020)

ONE

"Your time is limited, so don't waste it
living someone else's life." — Steve Jobs

ALICE

I'm roasting. The class valedictorian drones on and on about taking life by the short hairs, something she knows nothing about, while the pale skin of my forehead gets blowtorched. The diplomas haven't even begun to be handed out yet. At this rate, I'll resemble extra crispy barbecued pork by the time it's over.

From my seat on the outskirts of the audience, I glance over my shoulder and search the crowd. The view of the Santa Monica Bay from the side of the hill where the graduation ceremony is being held is surreal, picture perfect. The water Zen-like calm. The treacherous blue sky cloudless. The sight never gets old.

"Who you looking for?" Zoe queries on my right.

"I thought we agreed we weren't going to bring him up today?"

Am I surprised, however? No. As a general rule Zoe has never met an order she didn't love to trample under her

1

Chanel motorcycle boots.

"So you *were* looking for him."

I snatch the graduation program out of her hand and fan myself. It was probably a mistake to wear black but it matched my mood.

"No. Just bored," I casually answer without making eye contact. I don't even know why I bother. She's much too perceptive for her own good. If Zoe Mayfield ever decided to give a shit, she could rule the world.

"Riiight," she drawls while casually inspecting her short, dark nails. The sun catches the stacks of skinny diamond rings on her long fingers and returns a spray of light.

"I'm *not* looking for him," I mutter. A bold-faced lie. It's wrong how easily it trips off my tongue.

Meanwhile my neck heats, and a blazing path of pure embarrassment climbs over my face which has nothing to do with the Southern California sun. I can't bear to look pathetic anymore. It's time to move on. It's *been* time for a while now.

Expression completely blank, Zoe gives me the universal gesture for hand job and I snicker.

"I don't read sign language," I whisper.

"How about this? You read this?" She flips me the bird and I chuckle.

Two seats down, Blake leans over and glares at us. I shrug and point to Zoe. She shakes her head. No need to explain. She knows Zoe better than I do seeing as they've been best friends since junior high. Next to her, Dora rolls her eyes.

"What time does the party start?" I say in an attempt to drive the conversation elsewhere and fast.

"Nine at Shutters on the Beach—"

Two girls seated directly in front turn around and shush us. Zoe makes a face and crosses her tanned legs. The white Stella McCartney dress she's wearing hikes up to mid thigh, making them look like they go on for weeks. "We got a block of rooms so no one has to drive," she explains.

The two girls in front take it to the next level, graduating from shushing to giving us dirty looks. Filled with irritation, Zoe's gaze snaps back to them and I brace for the inevitable. I know that look. And more importantly, I know what comes next.

She rests her elbow on the back of her chair and swings her crossed leg. "Mind your own business, or I'll rip off those caterpillars glued to your eyes."

And there it is.

Horrified, the girls swivel around to face ahead.

"There's still time. Maybe he'll show up," she continues, completely unfazed by the exchange.

As much as I want to believe that, I promised myself that I was done pining like a war bride. It wouldn't be so bad if I knew he was safe and happy, living his best life. The life that he chose for himself and not the one mapped out for him. But I don't know. And I have to accept the fact that I may never know.

Looking into the sympathetic eyes of my well-meaning friend, I shake my head. "I haven't heard from him in four months."

"Do you want me to ask—"

"No—don't."

The hope in Zoe's eyes dims. And even though I can tell she wants to argue, all she does is nod. Curbing the urge to take one last look around, I force my attention onto the podium.

"So in closing, I give you the words of a truly inspiring First Lady, Michelle Obama—" Squaring her shoulders, the valedictorian beams, sunshine reflecting off her wide bright grin. *"It is absolutely still possible to make a difference."*

Applause explodes all around me. Everyone stands while I remain seated. This should've been his graduation day. In which case, I would've been on my feet, cheering him on. Except I'm not. Instead, I'm left to watch everyone else celebrate while a heavy weight settles in my gut.

"It's time to move on," I mumble more to myself than anyone else. I just want to forget. Except the yawning void where my heart used to be won't let me.

* * *

Ten Months Ago

Dammit. Dammit. Dammit.

I lift my forehead off the steering wheel and peer through the windshield of my brand-new, old car. Smoke billows up from the faded pistachio green hood of the '84 Jetta I purchased only two days ago.

I'm pretty sure this is how the term "hot mess" was coined.

Through the smoke, my gaze finds the brass plaque that reads **Malibu University** fixed to the stone pillars that mark the entrance on the south side of campus.

Just livin' the dream, Bailey.

Funny thing, despite appearances I am living the dream. I've been working most of my life to get here, to transfer from my small community college back east to this school. And it's taken everything and I mean everything I had—time, money, blood, sweat, and tears. A little thing like a smoking car is not about to dampen my mood. My mood is as dry as the parched earth of the Malibu hills.

On the passenger seat, my cell phone rings and my father's face appears, his handsomeness marred by the cracks on the screen. A minor miracle this thing is still working with how many times I've dropped it.

"Dad, I can't talk right now—" I say without preamble. Minor or not, I don't have the luxury of dwelling on miracles right now. Not when I have a major problem on my hands.

"Too busy for your old man already?"

"No..." My voice fades. I cringe because my father is nothing if not predictable. "The car crapped out on me. *Don't* say I told you so."

Two days. Two frigging days this jalopy lasted. Okay, yes, I only spent three grand. But two days? C'mon, it should've at least lasted three.

A heavy sigh comes through, then, "I told you—"

"I know—" I cut him off. "I know. But it was the only one I could afford. Can I call you back?"

Here's an interesting nugget, Los Angeles is sadly lacking in public transportation. The neighboring boroughs even worse, practically none to speak of. Compared to back east, it's a joke and nothing to laugh at. Pair that with the fact that Malibu is not the small quaint beach town most people imagine it to be. It's a sprawling thing, running along one of the busiest highways in America (Pacific Coast Highway). Ergo, a car, any car, is better than no car at all.

Unless it's a car that doesn't start....and has you stuck at the bottom of a mountain.

"Call me as soon as you get home safely. Love you, Button."

"I will. Love you too." Ending the call, I grab my purse and rummage inside for my sunblock.

I'm going to have to walk home. That's one grueling uphill mile. But safety first. Because I'm the safety girl. My mother died of cancer when I was five. I don't take my health lightly and the Baileys are staunchly Anglo and tragically pale. Sadly, I've inherited this burden. No tanning for me unless I want to look like a Roma tomato.

That said, I pull my extra large tube of sunscreen out of my bag and get busy applying it. It's not the amateur drug store variety, either. Nope. It's the all-natural, thick-as-paste and dense-as-spackle zinc one. The kind that no matter how much I try to rub it in still makes me look like a walking corpse.

I cover my bare legs all the way up to the frayed edges of my jean cut-offs. My arms to my shoulders where skin meets my black sleeveless t-shirt. And lastly, I smear a good amount across the bridge of my nose.

Once my armor is fully on, I tie my chin-length bob back in a tiny ponytail, shake out my bangs, and jump out. No need to lock it. Having this junker towed will undoubtedly cost me money that I don't have to spare. I can only pray someone comes by and steals it.

I slip on my backpack that carries my precious camera equipment and start the hike up the winding road that leads to my dorm.

Malibu University is built on a chain of hills and mountains overlooking the Santa Monica Bay. A labyrinth of snake-like roads connects the buildings on campus. It's heaven on the eyes and murder on the hamstrings. On the flip side, no need to bother with squats anymore.

Soon I'm sweating everywhere. It dribbles down my temple. Between my breasts. Down my back. My feet too. Good stuff (heavy sarcasm). They keep slipping out of my silver flip-flops, making the trek three times more arduous than it needs to be.

And it's hot. Sweet bee stings is it hot. Heatstroke is fast becoming a very real possibility.

I'm busy sweating when the loud purr of an approaching car gets my attention. I immediately perk up, hopeful that I could possibly bum a ride. Until a red BMW comes racing down the road and immediately snuffs out that dream.

It's a convertible. Top down. Filled with girls I've seen around campus. Hair whipping in the wind, they're laughing and singing along with Taylor Swift's *We Are Never Getting Back Together* at the top of their lungs.

Welcome to Wonderland. It is not a myth. Los Angeles is populated by a disproportionate amount of pretty people. A few weeks ago this would've had me staring with my jaw unhinged, but the sight has become so common it doesn't even warrant a second glance anymore.

Not a single one of them notices me as they drive by. My foot slips out of the flip-flop, making me stumble a few steps. Luckily for me, I manage to right myself before turning into roadkill.

I'm adjusting my backpack when I hear a second car

approaching. Out of the corner of my eye I catch a flash of black paint and an oversized, deep tread tire. A Jeep Wrangler comes barreling toward me and everything goes slo-mo, my life flashing before my eyes.

There's no time to think. All I can do is react. Instinct takes over and I dive for safety. It feels like I'm falling forever. Until, finally, I land on the grass running along the asphalt—and, unfortunately for me, slide to a stop on my face.

I'm lying motionless, trying to discern if all my parts are still attached to my body, when a series of sounds register. The screech of tires. A door slamming shut. And the soft thump of running feet.

"Are you okay?" a deep male voice queries. A big hand gently falls on my shoulder.

The only thing I'm absolutely certain of is that my face broke my fall.

"Does it look like I'm okay, asshole?" I barely manage to get out with my mouth smothered in dirt and grass. I can taste it. Disgusting.

I hear a quick snort. Then a murmured, "Don't move. I'm calling 911."

"No!"

I'm pretty sure the only thing injured is my pride right now and in no way can I afford any emergency medical care. I'm currently on the bare-bones-only-deploy-if-you're-dying plan and my savings account is allocated to other semi-important stuff like food. "Who taught you how to drive? Your blind nana?"

"You were standing in the middle of the road," the same voice asserts with undisguised amusement underpinning his bullshit claim.

He carefully pries my backpack off and I roll over, onto my back, blinking up at the head looming over me. Bad driver's face is obscured by the sun.

"I'm going to call campus security," he states with the confidence of someone who is seldom rebuffed, his voice deep and granular. Also, strangely soothing. That's weird but whatever. I probably have a concussion.

"I said no. It'll just be a waste of time." Time that I do not have to waste.

I attempt to sit up, and his hand moves to my back, helping to guide me. Brushing my hands off, I examine my palms—scratched up and dirty. My knees—skinned and bloody. Grass and dirt sticks to my face. I can feel it. Particularly to my lip gloss. This stuff is worse than superglue. I try to brush it off with the back of my hand to no avail.

"Wrong—I was standing on the *side* of the road." I refrain from adding, "dipshit," as I am apt to do when I'm angry, and in this case, in pain.

"Let me see your ankle."

As soon as he mentions ankle, it starts to throb. And I mean really throb. "Are you a doctor?"

The sarcasm is strong now, percolating behind every thought, simmering under every unspoken word waiting to be unleashed. I can control myself, however. I'm not a complete idiot. I'm stranded and injured and the stone-cold fact is that I need this guy's help right now. I'll save the verbal ass kicking for later.

"No, but my parents are."

His parents? I couldn't make this up if I tried. Let's get this out of the way—this school is filled with a bunch of pampered rich kids.

I glance up and at first the glare makes me squint and hide my eyes behind my hand. Then his head moves against the sun and I get a clear view of a face that would make even my cousin Marie consider going straight. A cleft accents his chin, nice lips, high cheekbones, a strong jaw line. In other words, features you usually find on billboards peddling underwear.

But his eyes…fucking A, excuse my French. Vivid green framed by thick dark lashes. A one-two punch to the sternum, knocking the wind right out of me. If I wasn't on my ass already, I would currently be in the process of falling on it.

I'm staring. I know I am and yet I really don't care. He almost killed me. Attempted vehicular manslaughter means I get a free pass to stare.

"So that makes you…what? A doctor by birthright?"

Just because my vagina is blinded by his good looks doesn't mean my head stops working. Although the throbbing sensation in my lower leg is another matter altogether. That's definitely inhibiting my ability to think.

"I'm premed if that makes you feel better."

"Not even a little," I grumble. A beat later I'm screaming in blinding pain. My ankle feels like it's being stabbed by a hot knife.

"I think you sprained your ankle."

"Thanks, Dr. Moron. Maybe try not poking it!"

He battens down another smile and rakes chestnut brown hair out of his eyes. "Let's go."

That's all the warning I get before I'm scooped up. One minute I'm on the ground and the next I'm hovering high above it, an infant cradled in the arms of a handsome giant. Who smells of chlorine? I'm fairly certain it's chlorine.

"Whoa." My head spins and I'm not sure if it's due to the heat, the near-death experience, or vertigo.

"You okay?"

"Yeah. I think so."

"I won't drop you," he says, readjusting his grip. "You can loosen the chokehold you have on me."

My gaze flickers to his. Traffic light green eyes flash amusement. I get stuck in that gaze for a while. His irises remind me of those cartoon swirling wheels intended to hypnotize.

Green means go. Green means go, Bailey.

I must've hit my head. That's the only plausible explanation.

"You're sure you're feeling alright?"

The rasp knocks me out of my spell. I peel my fingers off his neck and realize my fingers have left a red welt on his warm, bronzed skin. Jesus. "Sorry," I mutter.

"I'll survive."

Something feels off. I'm forgetting something. "My stuff!"

"I'll grab it. Let me get you in the car first."

Bad driver, as I've come to think of him, gently places me in the Jeep's passenger seat, careful not to bump my sore ankle. Then he leaves to retrieve my backpack.

In the meantime, I take stock of my situation. Swollen ankle that has been steadily growing larger by the second. A busted car that will cost me serious dough. No way to get to and from my off-campus job at the Slow Drip coffee shop—a job that pays a portion of my living expenses. Also, one that I only started a few days ago, which means I have no leverage with the manager.

My father works for the U.S. Postal Service and my stepmom's an emergency room nurse. Wealth and the Bailey name have never been synonymous. They're doing the best they can to help me out. I couldn't possibly ask them for more. It dawns upon me now that my parents will be worried sick with me so far away. Especially my stepmom. My mood is officially damp. I don't even want to contemplate the possibility of my ankle being broken. That would almost certainly signify the end of my dream. I would be forced to drop out.

"Here you go," bad driver says as he hands me my bag. I waste no time ripping open the zipper to check on my equipment.

The thought of it being thrown to the ground makes me twitchy. It took me years to save up enough to buy my collection of cameras, forgoing Rutgers University for a community college so I could use my savings to make the purchase. Not only is it absolutely necessary if I want to make independent films and submit them to production companies and film festivals, it also functions as my savings account. I have a ton of money invested in them. My cameras are my safety net in case of a catastrophe.

"What's in there?" He looks genuinely curious.

I shoulder-block his line of sight, shoot him a wary glare. I'm from Jersey—we think everyone is trying to steal from us. "My equipment."

"Cameras?"

I slide an assessing glance over him. He looks like a Disney prince. Clean-cut, close shave. Expression open, stare earnest. He even has the requisite dip in the chin. All he's missing is a red cloak.

The grimace comes naturally, so does suspicion. "Yeah." It's a rare occasion that I don't have some of it on me. At a minimum, I usually have my Leica in my backpack.

"Cool. Can I see?"

This prince is nosy. "No, you may not see."

Fighting a grin, his white teeth, stark against his tan, bear down on his lower lip. "You a film major?" This guy is awfully chatty.

"Yes, are you in the NSA?" I fire back and watch his lips tremble. I'm glad I can entertain him.

The Jeep shoots uphill, making me brace against the door. As tempting as the prospect of ending up in this guy's lap sounds, I'm starting to cold sweat from the pain in my ankle and getting anxious about the extent of the injury.

"Where are you taking me?"

He studies the open suspicion on my face. "To the medical center. Where do you think?"

"To dispose of what's left of the evidence."

He scans my face again and his gaze narrows in on something. It's making me increasingly self-conscious. "You have some, uh...dirt stuck to your lips." He motions with his index finger to his own mouth, pink and slightly fuller on the bottom. "And grass."

Scorching heat rolls up my neck and blankets my face, which I'm sure is the color of a baboon's butt. The Bailey curse. My pale skin keeps no secrets. Something I've learned to live with since the first grade when I told Brady Higgins that I liked him and he told me, and I'm paraphrasing, *to take a hike because I look like Casper the friendly ghost.* Last I heard, Brady's still unemployed and living in his mother's basement. Sometimes karma takes a while.

I flip down the visor and check the mirror. Not only does it look like I've been eating dirt and grass. He failed to mention the glob of white sunscreen stuck under my left eye. "Peachy. Thank you for so kindly pointing it out," I mutter as I wipe it away with my fingers.

"You're not from around here."

"What gave me away?"

A smile full of mischief now permanently fixed on his obnoxiously handsome face, he looks me over again. "Where from? New York?"

"New Jersey."

"Jersey," he echoes as he slow-nods. "That's…different."

"Why am I getting the impression that *different* is not a good thing."

"It's not a good thing," he clarifies, and for some strange reason my heart sinks a little. Gaze fixed on the road ahead, he adds, "It's a great thing."

TWO

ALICE

"I don't think it's broken," the campus medical center doctor, a middle-aged man with full cheeks and kind brown eyes, tells me while he examines my leg. "But I do recommend you go to the ER and get an X-ray. I'm sorry, what's your name again?"

From a prone position on the gurney, I snap up on my elbows, shaking my head before the doctor can even finish his sentence. "Alice Bailey and no, I really can't afford a trip to the ER." Without warning, he lifts my ankle to bundle it in a flexible cold pack, and as soon as it hits my skin, I squeak.

Bad driver is standing next to him with his legs spread apart and arms crossed over bulging chest muscles covered by a worn blue t-shirt. He's staring at the mottled red and blue thing, otherwise known as my lower leg, with his face screwed up like there's an answer here somewhere just waiting to be discovered.

Here's your answer, bud—there isn't one. Not unless you have a time machine we can jump into.

"How did it happen?" Doc asks. I'm not sure if the

question is directed at me, or the guilty party.

"My fault," bad driver mutters. I don't argue. We're in absolute agreement on that front. The embarrassed smile he returns is, I will begrudgingly concede, an endearing one. Or at least it would be under different circumstances. The throb in my ankle has now become so painful it feels like it's giving birth to a baby alien.

"How, exactly?" From the looks these two are exchanging, I take it they know each other pretty well. Doc pulls out cotton and a bottle of clear lotion and holds it up. "This shouldn't sting," he tells me right before he aims it at my skinned knees.

Never trust anything anyone says after "this shouldn't." Because sure enough, it frigging stings. Every time the antiseptic hits my cuts, a word bursts out. "He's...a terrible... driver. The fucking worst." My brown eyes latch onto green ones. "No offense."

"None taken." Bad driver turns away, chewing on his lower lip. Glad I can amuse him.

"She was walking up the street by the pool and I was coming around—"

"You hit her?" Doc finishes for him, looking justifiably horrified on my behalf.

Doc replaces the old ice pack with a new one and I nearly jump off the gurney. "I had to dive for safety—"

"You're in good hands now," the guy who almost killed me says. "Dr. Fred's our team doctor. He knows all there is to know about soft tissue injuries."

"Team?" Panting as the cold pack comes off and an ACE bandage is skillfully wrapped around my ankle, I'm reduced to speaking in single syllables. I couldn't care less what either of them are yammering on about, but I have to do something to keep my mind off the ankle.

"The water polo team." Dropping his arms, he points to his t-shirt. Emblazoned across it in faded orange...**Malibu U Water Polo** *How Wet Can You Get?*

"Umm..." is all I can come up with because—one, seriously? Two, who cares? Not me. Not this girl with the busted ankle, and the busted car, and a world of trouble. And three, the hell is water polo anyway?

My remark is met by two identical frowns.

"You know who this guy is, right?" Doctor Fred tips his head at bad driver as he's securing the bandage with a butterfly clip. My gaze slides over, and bad driver meets my scrutiny with a bright, expectant expression. Am I supposed to?

"I'm kind of a big deal," he deadpans with a smirk. "People know me."

Huh? For a minute I'm mired in confusion. Is he serious? Is he a screaming megalomaniac as well as a shitty driver? But then the words grow familiar. "Did you just...quote the movie *Anchorman?*"

Mr. Big Deal's gaze moves away, pink stains his cheeks. Roger that. I nailed it. Then again, I guess I should be grateful. Quoting the movie isn't half as bad as if he were serious.

He shifts on his feet and I catch sight of a tiny dolphin tattoo etched on the outside of his calf, hidden amongst the sun-bleached man hair.

"Reagan Reynolds," he finally mutters.

"Wait, wait...*The* Reagan Reynolds." My eyes go wide for maximum dramatic effect. I probably should stow the bitch card but my ankle hurts something fierce and this guy is the root cause.

The Reagan Reynolds gifts me with another one of his half-cocked grins. "You know who I am?" He's dropped the *Ron Burgundy* act. This is all him. He's a little surprised and a lot pleased that I may know him.

My face falls flat. "No."

Dr. Fred coughs and Reynolds's smile promptly disappears.

I can feel my forehead getting very clammy. "I don't know if the Tylenol is going to cut it, Doc."

"I'm afraid we don't dispense anything stronger. For that, you need to get to an ER."

* * *

"Thank you for waiting with me," I say as he parks the Jeep in front of my dorm two hours later.

"It's the least I can do," Reynolds replies through the tight set of his mouth.

It took a while for the painkillers to finally kick in, for me to feel more human and less *Incredible Hulk*, and once the pain became tolerable, Dr. Fred sent us to a medical supply store to pick up a pair of crutches. Reynolds insisted on paying and I didn't argue since I inconveniently don't have an extra fifty bucks sitting in my checking account.

Reynolds takes my new crutches out of the back seat and holds the passenger side door open for me. "You really should get that x-rayed," he insists, worry etched in the V between his pulled-together brows. I wave at him to step back and position the crutches to stand. In the meantime, he watches on, unsure what to do. The swagger he's been brandishing all afternoon seems to have deserted him, his expression steadily growing more troubled since we left the medical center.

I really can't. I have too much to contend with right now without adding this guy's "fragile male psyche" to it.

I hop ahead and hear him murmur, "I'll grab your stuff," at my back.

"I'm on the first floor," I announce awkwardly as I punch in the code on the knob to get in. "So, you know…there's that."

I force a broad smile in the hope that he'll lose the sullen attitude. More for my own peace of mind, seeing as he's making *me* feel guilty and I'm the injured party. No such luck. The gloom and doom persists. Oh well.

Turning, I hop down the hallway. Thick silence trails after us. When we reach my door, he gently places my backpack on the floor.

"Give me your phone and I'll punch in my number," he says, quietly. His open palm comes at me and all I can do is stare at it. It's huge and pale compared to the tan skin of the top of his hand, the topography marked by a series of calluses at the base of his long fingers.

"Why?" I don't mean to be difficult but, with the exception of my immediate family, I'm not used to people wanting to help me without an ulterior motive. As a matter of fact, I can't remember a single instance where that's happened.

His lips quiver with a tentative smile. Until he realizes I'm serious, then his amusement swiftly changes to confusion. "In case you need help—" He shrugs. "I don't know—with anything."

Yeah, the last guy that offered to help me was the manager of the car wash I worked at and he wanted a blowie in exchange. I'll pass, thank you very much. "I don't need help. I'm good, thanks."

His eyes widen and he pulls his hand back. Then he runs both of them through his hair, a move that lifts his shirt to reveal a tiny slice of heaven. A smooth, tan strip of skin with a teasing tail end of a V that disappears under the band of his low-riding basketball shorts.

Considering the circumstance, this should not get my undivided attention. And yet it does because, well, it's in my face and I'm a healthy, red-blooded woman. Also, it may have been a while since I've gotten naked with a man.

A clearing of a male throat lifts my eyes. Caught red-handed.

I expect some note of triumph on his face. It's glaringly obvious Mr. Big Deal's a major flirt and used to girls falling at his beautiful feet, and yet his expression remains strangely blank.

He backs away slowly, leans up against the front door of the dorm, and holds it open. "Yeah...so..."

"Yeah, this was fun. Let's do it again soon...ha ha. Or not."

I'm hoping for a smile, a chuckle, something, anything. Instead I get...nothing. He blinks, expressionless. Not even a ghost of a smile. Only an awkward, grating silence. Wow, that got weird real fast.

"See you around, Alice from New Jersey."

"Thanks for the crutches, *the* Reagan Reynolds."

He gives me a lazy salute, and a moment later he's gone, disappearing into the waning light of early evening.

THREE

REAGAN

What just happened? What in the fucking hell was that?

With my mind in overdrive, I pull the Jeep into the driveway of the beach house I share with three of my teammates. As if I don't have enough shit to worry about. Now I can add nearly running over a girl with my car to the list. I guess I should thank my maker that Alice Bailey isn't the dramatic type. Although she definitely has a tendency for anger and sarcasm. The memory of her smart mouth puts a smile on my face. Goes to show you how totally fucked my life is that some chick calling me Dr. Moron turns into the highlight of my day.

The garage is open. Two cars sit inside. Dallas's yellow Porsche and a white Range Rover I don't recognize. Cole and Brock are out—their bikes missing. Which means Dallas has some girl over. I love the guy, but his dick's given more rides than a N.Y. City yellow cab and I'm really not in the mood for company right now.

I park and stare at the phone sitting on the passenger seat. Anxiety climbs up my throat as I contemplate the call I have to make. Alice from New Jersey didn't ask for a police report—or a campus security one for that matter. Problem is, Doc Fred will most definitely call my father so I might as well get the ass chewing over with now.

I pull up his number and pause, my finger hovering over the button. I'll call him in an hour. After he's had his second scotch. He'll be in a better frame of mind then. Not a minute later, my phone rings and my father's name flashes onscreen. And if that's not a great big screw you from the universe I don't know what is.

"Hey, Dad."

"Have you called Jim Sullivan yet?"

Pat Reynolds has never met a greeting he liked.

"No, not yet."

"What are you waiting for?"

It's a forgone conclusion that I'm attending UCLA medical school next fall. It's never even been discussed, simply accepted as a done deal as soon as I was old enough to apply to colleges.

Legacy. A word bandied about often in my family. I come from a long line of accomplished doctors. My great-grandfather helped establish Cedars-Sinai. My grandfather holds two patents on surgical instruments. My father is the head of the cardiothoracic surgery unit—my mother the head of dermatology. You get the idea.

Everyone assumes I'll follow in my father's and grandfather's footsteps and specialize in cardiac surgery. An assumption I have done nothing to correct because the path of least resistance is the only way to keep the peace with my old man. And after the "great disappointment" my older brother has been to him, it all rests on me to "save the family name." I've heard that speech more times than I care to recall. All of it simply an effort to stroke his own ego—my dad cares for little else.

"He has my MCAT score and my application. I don't see why I need to call him."

"He's a friend and the dean of the medical school, Reagan. Do I need to spell it out for you?"

Frustration builds in my chest. I can't have this discussion with him now. Not over the phone. "Something happened today," I start, steering the conversation away from what is bound to turn into another ugly argument. My father and I have never been close, but lately it seem all we do is argue.

"What is it?" he spits out in a tone sharpened by irritation. He's always irritated. I'd be concerned if he wasn't.

"Nothing serious. I was in a minor car accident on campus."

"Is your car damaged?"

This line of questioning does not surprise me at all. That's dear old dad, for you.

"No, I didn't hit anything. But there was a girl...she sprained her ankle."

"Did you get a police report?"

"No, but—"

"Was anybody else present? Someone you can trust?"

My resolve to keep a cool head around him starts to slip. He knows exactly where my buttons are and goes after them every chance he gets. "No. Just the two of—"

"Then it never happened," he cuts in again. "It's her word against yours."

My frustration boils over. "You're not hearing me, Dad. She's not asking for anything, but I know she can't afford medical care and her ankle is really fucked up."

"Watch your language," he bites out. "And if the girl doesn't want anything, then thank your Irish luck and drop it."

"It's my fault this girl is injured. I was waiting for Brian to call. He texted that he needed to talk to me."

A heavy sigh comes through the phone. "I'm being paged. We'll talk about your brother later. Leave it alone, Reagan. And if she calls looking for a payout let me know immediately. I'll have to get Henry involved."

My family's lawyer. Less than a moment later, the call drops.

* * *

I pull in the empty trash cans from the curb, make my way up the front steps. Dallas's parents bought him this monster of a house our freshman year. Our school doesn't have dorm restrictions due to the lack of on-campus housing available. You would think he'd be stoked to live on a private beach next door to movie stars and pro athletes. I mean, who wouldn't, right? Dallas, that's who. He was always crashing on the couch in the apartment I shared with the Peterman twins. It took us a while to get it out of him, but he eventually admitted that he hated living alone. Once he did, we all moved in with him. Seemed stupid to let the house go to waste.

The front door opens and a tall brunette I vaguely recognize from the girls' volleyball team steps out.

"Hi, Reagan."

"Hi," I say to the tall chick whose name I can't remember.

Avoiding eye contact, she ducks her head and walks past me when she sees me checking out the stains on her neck, arms, and clothes. This has Dallas written all over it.

To put it bluntly, Dallas Van Zant is the team's resident fuckup. He also happens to be my best friend, has been since our freshman year when we beat USC by three goals scored by the two of us. From that day forth we were known as Thunder and Lightning, and like thunder and lightning we became inseparable.

Also like thunder and lightning, Dallas and I are profoundly different. I'm a straight-up team player, doing everything by the book, while D just likes to play. Being on this team is a means to an end for him. And that end is to accrue all the glory and the fun of being on a championship winning team without any of the responsibility. If he didn't have such mad skills, Coach would've kicked him off years ago. Not that I blame him. Responsibility is for chumps like me.

I walk into the kitchen to find D naked, with his back to me. He's focused on scrubbing the marble countertop. He's also, I note, covered in the same shit-colored stains as the girl who left.

"Do I wanna know what happened here?" I ask, dropping my backpack at the threshold and tossing the keys on the counter.

"Karen and I made a Nutella sandwich," he says, throwing a wad of dirty paper towels in the trash. He swipes a pair of basketball shorts off the kitchen floor and steps into them.

"You missed some on the refrigerator."

"Where?" he says, glancing up to inspect the stainless steel behemoth. Four athletes live in this house and growing boys need to store a lot of food. I motion to the spots and he grabs a handful of clean paper towels and starts wiping.

I slip onto the counter stool, rake my hands through my hair, and press the heels into my eye sockets. The pressure's been building since I dropped off Alice Bailey at her dorm. "Did you get any on the bread?"

"Yeah, no bread. We were the sandwich—" He glances up with a sly grin. "Very slimy, dude. No recommendo, amigo."

The instant he catches sight of my expression he stops cleaning and gives me his full attention. "Who stepped on your nuts?"

I need sustenance for this conversation so I get up, grab two Coronas from the refrigerator, hand him one. He'll tell me if I should be worried.

Despite the cavalier attitude, Dallas possesses an uncanny ability to read people. He's strangely intuitive about their character and has never steered me wrong. It took me three years to see past Jordan's bullshit. It took Dallas ten minutes of speaking to her. I don't know if this talent is a consequence of what his parents put him through, and from what I've heard it was pretty bad, or it comes naturally. Regardless, he has it in spades.

I pop the top off my beer, lean back against the counter, and exhale tiredly. "I screwed up today."

"Welcome to my life."

"I was driving down Severson after practice and I glanced at my phone for a split second, thinking it was Brian calling—

it wasn't, by the way, it was Jordan. And I almost ran someone over."

Looking unfazed, Dall takes a long pull of his beer. "Who?"

"New girl. Alice Bailey. A film major." A smile tugs my lips away from the edge of the bottle at the memory of the glare she aimed at me when I asked to see her cameras.

"And?"

"I took her to see Fred. She twisted her ankle, looks pretty bad. She might've torn something."

"Might have? Didn't she go to the ER?"

"She refused. Said she couldn't afford it."

He nods. "And you're worried she'll sue."

Leave it to Dallas to know where my head is, one of the reasons why we're so good in the pool together. I tip my beer bottle in his direction. "You're spooky. You know that, right?"

"Everybody has a gift," he deadpans.

Having money has its perks. No doubt about it. But it also has some major drawbacks. The minute we were born, my brother and I were taught to safeguard our reputation, our family name, and our trust funds. It was imprinted in our minds with all the subtlety of a jackhammer. And we were reminded of it every time we made a new friend, dated someone outside our social circle, or stepped out the door.

I'm not saying everyone I come in contact with has bad intentions. That's how my father thinks and I'll never be that guy. However, the suspicion that I could become someone's living blank check is never far from my mind. Especially after what happened to my brother.

"I don't know..." My gut tells me Alice Bailey is not

interested in money. "She didn't ask for a police or campus security report. I can't get a read on this girl. Except that she doesn't like me very much."

Most girls jump at the chance to stroke my ego. This one couldn't wait to insult me. And something tells me she was holding back a lot more. Recalling the mix of interest and repulsion on her face teases another reluctant smile out of me.

"She wouldn't even take my number, acted like I was a walking open sore to be avoided at all cost." A less confident man would've sustained a serious ego blow. Good thing I'm not that guy.

"Maybe she's not into dudes."

Pausing, I considered it. Then I recall her staring at my junk in the hallway. "I don't think so. She might hate me, but I definitely caught her checking out my package."

D nods thoughtfully. "Don't worry about it till it's time to worry about it."

He's right. I'm always looking to jump in and get my hands dirty. Maybe it's time I learn to keep my hands in my pockets. "Yeah, maybe you're right." I rub the back of my stiff neck.

"What are you gonna do?"

I think of what my father said. He's always there, hanging over me like a black fucking cloud. I have to pick my battles with him or lose the war.

"Nothing...for now."

The front door opens and Brock wanders in. He halts at the threshold of the open kitchen and takes in the scene.

"Nutella sandwich?"

A confused frown pulls at my face. How is it I'm the only

one not in the know here?

Dallas smiles and Brock adds, "Karen and Jill?"

"Just Karen. Jill had soccer practice."

Brock chuckles.

Two minutes later, Cole walks in and scans the walls and the refrigerator. Then he pins the three of us with a deadly glare. "Which one of you motherfuckers broke into my Nutella stash?"

FOUR

REAGAN

A nagging sense of guilt wakes me abruptly at 2 a.m. It's the third night in a row this has happened so there's no guessing why. Whatever that gene is that allows you to give a shit about other people—the gene my father lacks—I seem to have inherited double the Reynolds family's share. And presently, it's screaming in my ear with a megaphone that I'm the reason for this girl's problems and therefore somehow need to fix this mess if I ever want to sleep again.

I grab my phone, log on to Sharknet, the school's social networking site, and begin searching for any sign of Alice Bailey...and come up empty. Wtf.

Facebook? Her profile is on private. Snapchat? Yeah, she's not on Snapchat. Insta? Random artsy pictures. Not a single one of her. This might not even *be* her. There are like...a million Alice Baileys. Devastating because I am fairly certain I won't get a minute's peace until I sort this out.

I jump out of bed and march down to Dall's room, pound on his door. "Phone tree!" I move on to Brock's, then Cole's. "Wake up. Phone tree!"

They shuffle out of their bedrooms, rubbing the sleep from their eyes.

"What the fuck, dude? I have a history exam tomorrow morning," Cole gripes. "Today actually."

They make their way to the living room and crash onto the oversized couches.

"This better be good," Brock grunts.

"I need to track down Alice Bailey—"

"Isn't it a little late to be thinking with your dick?" Cole grunts.

"Not a hookup, asshole," I fire back. "This is important."

"Our boy, here—" Dallas takes it upon himself to explain. "Almost ran her over and can't stand to see this travesty of justice go unvindicated."

"That's not a word, bro," Cole mumbles, eyes closing fast.

"Which one?"

"Unvindicated."

"It should be." Dallas looks confused. "What then?"

"Unavenged," Brock offers. "You could use unavenged."

"That's not a word, either," claims Cole.

"Yes, it is, Merriam–Webster," Brock insists.

"Bullshit—" Dallas argues. "I got fifty bucks that says it is a word. Somebody check a dictionary app. Rea, you want in on this action?"

"Are you jerkoffs done?" I cut in, my patience wearing out with the lack of sleep.

"It doesn't sound like a real word," one of them mutters.

"Read it and weep, ladies!" Dallas holds up his phone as proof. "It is a word."

"Is this chick hot?"

"Search Sharknet," Brock says, speaking over Cole. At least, I think that's what he said. I can't make it out with his face smashed into the couch pillow.

"Checked all social media already," I tell him, bypassing Cole's question altogether. "I'm starting to wonder if she's in witness protection."

Is Bailey hot? Big dark eyes, full lips. Yeah, she's hot. Not my type but hot in her own way.

And these animals will never know.

That would complicate my life more than it already is and it's so complicated already you need a playbook to follow along. "I need you guys to call every girl on your phone tree and get me her digits."

"Seriously, what's the deal with this girl?" Brock's frustrated. I get it. I also know I've been there for each and every one of them when they've needed it.

"I'm responsible...this girl's in trouble because of me."

Sitting up, Brock nods, scrapes his hair back, and rubs his face awake. "Okay."

The three of them complain but get busy. Nobody messes with phone tree.

* * *

ALICE

I don't remember a time when I wasn't in love with movies. It started as a way to escape a quiet, lonely home. My father took my mother's death very hard. I don't remember much other than him retreating into himself. Hardly ever speaking. We could go days with only a few words exchanged. So I lost myself in old DVDs of *Lassie*, *Spy Kids*, *Coraline*, and more that my mother had purchased at garage sales around the neighborhood.

By the time I turned eleven the obsession had transformed from simply watching them, to wanting to create them. School notebooks were covered in dialogue. Dream boards, dedicated to the stories I had written, decorated my bedroom walls. There was a magic to it I couldn't explain, and a rush I couldn't get anywhere else.

Then my father bought me a Sony video camera for my twelfth birthday and the addiction went turbo.

I recruited kids that lived on my block to act in my amateur movies. I watched every online video there was on filmmaking, hit the library for books on the subject. Stole books on the subject. Yeah, let's skip right over that.

By the time I hit my teens I could tell you where you could film without a permit, how to get people to sign waivers, which high schools had strong drama clubs from which you could recruit actors willing to work for free.

So it's no surprise that every time I step inside the hallowed halls of the film and television building goose bumps ripple over my skin.

This is my church. The only church I worship in. The other one failed me when I was old enough to know I could ask for things. Not this one, though. The goose bumps, the shiver up my back—that's the universe telling me I'm right where I'm supposed to be.

"The deadline to submit a short for the James Cameron internship is the end of the semester. That's plenty of time to produce something if you don't already have something ready to go," Professor Marshall announces.

She walks back and forth, scanning all the ultra alert faces drinking in every syllable that falls from her knowledgeable lips. Marshall's is a master class in film and video production. People come from all over the world to take it and the crowded-to-capacity lecture hall serves as proof.

It also happens to be my favorite this semester and not only because it's the gateway to the prized summer internship with James Cameron's production company; Cameron not only known for being an Oscar-winning director but also a top cinematographer. I'm also hopelessly in love with this class because we get to actually film and edit, putting into practice everything we learn.

"Interviews start in November, people. Sign up for a time slot if you haven't done so already."

And I plan to nail it. This bitch is mine.

"Have you figured out what you're submitting?" Simon whispers, leaning over Morgan who's seated between us. Creature of habit like me, he chose his seat the first day of class and never moved. Looking uncomfortable, Morgan shrinks back.

A mop of dark wavy hair falls into his almond-shaped, chocolaty eyes and he flips it aside.

"I think so," I answer.

It's a lie. I'm a dirty, filthy liar. I really haven't. No clue whatsoever what I'm going to submit and it's kind of freaking me out. This is major-league important and I'm being indecisive and I am *never* indecisive. "Have you?"

"Still debating between a short film I submitted to Sundance last year and something I worked on over the summer, an indie film that a friend of mine directed and I worked on as DP."

He's cute and accomplished and he knows it. I should probably stay as far away from him as possible. "Wow. Trying to psych me out already? Let the *Hunger Games* begin." He chuckles and twin dimples pop up on his cheeks. I should stay away—*buuut* maybe I won't. I mean, a girl can't survive on passion for her craft alone.

I've always gone for the creative type. My high school boyfriend could be related to this guy there are so many similarities. Where Jack was moody and unpredictable, however, and as high-maintenance emotionally as you can get, Simon strikes me as much more easygoing. And easygoing is good.

He plays with the leather bracelets wrapped around his left wrist. "I was about to say if you need any help putting something together, all you have to do is ask. I have access to an Avid machine."

A professional editing machine? I suck in a breath. Sexiest words in the English language. "Now you're talking dirty."

He flashes me an Instagram smile and Morgan rolls her eyes. She's been low-key real-life trolling him since the beginning of the semester and I'm surprised he hasn't picked up on it yet. "I didn't see you in study group for Film Theory."

Right. The study group that I desperately need to attend, that I can't attend because it's on Thursday nights on the other side of campus and I don't have a car. That study group.

"My car died on me. And well, my ankle." I lift it for his viewing pleasure.

His face twists into an adorably troubled frown. "What happened?"

The question induces an image of a dolphin tattoo to pop up. My ankle is still sore and the lack of sleep is making me moody as hell.

Flipper happened. Instead I say, "Long story."

* * *

REAGAN

"What's up, Jersey," I say, pulling the Jeep up in front of the film and television building. Alice Bailey, a.k.a. the hardest woman on the planet to track down, is presently speaking to a guy dressed in skinny jeans. I immediately don't like the look of this dude.

Phone tree turned out to be an epic waste of time. No one I know knows this girl. Which is almost an impossible feat since I know everyone there is to know on this campus. No matter. Failure isn't in my vocabulary and so here I am.

Pausing their conversation, they both glance at me and frown. I stand through the open top of the Jeep. Smile and wave. There's no change in their expressions. It'd be funny if this guy hadn't already crawled under my skin and made himself unfuckingwelcome.

She says something else to him and he stares down at her with a wolfish smile. Very shady. I don't like it. Shady guy walks away and Bailey finally grants me her attention, a pointed look that lasts all of a second before she starts moving up the steep incline which leads to the Communications building. Naturally, I give chase, coasting the Jeep along the sidewalk.

"Did you fall down a rabbit hole?"

Her dark eyes flash. Yeah, she's not amused.

"Okay...okay, that was the wrong thing to say. I can see that now. Seriously, though, I've been looking for you everywhere and I mean everywhere. Are you in the mob? Because you're harder to track down than Whitey Bulger."

Circumstances dictated that I resort to some questionable tactics. Like stalking. I'm not proud of myself, but when I don't sleep shit gets real.

She stops, regards me curiously. I can see it on her face— she's gearing up to tell me off. So I jump in and backpedal before she gets the chance. "That sounded stalkery as fuck but I promise my intentions are true." My hand falls over my heart, as if I could dig it out and hand it to her as evidence that it's not completely black yet.

"What do you want?" she queries, tone not nice.

"To drive you to class."

"What do you *really* want?"

"I have a proposition for you. Let me drive you to your next class and we can discuss it."

"A proposition?" She smirks. "That's cute. Go away."

She starts back up the hill, attempting to speed past me on her crutches and it almost makes me laugh. Almost. After doing thirty minutes of eggbeater intervals and passing drills with a weighted ball, I'm dog tired and in no mood for a lengthy debate.

"You're getting a sunburn, Alice." Ignoring me, she keeps moving. Annoying her may not be the best plan, but it's all I've got. "Aren't you tired yet? Those crutches look hard to operate."

She bites her bottom lip to stop from smiling. Good news. I've managed to get a semblance of a smile out of her. The bad news is that it fades at record speed and she's back to glaring at me.

"Alice…Alice…Alice…"

"Stop—stop saying my name."

"Nope. C'mon, Bailey. Hear me out."

She stops, exhales a loud exasperated breath, and wipes her sweaty brow with the back of her wrist. "Give it a rest, dude. Haven't you caused enough trouble already?"

That one stung. I'm man enough to admit it. She's also proving a little more stubborn than I'd anticipated but whatever. Game on. I'm not known as the best two-meter specialist on the Sharks for nothing. "I haven't slept in three nights. You know why? Go ahead, ask me why."

"I don't care why."

"No, really, go ahead and ask me."

"I don't care."

"That's cold, Alice. But I'll tell you anyway."

Her lips quirk. "Please don't."

"I feel bad. I do. I feel bad that I crippled you, turned you into a gimp, and it's keeping me up at night."

Shaking her head, a full grin cuts across her face and I swear I feel it in my chest. This chick's smiles are so hard to come by it feels like I'm scoring the championship winning goal whenever I manage to get one out of her.

"It's not my job to make you feel better, Flipper."

Flipper? Now I'm smiling. Why am I smiling? I'm tired. That's all.

Behind me, a car horn blasts. In my rearview mirror, some douche waves his arm for me to move the Jeep. Fuck that. It took me two days sitting outside Bailey's dorm to find her. I'm not about to let her slip through my fingers now because this guy can't get his Hummer around my Jeep.

Raising my arm out the roof, I flip him off and tires screaming, he guns it around me, nearly missing a head-on collision with a Lexus coming down the hill.

People drive like shit around here.

Having reached her destination, Alice is standing in front of the communications building. She's rattled if the color on her cheeks and the way her small fists grip the crutches tightly is any indication. Add that to her dismayed expression and it's safe to say I won't be winning her over today.

"You're insane." She turns and walks away.

"But only in a good way!" I shout through cupped hands. "Let me at least give you my email address." There's no masking the rising desperation in my voice as I watch her retreating back. I need a good night's rest dammit, and this chick's obstinacy is standing in the way of that.

"That way we can work around our class schedules."

Too late. She's already gone.

FIVE

ALICE

"You coming over for dinner on Friday, sweetie?" my aunt Peg asks as soon as I answer my cell. She's my father's older sister and the only family I have in California. Notwithstanding my cousin Marie on my mother's side, she's the only family we have left period.

It's been four days since the incident and my leg looks as bad as it did the day it happened. Having to navigate the treacherous hills to get to and from class isn't helping for sure. I've got new bruises to show for it too. Under my armpits. And one should never have bruises under one's armpits.

"Can't. Sorry, Aunt Peg," I answer while trying to gingerly descend three measly steps that lead back to my dorm.

My good leg is sore. My arms are throbbing and useless. Three steps take me forever—they may as well be Everest. "The car died and I might have broken my ankle."

Across the quad, I catch sight of Reagan Reynolds laughing it up with a girl in little more than a scrap of material over her bikini top. He almost caused another accident this morning. What's his deal with wanting to drive me around

41

anyway? I can't figure out what he wants from me and it's making me nervous.

"Broken? Are you sure?"

"No, I didn't go to the ER. I can't afford to right now."

"Order the Uber—I'll pay for it. That way Wheels can have a look."

Arthur "Wheels" Webster, my aunt Peg's live-in boyfriend. Wheels is called Wheels because he's been in a wheelchair since getting into a car wreck twenty years ago. How do I know this? Because when we met, he shook my hand and said, "The name's Artie but everyone's called me Wheels since I got in a car wreck. You should know that I live here with your aunt Peg even though she and I aren't married. Tried to marry the woman but she won't let me. I apologize if this causes you discomfort."

"Why would he take a look at my ankle?" As much as I love Aunt Peg, she's always been a little "out there."

"Wheels is a doctor—was a doctor. One of them highfalutin types too. Well, before he got pinched for selling prescription drugs and did time."

Right.

Picturing the quiet, silver-ponytailed man with gnarled leathery hands that's often tending the small garden out back when I visit, I can't keep the disbelief out of my voice. "Wheels? A doctor?" *And a drug dealer?* I leave that last bit out.

"Don't sound so shocked. Come over. He'll tell you what's wrong with it."

The foot of the crutch catches on a rock. I almost fall and in the process stab myself in the armpit. Tears of frustration prick my eyes as I adjust the crutch under my aching pit. When I don't answer, she presses, "Alice?"

"Life sucks rotten eggs." My voice breaks as I fight back tears of frustration.

"Oh, sweetheart. Take life with a grain of sugar and it won't seem so bad."

"You mean salt?" I say wiping a stray one away with the back of my hand.

"No, I mean sugar. Life's salty enough, dear."

* * *

REAGAN

"Yo, Rea," Cole yells from the other side of the Cantina, the bar overlooking the beach were we usually hang. It's got peanut shells covering the scuffed-up wood floors, large television screens strategically placed around the bar, and the kind of vibe that makes you never want to leave. The nachos also happen to be awesome.

He waves me over to a table already littered with beer bottles. All the guys are already here. Brock and Cole Peterman. Dallas. Warner Moss, a recent transfer from UCLA and probably the most naturally talented player on the starting lineup. Shane Westbrook, a sophomore who earned a spot when three of our top players graduated. And lastly, Quinn Smith, our notorious goalie.

Tuesday is twofer night so the place is packed, filled to capacity with girls looking to hook up with all the athletes and the occasional celebrities that hang here.

I fall in an empty chair next to Dallas and eyeball a clip of last weekend's UCLA Bruins game on the television over the bar.

"Well?" Cole starts. Uncrossing his arms, he holds them open and makes a face that says *get on with it*. "We're waiting to hear what happened with phone-tree girl."

Cole and Brock Peterman are fraternal twins, two of the best defensive specialists in the country, and as opposite in every way as two brothers could possibly be. I've known them since elementary school, their father being the minister of the church my parents attend.

Brock is twenty-one going on eighty, quiet, and laid-back. I'm almost one hundred percent certain he has never in his life strayed from the righteous path. At least, I've never witnessed it and I've been around the guy most of my life.

His brother, to put it nicely, is a machine. Competitive to the point of being obnoxious, and completely untrusting of any human that was not born with a dick—a mystery I have yet to solve.

I assume it's the handywork of the girl he dated in high school, but he's never spoken of it to me. He'd throw down for any one of us, though. The stories of his loyalty are legendary. Which is why we all put up with his bullshit.

Blowing out a deep breath, I stretch my neck side to side. "Shut down, man. She shut me down." I've never met a girl so desperate to be rid of me.

A bunch of snickers come from the peanut gallery. One comedian shouts, "*Crash and burn, Mav?*"

"Man—" Cole shakes his head, presses down a smile. He crosses his arms again, jams his hands under his pits, thumbs over his pecs. His chair tips back, balancing on two legs. "Never thought I'd live to see the day. What happened to *always be closing?*"

"This isn't about my dick, bro. I'm just trying to help the girl out."

"So says you."

Whatever Cole thinks he's onto, he's dead wrong. As soon as I correct the damage I've caused, I'll put this entire business—including Alice Bailey—behind me. This is the last year that belongs to me and only me. To do *as I wish*. Next year there will be medical school, and my father riding my ass for the following eight to ten. It's not like I'm planning to burn through co-eds like Dallas and Cole, but I'm also not about to squander the time on a relationship that won't last.

I level him with an irritated stare. "Yeah."

The attention leaves me when highlights of the Bruins game show their star running back, a projected first-round pick in next year's NFL draft, fracturing his leg. The injury gnarly as he hyperextends it in the wrong direction. That guy's whole world just ended.

Welcome to the glamorous world of college sports.

Most people have no idea the sacrifices we make. Of our time. Our bodies. All the injuries. Most of which do have long-term effects. Then again, it's the only means of escape some of us have.

Dallas leans in. "What are you going to do now that Penny's gone?"

Penny was last year's convenience lay. Over the summer she moved to New York to get married. She said she was sure her fiancé had a piece on the side too. Whoever tells you long-distance relationships work has never been in one.

We met when she was the TA for my advanced biology class. Hot, uncomplicated, smart enough not to give a single shit about me with the exception of my body, and career driven. My favorite type of woman. I'm already missing the hell out of Penny.

"I don't know." But I better figure it out fast because Bailey's dark gaze has been invading my dreams lately. The little I've had, since I'm not sleeping all that much.

* * *

ALICE

I pry up the top of the page I'd slapped facedown the minute they handed them out, and stare at the big fat **D** on my Film Theory and Criticism exam. No, I wasn't hallucinating. It's still a **D** for dumbass.

I'm not one of those people that breezes through school. I'm more of an abstract thinker. Unless it's visual information it's receiving, my mind tends to move sideways, in tangents. Which means the linear mental process needed to accumulate knowledge and regurgitate it in test form is, bottom line, a struggle. I need to apply myself to keep my grades up and sometimes I need extra help.

I knew I hadn't aced it—we took it the day after the ankle incident so I didn't get much studying done because I was distracted and in pain—but I didn't think I bombed it, either.

"How'd you do?" the girl next to me asks. Morgan's piercing, the one on her eyebrow, glimmers under the floodlights. I wonder if it hurt. Why did she get it? Does she regret it? Does it have meaning to her? See what I mean about tangents?

Exhaling a deep, frustrated breath, I run a hand over my head. My bangs stand up so I shake them out. "Horrible. How 'bout you?"

She tugs on the ends of her short, pink hair. "B plus. I don't know how, I barely studied. I hate Bertolucci. Such a misogynistic pig."

I don't care either way about Bernardo Bertolucci. What I do care about is my average. I can't afford to do poorly in any class. My scholarship demands I maintain a B plus, and everything I've ever worked toward is at stake if I can't do that. Chewing on the tip of my thumb, I glance around and find Simon staring back at me. He sends me a coy smile. Which forces me to return one that lacks sincerity. God, I hope he doesn't ask me how I did. That would be twice as mortifying.

"*Last Tango In Paris*. Classic," he says with a leer.

Morgan turns away from him and mimes a gag, drawing a dry burst of laughter out of me. I'm definitely with her on this one. The movie is basically cheesy soft porn peddled as an art house think piece. And the *profound* moral of the story? Women are incapable of handling sex without an emotional attachment. They become hysterical, maniacal, and ultimately resort to murder.

See, I know my stuff. I just don't do so well on tests unless I put in a lot of extra time.

"I rarely do this, but since quite a large number of you did poorly on this one I'm going to offer an elective make-up exam," Levine, the professor, announces.

A bunch of murmured "Thank Gods" circulate the room. The tension in my shoulders eases a fraction.

"Come to study group and I'll help you out," Morgan says. I glance over and discover a flicker of apprehension on her round face. I don't think she has many friends here. She only ever speaks to me in class.

"Where is that again?"

"Tomorrow night at the library. Study room B."

"I'll be there."

A brief smile lights up her face and the butterfly tattoos on her neck flap their wings.

* * *

The following evening I'm sitting on the toilet in the communal bathroom, in the middle of gingerly rewrapping my ankle after soaking it in Epsom salts for half an hour, when my stepmom calls.

"Hey, sweets. How's the ankle?"

"Getting better. I've been soaking it every day and it's helping." It's marginally better. She doesn't need to know that, though. She's worried enough as is. "Are you taking arnica?"

"Not yet. I haven't been able to get to the store." I'll have to rectify that tomorrow, ask Zoe to drive me when she has time.

"I still think you should get an X-ray."

"Button? It's me, Dad."

As if anyone else on this planet calls me Button. He does that, steals my mom's phone when she's in the middle of a conversation. Yeah, she loves it. I wouldn't be surprised if they find him bludgeoned to death by iPhone one of these days.

"Hi, Dad."

"How are those California fruits and nuts treating you?"

"Awful. They say hello all the time. Like, for no reason. Even strangers. And smile. They even have the audacity to make eye contact. I'm a little freaked out."

His deep chuckle comes through the phone and a sharp pang hits my heart. I miss them. One of the downfalls of being an only child is that you develop an unhealthy attachment to your parents.

"What happened with the car?"

"It cost me a couple hundred bucks to have it donated."

"You live and learn, kiddo."

"Please don't say I told you so again."

"Okay, okay. Here's your mother. Love you. And I told you so."

"Love you too."

"Sweetheart?" my mother cuts in a moment later.

"I have to get going if I'm going to make it in time for study group."

"At this hour??" she exclaims.

"It's only seven thirty, Nance. Chill." Though it will be late by the time I get out. "If it makes you feel better, I'll take an Uber home."

I won't. Can't afford it. But I can't have her worrying about me walking around in the dead of night on crutches.

"I don't know, Alice. This is making me increasingly uncomfortable. Maybe I should come out for a few days. Until you're better."

"Mom, stop. I'm fine. Gotta go. I'll call you tomorrow."

Despite seeing blood and guts on a nightly basis at one of the busiest hospitals in Newark, New Jersey, Nancy Bailey is a fretter when it comes to her only kid. She's also repeatedly said that she didn't fret a day in her life until she met me and fell in love.

"Call me tonight. I mean it. Call me or I won't sleep."

"Fine," I grumble. "Love you, bye."

We're big on the *I love yous* in my family. After my birth mom died, Dad started to say it all the time. Then I started saying it all the time. And then he met Nancy who says it more than me and Dad combined.

"Love you more."

An hour later I'm cursing my stupidity. Sweaty and in pain, I'm in a foul mood by the time I reach the library. Only to find a note on the door of study room B explaining that it's been moved off campus, an address attached, due to a broken pipe that flooded the room.

I want to die.

Anyone who forgot to list their cell number on the sign-up sheet can do so here, it says at the bottom.

As a general rule I don't write my cell number on something as public as a sign-up sheet, and judging by the list of numbers written on here now, quite a few of us hadn't. The joke's on us. Without pause, I take out a pen and scribble it on the designated line. This can't happen again. My mental health won't allow it.

As I'm leaving, to begin the torturous journey back home, someone I recognize from class rushes in. "Group has moved off campus. Room is flooded. There's a sign-up sheet if you forgot to leave your cell number."

His shoulders slump. "Shit," he grumbles under his breath.

I know what you mean, bud. I know what you mean.

SIX

ALICE

Being a transfer student, I've been exiled to the dorm of cast-offs. I share a suite with six other girls. Each of us with a single room since we're all upperclassmen. Out of the six, four of us have struck up a fledgling friendship, bonding over our mutually obsessive love of reality television, Netflix, and sarcasm.

Here's the rundown: Zoe Mayfield, tall, blonde, extrovert (to put it mildly), likes to curse a fair share, grew up in Beverly Hills and is presently slumming it in the dorm as punishment. Some business about being kicked out of her mother's ritzy beach condo for throwing a party, during which somebody walked away with her mother's favorite Andy Warhol painting. A real one. That's the abridged, sanitized version. Zoe's was a lot more descriptive.

Blake Allyn, medium height, bears a striking resemblance to Halle Berry with long braids. She's another rich kid from Beverly Hills, reserved, the total opposite of her best friend. From what I've observed, they balance each other nicely. Operating in lockstep, Blake is the conscience of the two, and the only thing standing between Zoe and the possibility of a mug shot. She was living with Zoe in the condo, and from what I've been able to suss out, she's only here out of friendship. Which is seriously admirable considering the mattresses (relentlessly hard). She also wears a medical bracelet and I haven't worked up the nerve to ask why yet.

And then there's Dora Ramos. Shy, studious to the point of being obsessive. Small, curvy, redhead. Has a tendency to stutter. Dora, like me, is a scholarship kid.

Together we're the merry bad of misfits.

On Friday, I hobble back to the dorm and go in search of Zoe, the only person I know who has a functioning car. Hearing the sink running, I knock on the bathroom door in our suite.

"Zoe, you in there? Can you give me a ride to the trailer park?" The unmistakable sound of a sniffle rides above the running water. "Zoe? You okay in there?"

The door bursts open and out steps miles of long tan legs set off by a tiny denim miniskirt. Her large, heavily lashed hazel eyes glisten with unshed tears and her slender nose looks rubbed raw.

Zoe's supermodel features are so distracting that most don't see the odometer reads a thousand hard miles in the depths of her eyes. There's a weight to her stare that says Zoe's seen and done things she'd rather not have. I don't know... maybe it takes someone who's faced their own dark matter to recognize it in another.

"Are you crying?" her red-rimmed eyes compel me to ask.

Dabbing at the corners, she gives me a look that says *are you high*? "Allergies." Avoiding closer scrutiny, she looks down, adjusts her off-the-shoulder t-shirt. I don't press her for more. I don't know her well enough for that.

She pulls out a tube of lip gloss from the micro Chanel purse hanging across her slim torso, swipes some on, and exchanges it for a set of car keys.

"You wanna take my car?" A Mercedes fob is thrust in my face. Her car costs as much as my dad's saltbox house in New Jersey. No, I do not want to be responsible for her car.

"Not a chance," I say, expression horrified.

"What's the big deal?"

"What's the big deal? What if something happens to it? It would take me till I'm dead to pay you back."

"It's just stuff," she tells me, her tone implying I'm the densest idiot on the planet. "Come on." She motions for me to follow her out the door.

Minutes later we're barreling down Pacific Coast Highway in her customized AMG black-on-black Mercedes G wagon.

"Slower!" I practically shout as I cling to the door handle with a death grip. "Do any of you California drivers have any respect for the basic rules of the road?"

Ignoring my harried expression, Zoe's gaze darts to the ACE bandage on my ankle. "What happened to you anyway? You never explained."

The last few days have been an exercise in sleep deprivation. Every time I move, my ankle reminds me it's injured. And I'm one of those people that needs at least seven hours to function. The consequence of this lack of sleep is that I've been steadily growing grumpier by the day. It was so sore when I woke up this morning to leave early for class—having prepared myself for the extra hour it was going to take for me to get there on time—that when I passed Zoe going into the shower I basically growled at her.

"The short version is my car broke down at the bottom of the southside entrance and a water polo player almost ran me over as I was walking home."

Her face goes unnaturally still. "A water polo player?"

"I don't think it's broken, but it's still really swollen and sore. So now I'm crippled and without a car."

"Which one?"

"Reagan Reynolds—"

She gets quiet for a beat, the tension in her shoulders softening. "Word of caution if you plan to sue, the water polo players are gods on this campus."

"Sue?" I practically shout, my heartbeat suddenly racing as fast as Zoe's G wagon down Pacific Coast Highway.

I hate conflict. I hate it. It would never even cross my mind to do such a thing. "I would never...I...I mean, regardless of who he is. I can't...I couldn't—"

"Relax, Alice. I only mentioned it because Reagan's parents are well-known Beverly Hills doctors." Although she shrugs casually, there's nothing casual about this conversation. The weight is back in her stare. "Every one of us who's grown up with money has been drilled since birth that anything we do could bring on a lawsuit."

What an awful way to live. Never knowing what someone's true intentions are. Never knowing if all you're valued for is your money.

"Do you know him?" I have to know if he's anticipating me coming after him for money. If that's the reason he's been charming me. Or, whatever—stalking me.

"My mother knows his parents. She's sold them a lot of art."

Zoe had mentioned that her mother was one of the biggest art dealers in the world.

"But I don't know him personally, if that's what you mean. Only of him. Everybody does. He was on two championship winning water polo teams. The first when he was only a freshman, and he scored the winning goal against UCLA." Then gleefully adds, "And he's hot as fuck, so pretty much every girl on the West Coast knows who he is."

"I guess." Staring out the passenger window, the side-by-side beach houses, most of which look like they were built in the seventies, blur into a streak of color.

"You guess?" She's all big eyes and feigned outrage. "Have you seen that face? Have you seen that body?"

The reverence in Zoe's voice makes me chuckle. I've never been much for school athletics. I don't get the crazy obsession with it. And I definitely didn't peg cynical Zoe as a Speedo chaser.

"Fangirl, much?" I tease.

A slow grin transforms her face. "We have baseball, basketball, soccer, and water polo teams at this school and only one of those has won seven national titles. Those guys get a lot of love."

"Warm fuzzies, or bumping uglies?"

"Both."

"What's his deal anyway?" I can't deny I'm a little intrigued—regretfully.

"Who, Reagan?" Zoe clarifies and I nod. "Sounds like someone's nursing a cru-hush."

This earns her an exaggerated eye roll. I'm not crushing on anyone. It's a mild interest. A fleeting curiosity. I haven't entertained a legit crush since the third grade. I had one long-term boyfriend in high school and we parted ways as friends because we were both smart enough to understand that there was a life to be lived out there, somewhere, and hanging on to each other would've only held us back. Since then I've had one thing on my mind and one thing only. Get my film degree. Live my dream.

"Hey, don't get me wrong. I one hundred percent agree. I fully support your mancrush." She raises a manicured hand, stacks of skinny sparkly rings on her long fingers. "He can run me over anytime."

"I don't have the time for a crush. I have two years and just enough money saved up to graduate. It's that he's been super eager about giving me rides to class since the accident and I want to make sure I don't need to invest in pepper spray and a set of brass knuckles."

She snorts. "He's a good guy. I've seen him with a couple of different girls in the last two years, but not the worst by far in that crew." A sneaky smile appears. "And FYI, I have a Taser gun in the glove compartment in case you ever need it."

Zoe pulls the G wagon into the trailer park. Yes, there's a trailer park in Malibu. Granted, it's rather ritzy for a trailer park. The trailers look more like cute little bungalows. Some famous people even live there from time to time. Still a trailer park, though.

"We're going to the next home game," she tells me. "If you're going to be here for the next two years, you should at least see one."

In a momentary bout of madness I picture Reagan Reynolds in a Speedo. "I'll think about it."

* * *

I knock on the sliding glass door to my aunt's royal blue trailer with white trim and get no response. The minute I let myself in her scarlet macaw squawks. That bird hates me. I'm no bird expert but I'm almost positive he's hurling parrot profanity.

A voice coming from the back room breaks into the squawking. "Oh, don't...no, don't do that. Goodness' sake..."

"Aunt Peg?"

"Alice? Is that you?"

"Hi."

"Back here, sweetie, I'm watching the *Outlander*."

In the den I find her seated in her favorite armchair. My aunt Peg is a big, beautiful woman and her home and clothing definitely reflect her style—a mash-up of seventies Hawaiian prints and eighties fluorescent colors. Somehow she makes it work.

Unlike me, she's a real girly girl. She works from home as a virtual assistant and yet she's got on a full face of meticulously applied makeup, her red chin-length bob is perfectly blown out, and she's wearing what can only be described as a very fancy caftan in a jungle print.

Smiling brightly, she stands to her full five-eleven height and sashays over to me with open arms. Then her head whips around, something on the television screen catching her attention. "What a little brat that daughter is."

I'm fairly certain she's speaking to the television. Aunt Peg does that a lot. Her smile dies as her gaze falls to my crutches.

Hugging me, my face buried between her breasts, my senses drowning in roses and vanilla, she rocks us side to side. "That bad, huh?"

"I can't put any weight on it."

She pulls out a kitchen chair and pats it. "Have a seat. We'll have Wheels take a look." She makes her way to the refrigerator. "Want something to drink?"

"Water is fine."

"No soda?"

"No...I try to eat healthy."

Grabbing a pitcher filled with water out of the refrigerator, she sets it on the table before opening the cabinets to retrieve a couple of glasses. No sooner has she set those down that she opens the window right behind her chair at the kitchen table. "Wheels!" she shouts. "Alice is here and she banged up her ankle. Come take a look."

"Aunt Peg, I don't think—"

She purses her bow-shaped lips and waves her polished red nails at me. "Don't be shy. He worked for the Dallas Cowboys as the team doctor, knows a thing or two. He can tell you what's wrong with it." Joining me at the table, she regards me with an indecipherable look on her face. "How's your father?"

The way my father tells it the nine-year age gap between my aunt and dad was a big enough difference that they grew up virtual strangers. Then, at seventeen, Aunt Peg ran off to California to join a hippie commune and that was the last they heard of her for a good long time. That was, until she was arrested for dealing pot and sent to the "big house"(my father's words) for five years.

"Good," I answer. "He and Mom may come out for Thanksgiving."

"It's nice that you think of Nancy as your mom." Peg's gaze grows distant. As if she's dredging up all the regrets she's tried to forget. "You know I've always felt terrible that I couldn't help when Jennifer died."

Aunt Peg was a guest of the California Department of Corrections when my mother died so my father had to fend for himself. Working full-time and raising a five-year-old was nearly impossible, as he tells the story. Two years later he met Nancy.

"I know," I say to soothe her guilt.

Her gaze slides over my features. "You look so much like her..." Her smile is weak and sad. "Anyway..." Clearing her throat, she pokes her head out the window again. "Wheels!"

"I'm comin', goddamnit. Got myself stuck in the mud!" drifts in through the open back door. Wheels enters, gives me a curt nod. "Alice."

"Hi, Wheels. You don't have to—"

"Nonsense." He pushes the wheelchair to the kitchen sink—now that I take notice I see it's lower than a regular kitchen sink—and washes his hands. A moment later he's by my chair and pats his lap. "Let's see whatcha got."

I place my injured leg on his jeans-covered lap and watch as he removes the ACE bandage and prods the swollen ankle. In the process I get a bunch of "Hmms" and a few nods.

"Well?" Aunt Peg prompts.

"Not broken. Looks to be severely sprained, however. Grade two..." His gray eyebrows hike up. "Could be six weeks recovery—four, at the very least."

I'm stunned. And lightheaded. "You're sure?"

"Yep," Wheels confirms before he wraps my ankle back up.

I want to cry. What am I going to do about my job? I've called out sick for the last three shifts. I can't stall much longer. "What do I do in the meantime?"

"Stay off of it. Soak it three times a day in Epsom salts. Take arnica—that'll help. But mostly it's a matter of time."

SEVEN

ALICE

"Mr. Howard, it's only a sprained ankle."

The *thump, thump, thump* my crutches make as I follow Mr. Howard, the manager of the Slow Drip, the coffee shop where I work, is the drumroll reminding me that if I don't get back to work soon I'll probably go broke and be forced to drop out of my dream school.

"I'll be off the crutches in a few days," I add. Granted it's a lie, a bald-faced lie—diagnosis courtesy of one Artie "Wheels" Webster, former MD—but I'll say anything to keep this job.

Howard stops short and his hipster haircut, a blond shellacked wave of hair, sways. He takes a good hard look at my injured leg then slips behind the counter and starts cleaning out the multiple coffee machines lined up against the wall.

"I need someone that can actually do physical labor," he tells me in a flat tone, not bothering to give me his undivided attention as he dumps used coffee grounds into the trash.

A marked heavy pause happens. Instigated by me. Because what's there to argue? He's right. How *am* I supposed to maneuver on crutches behind the bar with three other baristas? Impossible. Not to mention this place is always wall-to-wall packed with customers.

"Let me get your check." Without waiting for a response, he walks away, toward the back office.

Standing behind the counter at the cash register, Josie, the girl I usually work with, gives me a sympathetic smile as she hands the surfer dude picking up his four megabeverages his change.

"How are you, Alice?"

My entire life is on the precipice of destruction. That's the ugly truth about poverty. Even when you have a job, you're only a paycheck away from total annihilation. The anxiety never goes away.

I'm legit about to start hyperventilating when Peg's words come back to me. "Take life with a grain of sugar, Alice." It's a marvel how she always manages to see the glass as half full, despite her personal experiences.

"Wonderful. You?"

"I'm working a double." Looking put out, she shrugs. Josie's the type to stand around picking away at her lilac gel nail polish rather than do a minute's worth of work. I don't mind Josie. She's not a bad person. I just won't miss working with her.

Gaze aimed at someone beyond my shoulder, her eyes stop blinking. She sweeps away a stray corkscrew curl and performs a quick inspection of her nails. That and the fire-engine red flush makes me think it's a boy she likes.

"Rea, get me an extra large with a triple shot," an unfamiliar male voice yells over the others. I may not know the voice but I do recognize the name.

With as much nonchalance as I can marshal, which isn't very much at all, I glance over my shoulder and find Reagan Reynolds parting the crowd in the coffee shop. And he's headed straight this way.

Necks start snapping in his direction. "Reaaa, great match last weekend," unfamiliar voices call out.

"Thanks, dude," I hear a couple of times. He drags most of the attention in the place with him.

I turn my back, curl my shoulders inward, pray he doesn't see me.

Howard returns, holding up an envelope. "Look me up after the ankle's healed," he offers. "If I haven't filled the position, I'll take you back."

Hard to believe when there's zero sympathy anywhere to be found in his expression. Besides, with campus only a mile away it's unlikely this job will be here in the next thirty minutes let alone in six weeks. Plenty of able bodies around to fill my shoes.

"I had to dock your last check for the three days you called out sick." He hands it over.

I take it from him with a heavy heart. I've finally hit bottom. There's my sugar. My day can't get any worse. I've officially lost my only source of income and I can't even call my parents because they will stress, and in turn, I'll stress even more.

A whiff of chlorine and laundry detergent tickles my nose. As I'm rubbing it, the sudden, obvious presence of a tall person standing much too close for comfort draws my attention to the left and up, up, up. Where I'm met by a set of blazing green eyes staring back at me. My attention falls to lips molded into a sulky frown.

My day just got worse.

"What?" is the only thing I can think to say under scrutiny so intense it could strip paint off a car.

"Hi, Reagan," Josie says a bit too loudly, compelling both of us to glance her way.

"Hi, Josie," he returns with a crooked smile.

My gaze skips between the two of them. Then takes a full lap around the joint to find a stifling amount of attention—mostly female—attached to the guy standing next to me.

Spare me. Fine, okay, he's hot. No question. And maybe if my life wasn't crumbling around me, I would be trying to stuff my panties in his mouth the same way Josie is clearly thinking about doing.

But these girls? I'm just going to say it—some of them look concussed. Josie included. I am almost one hundred percent certain I've never worn a concussed look over a boy and if I ever do somebody needs to slap me.

"Rea! Call me so we can make plans," one of the glamour girls sitting in the corner shouts. She's so perfect she looks Photoshopped.

Delete. Delete my prior claim. This guy is way out of my league. The only way my panties would ever get near his face is if he had a gushing head wound and I needed to stop the bleeding to save his life.

He gives Photoshopped girl an absent nod and returns to bore holes in my head with his hot stare. "You lost your job?" he asks with unmistakable concern in his voice.

It's my turn to frown. "Were you eavesdropping?" The

guilty look he gives me is all the answer I need. "Great."

Now that my humiliation is complete, it's time for a speedy departure. I hobble away from the counter, last paycheck firmly grasped in one hand, and push through a wall of guys. Members of the soccer team, judging by the uniforms. The inconsiderate jerks barely make room for the girl on crutches. I head for the exit with Reynolds on my heels.

The urge to ugly cry is strong and this guy is not allowed to watch. I've never been a fan of messy public displays of emotion and right now one is imminent.

"You've got that determined, stalkery look about you, Reynolds. Stand down," I grumble under my breath and hear him chuckle.

"Determination is implied in stalking." I stop and shoot a glare over my shoulder because...really? "You might want to use another adjective is all I'm saying."

I blink. He smiles.

"How about annoying?"

"That works."

In my haste to be gone, I bum-rush the door and almost lose my balance. My life has officially become a comedy of errors.

Thankfully, strong hands reach out and set me safely back on my feet—pardon, my foot—before I get a taste of the cement sidewalk. "Thanks," I mutter.

"You're welcome," my stalker replies in a semi-amused tone.

A marine haze hugs the shoreline, making the overcast sky the color of opals. Something to be grateful for since I have to wait for the campus shuttle and I forgot to spackle on the SPF

50.

While I wait for a convertible Bentley with a surfboard sticking out of the back seat to drive by before stepping off the sidewalk, I sneak a side-eye and find Reagan staring straight ahead. I'm assuming he's going to his car while I'm headed to the shuttle stop.

I am dead wrong. He's a barnacle. A monkey on my back. Toilet paper stuck to my shoe. All the metaphors for shit you can't get rid of. I pick my way between cars to reach the other side of the Malibu Mart parking lot with him riding my every step.

"Why are you still following me?" And he has, all the way to the shuttle stop. Nowhere near his Jeep. "Your car is that way," I helpfully point out.

"You lost your job because of me."

His voice sounds dull, lacking its usual snappy charm. There's something wrong about it. Like a lion with no mane… or no roar. Whatever, it sounds wrong.

When I reach the shuttle stop, I glance up and find his gaze remote, as if he's not seeing me, and while he's lost in thought, I take the opportunity to study his face. Something I haven't done yet because frankly it's like staring into the sun, way too intense and only to be attempted in small doses. Closely shaven, the sharp line of his jaw is stiff. His angled brows pulled low over traffic light green eyes. There's a small scattering of barely noticeable freckles along his sculpted cheekbone. I wonder if he wears SPF 50. He's so tan I doubt it. He should though. He definitely should. Melanoma kills.

His hands come to rest on his hips and his sensual mouth purses like he's mulling over a serious dilemma. Except the dilemma isn't his to solve. He doesn't have a high GPA to maintain to hold on to his scholarship. He doesn't have a car that's more valuable as scrap metal. He doesn't have to work to pay his living expenses. Mr. Big Deal doesn't have a worry in the world.

My emotions are presently everywhere on the scale: annoyed, crushed, overwhelmed, scared…so scared I don't dare answer. I'm liable to say something I'll regret in my present state, and it would be really unfair of me to unload on him during this freak-out.

"You did, didn't you?" He gestures toward the Slow Drip with a tilt of his perfectly shaped chin.

Did I mention that the dimple in his chin is cute? Yeah, well, it is darnit. Which annoys me. Chins like his should only be dispensed to movie stars and billboard models. They're too dangerous for ordinary civilians to possess.

"Because of me," he continues, nodding to himself. His gaze latches on to mine and gets squinty. "Do I have something on my chin?" He brushes it with the back of his hand.

"No," I huff. Because nothing screams I'm innocent of whatever you assume I'm up to like acting bitchy. "And yes. I lost my job. I have a sprained ankle. How am I supposed to work behind the bar with three other people on these?" I stomp the crutches for a fleeting moment of juvenile satisfaction.

He frowns, his flawless face crowded with guilt.

"Anyway…" My voice peters out, my shoulders fall. I'm suddenly exhausted. I'll have to sell one of my cameras. The mere thought of it makes tears prick my eyes and stuffs up my nose. "It's my problem. Not yours. And—" I glance away. "I guess food isn't absolutely necessary." A burst of dry laughter comes out. It's strained, humorless. Awkward. "I'll be fine."

He exhales harshly. "Jesus." It's safe to say my joke bombed. His hands rake back and forth through his sun-painted hair.

"I'll sell a camera," I barely get out, wracking my brain for a happy thought to stave off the tears welling in the corners of my eyes.

Babygoatsbabygoatsbabygoats

My cameras are the only things of value I possess in this world. It took me seven years of working the worst jobs on the planet to pay them off.

Cleaning cages at the animal shelter? Been there. The cleaning was easy compared to seeing all those distraught furry faces behind bars. Many a night I drove home in tears.

Working at the car wash in the middle of a northeast winter? Done that. Don't try it. Not unless you're keen on frostbitten nipples. The sexual harassment wasn't a whole lot of fun, either. Which served as a springboard for the next horrible odd job.

Transporting vats of used grease from fast food joints and diners to recycling. Yep. Unfortunately, I've done that too. My least favorite. I still won't touch fried food with a ten-foot pole. My gag reflex trips automatically if I even catch a whiff of used oil.

And yet I would go back and do it all over again for my cameras because they are life. The tools of my trade. The instruments of my passion.

"Your camera?"

"Never mind."

"Let me drive you back to campus," he implores softly.

Even though it's well in the eighties, I'm chilled to the bone. That's easy enough to explain. I'm tired and stressed. That's all. What I can't explain is how his low voice warms me from the inside out. A ray of sunlight bathes my eyes. The sun is starting to burn through the marine haze. I nod because anything is better than standing here for another minute.

EIGHT

REAGAN

"Email me your schedule."

"You're like a dog with a bone," she murmurs impassively.

I look over at the quiet girl sitting in the passenger seat of my Jeep. You'd never know by looking at her what just happened. She lost her job because of me and I don't think this girl has much to fall back on. As if I didn't have enough to keep me up at night. Now I can add getting her fired to the list of things I need to atone for.

Staring out at the coastline, expression calm, she pushes her sleek dark hair behind her ear. Bailey is delicate, her features angular and tiny with the exception of her eyes which are big, dark, and expressive. She's beautiful—I won't deny it. As soon as I stepped into the Slow Drip and saw her face, I forgot why I was there in the first place. She's got that girl-next-door thing nailed. Except Jersey's got an edge that makes her...Interesting. Sexy. Something more. My eyes slide over her bare thigh, her shapely legs. Definitely sexy.

"Sharkattack101@gmail," I throw out and get no reaction at all. My attention shifts from the road to her. She's in a zone, hasn't heard a word I've said. "You're not writing this down."

Her sharp brown gaze finally seeks me out. Heavy suspicion lurking there.

"I'll drive you to class. And if I can't, I'll have one of the guys on the team do it."

"No—"

I sigh tiredly. I've never met anyone so unwilling to accept help. "Immovable mass, meet an unstoppable force."

"Unstoppable arse, you say?" A sly smile tips my way.

"Ha. Not funny. And that would make you an immovable ass," I gladly point out. She smirks. "I've never had to beg a girl to let me drive her around before." I soften my voice, coax her with humility. Ego has no place in this. I genuinely want to help her. "But I'll do it if you want me to." She watches me closely. I've got her full attention. "Think of it as my soul's absolution. Allow me to squire you around, Alice."

She bites down on her bottom lip and heat shoots up my neck. Then it ricochets all the way down to my balls. The fuck was that?

Abstinence. That's what it is. Something I have to remedy quickly.

"Did you just quote *The Legend of Ron Burgundy* to me for the second time since we've met? Did that really happen?"

A stupid smile spreads across my face. I knew I liked this girl. Any female that's seen *Anchorman* and can quote lines gets a vote of confidence from me. "Best movie ever."

"Wow, brutal honesty. And you're not even in the least bit embarrassed. Just owning it. Owning that shame."

"I'm man enough to give it a bear hug, even."

She looks away, hides the full-blown smile sliding across

that fine pale skin of her beautiful face. Seeing that smile makes the load I've been carrying around the past few days feel a little bit lighter.

"I'm impressed," she tells me.

"Really? If that's what it takes to impress you then 'you're a smelly pirate hooker.'" A burst of laughter rips out of her. It's full-throated. And God, yes, I'll have another. "'Why don't you go back to your home on whore island.' I could do this all day."

"Please don't," she laughs.

I pull the Jeep over in front of her dorm and park. "I'm going to make it my mission to make you laugh more, Bailey."

Her laughter slowly dies down but her smile remains as she studies my profile. She doesn't want to like me. I can feel her resisting the pull. What she doesn't understand is that I'm a natural-born competitor. I live for a challenge and she's just issued a major one. It only makes me try harder to win her over.

"Don't fight it. My suggestion is that you let yourself like me. It'll be easier for you that way."

Rolling her eyes, she chuckles. "So modest. So humble." Her dark eyes sharpen and narrow as we exchange a sixty-second stare-off. "So sure of yourself."

"That I'm a likeable guy? Yeah, I'm sure."

Shaking her head, she tamps down another grin. "First of all, I find it incredibly creepy that you stalked me all around campus."

"I prefer to think of it as moxie."

"Moxie is for mousy twelve-year-old girls yearning to make it on *American Idol*. What you did was borderline cause for a restraining order." She studies me. "Why do you want to drive me? Seriously, why insist? You can walk away from all of this. I'm happy to let you."

Tension rides up my back. "Isn't it obvious?"

"Obviously not, or I wouldn't be asking."

"You can't get around this campus on crutches."

"I mean why do you care, Reagan?"

Two things happen at once. Something inside of me wakes up from the dead at the sound of my name being spoken in her voice, and that something travels straight to my dick. I shift, pull the hem of my t-shirt over my shorts.

Then my father's face crops up. Those two things should never occur at the same time and yet sadly they have.

My smile loses its shine because the prior makes me hard as Valyrian steel, and the latter kills my boner instantly. I don't think a girl's voice has ever made me hard before, but I guess there's a first time for everything. The second would kill anyone's boner. Probably won't be the last time, either.

No one on this planet knows the real story of the family Reynolds and it's going to stay that way. Deflection is the name of my game and I mean to play it to the bitter end. I can't tell her that I'm ashamed of my father. That he's everything I don't want to be. So I whittle it down, reduce it to something that will make sense to her.

I send her a casual smile. It's become second nature and therefore not hard to summon. "I feel responsible. It's my fault you're in this mess and I need to fix it."

The weight of her stare on the side of my face is palpable. I'm seconds from piling on more bullshit to my explanation when she speaks.

"Okay," she quietly concedes. So quietly I have to look at her face to make sure I heard her right.

"Yeah?"

"You can drive me to my Thursday night study group. It's off campus, on PCH. That's more important. But *only* on the condition that you drive me. I'll fend for myself on the days you can't."

"Deal." A grin spreads across my face. A real one. "Now email me your schedule."

NINE

ALICE

"Why aren't you ready?" Zoe asks as soon as she and Blake step into the suite. Zoe places a tray with four iced coffees on a side table and we all reach for one.

Have I mentioned the suite? It's decked out like a penthouse at the Four Seasons. Or what I imagine a penthouse would look like. 60-inch flat-screen television with cable and Netflix, abstract art prints on the walls, rugs, and a feather-stuffed couch. All courtesy of Zoe's decorator. Not kidding.

It stinks like school spirit today because both of them are wearing tight-fitting **Malibu U Water Polo** t-shirts and frayed jean short shorts. I glance at Dora and find her stuffing a powdered donut hole into her mouth. She shrugs and pauses the show we've been watching.

"Ready for what?" I ask.

Perching her pink mirrored sunglasses atop her head, Zoe gives me and Dora the once-over. "The water polo game." Her tone suggests I'm an idiot, her expression says more of the same. "You said you'd come."

"I said I'd think about it."

"We don't have time to debate details. We're playing Cal today. It's gonna be jammed." Zoe's scrutiny moves to Dora, giving me a precious moment's respite. "You too, Red. Let's go. Chop, chop. Out of the maternity clothes."

"But…" Nose crinkling, powdered sugar dusting the corners of her lips, Dora looks adorably put out. "We're watching *Gigolos*…and the guys forgot Steven's birthday." She examines her oversized teal-colored sweatpants and frowns. "And these are really comfortable."

"Yeeaah," is Zoe's answer to that. "Time for an intervention. You've been mainlining that show since you discovered it and enough is enough. Go put on some clothes that don't make you look like a middle-aged third-grade teacher from Poughkeepsie who gets off by creeping on her young, shirtless neighbor from her upstairs bedroom window while he's washing his car."

"Wow." I choke down a burst of laughter. "That's a mouthful. You put *a lot* of thought into that one."

"Sounds like someone is speaking from experience," Blake snickers.

Dora pops another donut in her mouth, this one glazed. "Have you ever even been to Poughkeepsie?"

Zoe blinks. And blinks. "Do you want to die a virgin, Ramos?"

Dora freezes. She's the epitome of wide-eyed innocence. "How do you know I'm a virgin?" The note of challenge in her voice makes me smile. She so seldom sounds confident that it's nice to see her flexing some muscle.

Zoe crosses her slender arms and cocks a hip, her glossy lips lifting in a smug smile, and with each silent moment that passes, Dora's confidence fizzles.

Swallowing the last mouthful, she puts down the box of donuts and sighs. "G-gimme a few minutes to get changed."

A few minutes after that I hear Zoe's voice coming from Dora's room. "No, you're not wearing that…because you're not…because…Blake, explain it to her."

"Nuh huh, keep me out of this."

"Because it makes you look like *Mr. Rogers*. Okay. There, I said it. Now take it off."

I button my worn Levi's, grab my Yankees hat, and make my way there. Inside Dora's room, I find Blake with her lips curled around her teeth, a burst of laughter imminent, while Zoe stares into Dora's closet like she's staring into the bowels of hell.

"Khakis. It's all khakis. Button-downs and khakis," she mutters.

"I don't like to think about w-what I'm wearing." Dora shifts uncomfortably from foot to foot, her cheeks flushing pink.

"Clearly." Zoe looks down at the bottom of the closet. "Are those actual *pennies* in your penny loafers?"

Dora chews on her lips but the corners of her mouth are already lifting. "Umm, maybe."

Zoe throws up her hands. "This wardrobe has officially put me in a sad coma."

* * *

Half an hour and three wardrobe changes later, my crutches earn us seats in the first row of the bleachers around the outdoor pool. The stadium is packed with screaming fans, a highly disproportionate percentage of them female. I'd have to be blindfolded not to notice—and wearing noise-canceling headphones to safeguard my ears from all the trash talk around me.

"I'd do him," one snickers.

"I'd do all of them at once," the other serves back.

Next to me, Dora makes a face and squirms. The tight designer magenta top and white shorts she's wearing are not hers. Quite frankly, watching Zoe harass Dora into borrowing her clothes—in which she looks amazing—was worth the price of having to sit under the blazing sun for an hour.

As soon as we get settled, I go through my routine: adjust my Yankees ball cap low over my eyes, fish the SPF out of my messenger bag that's tucked against my Leica D-Lux, and slather it over my arms and thighs.

Zoe squeezes her skinny ass in between me and Dora and announces, "One game and you'll be a fan for life."

"I'll keep an open mind," I reply dryly, but the truth is I'm already having a blast and the game hasn't even begun yet. I've never had a group of girls to hang out with and damn if it isn't underrated. I haven't had this much fun in forever.

"I love that you think I'm exaggerating right now," Zoe continues, bouncing in her seat. Her giddy delight is starting to rub off on me. "Wait till you see all the tan, wet muscles. All the touching and ass grabbing that goes on."

"What are the r-rules?"

"Similar to basketball."

When neither Dora nor I respond, Zoe rolls her eyes. "Okay, here are the basics: six on six plus the two goalies. You can move the ball by *dribbling* it, which in water polo means swimming with it in front, or they can one-hand pass it forward, sideways, and backward. You get thirty seconds to score. You can't foul by taking someone under, or the ball, but shit happens underwater all the time."

"I'm getting the impression you've attended a few of these?"

Zoe blushes. Actually blushes, something I never thought to witness. "Only the goalie can touch the bottom. The rest have to tread water for four quarters, which are each eight minutes long. And most of the time they last even longer."

Both teams file out of the aquatics building and with the way the crowd goes wild you would think we're at a *One Direction* reunion concert. Among the rabid fan base are Zoe and Blake who raise their arms and shout at the top of their lungs, "Go Sharks!" Then they smash together to take a couple of selfies. When they try to wrangle me and Dora into taking one with them, I steal the iPhone out of Zoe's hand and snap away. I'm an introvert. There's a reason I live behind the camera and not in front of it.

In the meantime, the teams go to their respective benches and start divesting themselves of their clothing. Some of the guys are wearing rip-away track pants and each time a pair comes off the girls around us scream. If I had any doubt whether this was by design, watching the guys smile broadly answers that question.

"Was I right? Am I right?" Zoe squawks over the ruckus, a perfect grin prying her bee-stung lips apart. Her mad enthusiasm has me grinning from ear to ear.

My eyes move to the home bench of their own volition, taking cursory stock of each and every player until they reach the last one. Reagan's head comes up and our eyes lock. For a moment I'm trapped in that gaze, unable to move a muscle as some heavy-duty vibes fly between us. Well, this is inconvenient.

A knowing grin cuts his face in two and I'm jolted out of my trance, my gaze flitting sideways, finding something else to stare at. I'm a coward. I fully admit it. Those go-green eyes have the power to pluck every thought from my head and seeing as some of those thoughts involve him I'd rather keep them to myself.

One by one, the guys jump in the water. Reagan is last. I catch sight of the body Zoe was raving about and holy hell I really need to give the girl some credit. He's a diamond, cut to exacting precision. Broad shoulders, a powerful chest smattered with hair that tapers down to a set of cobbled abs, narrow hips, and muscular thighs. My entire body bursts into flames and it has nothing to do with the blazing SoCal sun.

The players begin swimming warm-up laps, raw power cutting through the water with grace. The screams reach an eardrum-shattering level. The camera comes out. I hold it up, snap away indiscriminately. Some of my favorite shots have been happy accidents and between the colors and all the kinetic energy this moment is rich with possibilities. "I can't believe I'm going to say this but you're right," I begrudgingly admit.

"Of course, I'm right." Zoe grins, full of herself.

"Look at Red—" Blake snickers and hooks a thumb at Dora whose eyes are pinned wide open. "She's in a trance. Can't even answer. Red—"

Leaning over, Zoe snaps her fingers in Dora's face. Dora

swats her hand away and laughter breaks out. "Red, are you breathing? Do you need CPR?"

"Beat on her chest, Zo," Blake yells.

"Those swim trunks are s-small," Dora mumbles.

"And tight," Blake adds, her sculpted eyebrows waggling.

"No Jiffy P-Pop," Dora adds.

"Like the popcorn?" I query, confusion stamped on my face as I picture the tin pans my dad used to use to make popcorn on movie night when I was a kid.

Dora flushes red to the roots of her long auburn hair. "You know…" She chews on her lips, eating away all the gloss. "When you have too m-much hair down there and the suit…"

A dry burst of laughter rips out of me. The ability to visualize in high definition can be a curse sometimes. "Ohhhhh."

"Some of them shave their entire bodies," Zoe remarks with an expression of maniacal reverence. The image this elicits instantly floods my face with heat.

Reagan's silky-smooth junk.

Eyeballing me, Zoe snickers. "You're picturing it, aren't you? I know you are. Don't bother denying it, you filthy animal. I can see it on your face."

Which makes me laugh, overriding any embarrassment.

"I guess I-I'm filthy too, then."

"Ramos—" Zoe holds up a palm and Dora high-fives her. "Welcome to the club."

* * *

REAGAN

As soon as the buzzer sounds, I jump out of the pool and

head to the bench to towel off with the sonic boom of the cheering crowd trailing after me. I am bone-tired. The goal I scored plus Warner's and Dall's led us to beat Cal by two. Part of the reason may or may not have been that I played with a little more motivation than usual.

Alice Bailey.

I never expected to see her at one of my games. Not today, not ever. She doesn't strike me as the type to enjoy athletic competitions of any sort. And yet what did I find as I absently scanned the crowd? The girl who's been keeping me up at nights sitting in the first row of the bleachers with a Yankees ball cap pulled low over her eyes, and those long bare legs stretched out before her. Nice try with the hat, but I'd recognized that face anywhere. I'm having a hard time closing my eyes at night without her flashing dark eyes and heart-shaped ass invading my personal headspace. Which is a major fucking inconvenience since there's no way I can scratch that itch. If I don't find a distraction soon, my dick will go on strike.

I'm in the midst of throwing on a t-shirt and shorts when a commotion at the opposite end of the pool gets my attention. The crowd is slow in leaving the stadium, the usual Speedo chasers hanging around waiting for the guys to leave the aquatics building. A group of people part and a guy stumbles through. My lungs arrest. I can't draw a single breath because it's not just any guy—it's my brother.

He stumbles around in a state of anxious confusion while I'm frozen, rooted to the cement beneath me in shock. My hands shake from an adrenaline rush, the only sign that I can still move my limbs. I can't tear my eyes away from him. His t-shirt, torn and stained. His jeans, worn-out and filthy, look ready to fall off his hips. He's shoeless and dirty and thinner than I've ever seen him.

I haven't seen Brian in three months and not for lack of trying. I've been chasing him all over the damn city. I've got people I've developed relationships with, some I pay to call me if they spot him. And according to them they hadn't seen him either lately. Which was making me think the worst had happened. It's always there, the fear, lurking in the back of my mind.

"Rea…" Dallas murmurs from somewhere behind me. Every set of eyes left in the stadium is staring at him. At my brother the junkie.

"I know," I tell him. He's got my back if I need him but this is my burden to carry. Snapping out of a daze, I make my way over to him, taking with me all the attention in the stadium. Of the spectators. The Speedo chasers still here hoping for a chance to talk to me. The coaching staff. It's about as comfortable as getting a tooth drilled without Novocain.

Brian staggers past them, and on cue the glares and sneers start. His blue eyes are wild as he searches for me amongst the crowd. Hushed whispers and giggles build into open ridicule.

"Who's that?"

"Gross."

"Oh, God. He smells."

"Total junkie."

"Crack kills."

"Lay off the bath salts, dude."

It no longer upsets me the way it used to when I was in high school. I've learned to tune them out—the haters. I've learned to stop throwing punches.

These people don't know him. They don't know that my older brother used to be my best friend. That he was an honor role student, a world-class swimmer, and an exceptional water polo player. Brian's the reason I got into polo in the first place. I wanted to be just like him. Until he met Jessie and everything went to shit. These people have no idea how he got to be a junkie and yet they judge him.

"Brian."

At the sound of my voice he glances my way and relief spreads over his face, which is looking worse for wear these days. His eyes are sunken in and skin leathery from living on the streets. Beard heavy and hair matted. Twenty-four going on a hundred and five.

"Rea—Rea, I need money, man. I need it bad," he says talking fast. He fidgets with his hands, alternating between running them through his matted brown hair and stuffing them in his front pockets. He shifts on his feet. Pupils blown out.

I'm not surprised that he's high. I'm only surprised at how gut-wrenchingly painful it still is to see him like this. After all these years you would think I would've grown accustomed to it.

"Okay, Bri. Come with me and we'll talk."

"I need the money," he insists, his eyes nervously shifting around. Never landing on anything or anyone for too long.

I go to grab him and my hand swallows up his bicep, my fingers completely curling around his arm. It's another stab of pain. A gut check. This time it's coupled with the knowledge that time is running out. That I may not be able to save him from what is starting to look like the inevitable.

I lead him away from the pool, toward the back of the aquatics building where my Jeep is parked. The collective attention of the crowd follows us until we're out of sight, the feeling palpable.

Brian comes reluctantly, mumbling that he needs money, while I keep reassuring him that I have some in the car. I need to get him back to my house and fed. Maybe with a little luck cleaned up…if he'll let me.

"Come home with me and you can have something to eat. Maybe take a shower. I'll give you my clothes…"

He shakes his head and scratches his neck. He's twitching, in need of a fix. "I got people waiting. Maybe next time."

I can't keep the fear out of my eyes. I know it's there as blatantly as I know he doesn't see it. "Brian, c'mon, man. Do it for me. I'm worried about you."

He shakes his head fast, gaze cast on the asphalt. He always hated disappointing me when we were kids. Not everything's changed. "You look like shit. I'm saying this because I'm scared you're going to end up like Jessie." My throat feels thick, swollen with the feeling of helplessness that comes up every time I talk to him.

At the mention of his dead girlfriend his eyes lift and come to life.

"I live in a constant fucking state of fear that I'm going to get a phone call. Don't do that to me, bro."

His face cracks into an awkward smile and I almost find him in there, the brother he was before all this got started.

"I'm…I'm begging you to try rehab one last time."

"Nah. Nah, man," he says, shaking his head really fast and shifting from foot to foot. I look down and notice a deep laceration on his left foot.

"Just one last time. One more chance and I'll never ask again."

"You got the money? I need the money, little brother."

He won't even make eye contact. He's already shut me out. More of the same. This is how it always goes with him. Depressing as shit.

Reaching into the back seat of the Jeep, I pull out a pair of brand-new, limited edition Nikes and hand them over. "Put these on first...and you need to have that cut looked at. It's going to get infected."

Brian quickly drops to the hard ground and jams his dirty, bleeding feet into the shiny, new kicks. Once he's done tying them, he stands and holds out his dry cracked palm. I pull out two fifty-dollar bills and hold them up.

"Do *not* sell those kicks. Call me if you need anything."

He nods. His blue eyes flicker to me and away, to the horizon. I place the bills in his palm and he crumbles them up, stuffs them in the front pocket of his jeans.

"Reynolds—everything alright?" Coach Becker's voice breaks into our quiet moment.

"Yes, sir."

I glance behind me for a split second and that's all it takes for Brian to make a run for it. He's wired, hopped up on meth, and after playing a tough game, I'm exhausted. I take off after him, booking down the grassy hill, but he easily leaves me in the dust. I watch him disappear down the rolling lawn that abuts the highway.

"Brian!" I yell. I don't know why. All the screaming in the world hasn't gotten through to him yet. I should know better by now.

TEN

ALICE

"Which one of you two wants to be designated driver?" Zoe asks me and Dora as we pour out of her car.

Dora and I exchange a look that says *you do it* and not because either of us was planning to get wasted tonight but because neither of us want to be responsible for driving a car that costs close to four years of our college tuition.

I glance at Blake and she raises her wrist and jangles her gold medical bracelet. "I don't drive."

"I'll do it," Dora pipes up and I breathe a sigh of relief.

Music can be heard over the busy traffic racing up and down Pacific Coast Highway. A heavy bass pours out of the house and fills the air around us, making my blood hum. Cars are parallel parked up and down the street, signaling the party is well underway. Zoe insisted we come to this party. Insisted is putting it lightly; she practically dragged Dora and me by the hair and threw us into the car.

The only reason I'm here is because of what I witnessed at the end of the water polo game. One minute I'm laughing with the girls, having a great time, and the next I'm fighting tears.

Because the look on his face, of utter devastation when he saw his brother standing at the side of the pool surrounded by people mocking him...that look split my chest wide open and ripped my heart out.

I'm worried. I know I shouldn't be—he's not mine to worry over. We barely know each other—and yet I can't seem to stop.

Walking down the narrow street, we pass house after house crammed together side by side and hidden behind security walls. Each one bigger than the next. We finally reach our destination and it's not a house. It's a freaking mansion— on the beach. Light pours out of every floor-to-ceiling window overlooking the road. People smoking loiter on the front steps. A group I recognize mill about the small patch of front lawn.

"Stop gawking. It's only a house," Zoe commands. Easy for her to say. She's been around this all her life.

Blake pats my arm and smiles softly. "You'll get used to it."

"Doubt it," I tell her as we file into the jam-packed foyer after Zoe.

"W-what's that smell?" Dora demands to know, her face twisting in a disgusted grimace.

Zoe's feet halt in their tracks. She glances over her shoulder with an expression of utter shock. "You can't be serious?" Her face changes from dubious to confused. "Can you?"

"It s-stinks. I think someone got sprayed by a s-skunk. What's there to joke about?"

"Were you raised in a time capsule from the eighteen hundreds? It's pot, Ramos. You've never smelled pot before?"

Dora's eyes practically bug out of her head and she swiftly pivots on her borrowed heels and turns to leave. Not fast enough, however. Catching her by the shoulders, Zoe stops her before she can make it down the front steps.

"My father's a DEA agent!" Dora whisper-hisses. "I'll get high off the secondhand fumes. We all will!"

"With any luck," is Blake's quick comeback and Zoe and I snicker.

On level ground Zoe has a good four to five inches on Dora. Tonight she's wearing four-inch Louboutin booties with the spikes on them so the disparity is hilarious. Ducking down so they're face-to-face, Zoe calmly says, "First, let's scale down on the melodrama. Second, you're not leaving, Red. You're going to board that courage train and ride it all the way inside the party."

Dora glares. There's a moment of silence, in which Zoe feels compelled to add, "Do you want to be the *40-Year-Old Virgin*? Is that on your vision board?"

Without another word, a sullen Dora drags her feet back into the house, a hand covering her mouth and nose.

"Outta the way, crutches coming through," Blake yells as she splits the crowd. Her long braids swaying down her slender back. She's wearing a body-hugging white t-shit dress that hits mid thigh and tan high-heeled sandals. The stark white against her brown skin makes her look like a living statue. Too good to be real. Necks snap as we follow her across the living room. She's got so much natural, unintentional sex appeal that it's impossible not to stare at her.

There's so much to take in, my eyes don't know where to look first. You could park a small airplane in this place it's so big. This is definitely a party house. Wide-open spaces. Furniture sparse and large to accommodate the size of the guys who live here. Zoe said it belongs to one of the water polo players. Whoever he is he definitely wants for nothing.

A series of glass panels span the entire back of the house that overlooks the patio. All of them wide open. The crowd spills out around a pool lit up in orange, one half of Malibu U school colors, and down to the beach.

I'm gaping. I fully admit it. I've seen ridiculous displays of wealth. Living so close to New York City, it's hard not to. This, however, is silly rich.

Lil Tjay's *Goat* pumps loudly out of the state-of-the-art sound system. Bodies move, swaying to the beat. Arms wave in the air. Solo cups filled with alcohol slosh over the sides, spilling down shirts. Girls laughing. Guys shouting at an enormous wall-mounted television where a basketball game plays.

"This party is lit! Let's head out back," Zoe yells over the music. I can barely hear her. She motions us in the direction of the patio and ventures deeper into the crowd.

We find some open space the size of a postage stamp and park ourselves there. Dora fidgets with the short skirt Zoe made her wear, pulling on the hem, while her eyes dart around in wonder, not sure what to take in first. I'm almost as awestruck. Though I do a better job of concealing it.

"Incoming—mythical creature," Zoe mutters through a fixed smile, the first time I've ever seen her look even remotely uncomfortable.

"Mythical creature?" I repeat with a curious glance at Blake.

"It's a well-known fact that Brock Peterman is a virgin," she explains, her lips tilting up on one side. "Every girl on campus is gunning for him."

A guy approaches, a head taller than just about everyone else and therefore easy to spot. He's wearing a faded blue **Sharks Water Polo** t-shirt, a deep tan, shorts, and flip-flops.

I'm starting to sense a trend here. Do any of these guys ever wear anything else? Is it a rich boy thing, or California thing?

"Well, I'm not," I clarify. No matter how handsome he is. And that, he is—with intense, dark blue eyes and full lips that soften his overly angular features.

"N-neither am I," Dora concurs.

"Me three," Blake adds.

The only one conspicuously silent on the subject is Zoe who is presently surveying the crowd in an attempt to pretend she didn't hear us. Her face grows tighter the closer he gets.

"Zoe—" Peterman calls out and Zoe's head whips around, her shy smile blossoming into a full one. I've never seen her look so...vulnerable. Or genuinely happy for that matter. Which answers some of my questions and produces more.

"Hey, P.K."

Set in a severe line, his lips part to reveal optic white teeth while his warm gaze takes its sweet time moving over her face. "Wanna go over notes tomorrow?"

His deep, smooth voice makes something as boring as studying sound sexy. And going by the look on Zoe's face, I'm pretty sure I just heard her designer panties go up in flames.

A beat later he seems to recall that they are not in a bubble. His indigo eyes move to me and Dora and a question mark appears in them. One Zoe is quick to answer. "Brock, this is Dora and Alice. You know Blake."

His chin tips up. "Ladies." His attention immediately returns to Zoe. "How's late afternoon? We can meet at the library?"

She looks up at him with so much undisguised awe that it almost feels like we're intruding on an intimate moment.

"Brock—" yet another deep voice murmurs.

A tall black guy walks up and I'm instantly struck by his eyes. Large, golden, and rimmed in something darker. I can't get a good read on the color because it seems to change with the way they catch light. They're mesmerizing. And he just caught me staring. Great.

"Shane—Zoe, Dora, Blake, and…"

"Alice," I finish for him.

Shane's questioning gaze tags Brock's. "Phone-tree girl?"

Phone-tree girl? I'm confused.

One corner of Brock's mouth hikes up and he nods. Which only confuses me more. Shane smiles. It's brief and brilliant, and so precious I can see why he doles it out in very small portions. "'Sup, ladies." His attention immediately returns to Brock, expression turning grim. "Caught a couple of dudes doing bumps in the bathroom."

Brock's face darkens. "Ours?"

Shane shakes his head. "Never seen them before."

"Do me a favor and toss them out." Shane starts to leave and Brock catches him by the arm. "Take Quinn and Cole with you."

Shane nods and a beat later he melds into the crowd.

"I am a golden god!" someone shouts from the second-floor balcony.

All heads tilt back to witness a guy standing on the railing. Wild curly blond hair. Chest bare with his arms spread wide. His body is a patchwork of carved muscles that descend into a deep V at the edge of his low-slung board shorts. An intricate tattoo covers his left pec, snakes over his shoulder, and down his arm.

"Way to rip off *Almost Famous*, dude," a male voice emerges from the crowd.

"I fucking hate these parties," Brock groans.

"Jump, jump, jump," the chants start.

Scowling, Brock brackets his lush mouth with his hands and shouts back, "Do NOT jump. You'll break your neck, asshole." He glances back at Zoe and says, "Be right back," before walking off to deal with his friend.

"Dallas Van Zant is a certified idiot," Zoe mutters.

"He's not that bad," Dora counters.

Well, this is curious. All three of us turn to stare at her. Wide and innocent, her big brown eyes dart back and forth between us.

"What? We have English lit together." She shrugs. "He's a lot smarter than people think."

No stutter. Her adamant defense of him also noteworthy. Hmm.

I bookmark it, save the questions for later because Dallas (smarter than people think) cannonballs into the pool and displaces most of the water onto the people crowded around it. We scrabble away in time to avoid getting hit. The group of girls standing nearby, however—not so lucky. They scream as they bear the brunt of it.

"Most of the time," Dora amends.

"Zo-ho, trolling for dick as usual," a male voice calls out, loud enough for everybody around us to hear.

Zoe stiffens. Her hard stare veers to a guy who slowly approaches with two others right behind him.

He's stocky. With espresso dark hair and even darker eyes hidden beneath the flat brim of a Malibu University Baseball team cap. All three are wearing Under Armour shirts painted to their ripped chest, silky shorts hanging to their knees.

Brock returns almost simultaneously and wedges himself between Zoe and the trio, essentially creating a human wall.

Zoe flips the troublemaker off and he returns a sly half smile. More of a leer. This guy is objectively attractive, but seems almost a cartoon villain with all the posturing.

"The bird? Really, Zo-ho, that's the best you can do?" he says with a humorless chuckle.

Zoe tilts her head, slouches. The epitome of lazy indifference. "I wasn't flipping you off, Kellan. I was showing the girls the size of your dick." Scanning our frozen expressions, she showcases her finger. "This is what it looks like hard. I can't recommend it."

Strangled bursts of laughter come from Kellan's entourage and the pretense of a smile he's wearing quickly transforms into an expression of barely leashed rage. He takes a step closer and Brock stiffens, looking down on Kellan with clear warning in his hard stare.

"Take another step and you'll get these straight in the sphincter," Zoe calmly states. She points to the Louboutin heels she's wearing, the ones with the tiny studs on them. "Although you might like it and we both know what I mean."

Then she lifts her hands in a gesture of surrender. "No judgment."

Kellan turns cherry red.

"Keep walking, Blythe," Brock orders. At the same time he pins Zoe with a silent command to stop, a flare of anger turning the sharp edges of his cheekbones pink under his deep tan. "Keg's that way." He points to the far side of the patio. "Move, or I'll escort you out."

Kellan's furious glare shifts between Zoe and Brock. He mutters, "Bitch," as he walks away with his friends. This is better than binging on an entire season of *Gigolos*.

Brock's frown persists and it's aimed at Zoe.

"What?" she says, uncertainty drawn on her delicate features.

He shakes his head. "That was harsh."

Zoe's eyes go theatrically wide. "Did you hear what he called me?"

"He's an asshole," Brock practically growls. "Everybody knows it. Why can't you ignore him?"

I can feel the weight of his judgment and it's not even directed at me. Zoe's face falls, her confidence wanes.

"I didn't start it—" she argues quietly.

"You bait him."

"Brock…"

He exhales loudly, tugs at the collar of his t-shirt. "You're better than that." He turns to leave and Zoe blanches.

"Brock…"

Casting one last disappointed look at her, he walks away. And leaves behind a vacuum. The silence stifling. We all exchange looks while Zoe stares after his broad, retreating back. Her body stiff, her hands fisted at her sides, eyes glassy.

"You're designated driver, Ramos." Her voice sounds flat. No sign of the kick-ass Zoe I've come to love and appreciate. I hate seeing her like this.

"Sure...y-yeah."

She holds up her keychain. Dora takes it and Zoe turns to Blake. "Let's party."

ELEVEN

ALICE

By midnight, the luster of the party has worn off and I'm ready to go home. While Zoe is hammered, Blake's not quite there yet. For the past hour, the two of them have been taking turns playing an arcade video game with a couple of random guys in the game room (yes, this house has a game room) while Dora and I have been watching from the wings.

"Three out of five," one of the guys announces while Blake and Zoe celebrate another victory by high-fiving each other.

"Didn't they say that when they lost the last two sets?" I toss out.

"Last three," Dora corrects.

"Do you want to get out of here? My armpit is starting to hurt again."

She nods enthusiastically, which makes me chuckle. It wouldn't be a stretch to say Dora's here against her will. "I'm heading to the bathroom. Be right back," I tell her as I push away from the wall behind me.

It's nearly impossible to move around the packed house. I get jostled and pushed around. The sweaty bodies buttressing me are the only reason I'm still upright.

Reagan's nowhere to be seen. Makes sense. I doubt he was in the mood to come out for a party tonight. Win or no win.

Halfway across the room I pass Brock, who's deep in conversation with the blond guy, Dallas. His expression serious, big hand gripping Dallas's shoulder. "I'm worried about you..." I hear him tell his teammate.

I catch his eyes and ask him where I can find the bathroom. Meanwhile the blond conducts a blank-faced inspection of me, his bright blue eyes sharp and assessing. Nothing about his demeanor indicates he's high or drunk so I assume the reckless behavior comes naturally.

"End of the hallway on the right," Brock shouts back and returns to his conversation.

Getting through the crowd takes forever. When I finally reach the hallway, it's blessedly empty. And long. Door after door confuses me.

Did he say last door? On the right or left? I can't think straight with the music blasting. Consequently, I pick a random door on the right and push it open.

Wrong door. Definitely wrong door.

Two girls and a guy occupy a large bed. He's lying prone. One girl, a blonde, rides his dick and the other, a brunette, his face, which is obscured save for the dark hair against the pillow.

A creepy sensation rides across my skin.

The blonde girl moans. The other shouts. Meanwhile I can't move a muscle. I'm rooted to the floor for what feels like forever, long enough for the chick on his face to come loudly.

My gaze lowers to the tiny dolphin etched on the outside

of his calf. The girl riding his dick turns and giggles and his big hand squeezes her thigh. I think to myself, *she sounds drunk*. Which doesn't matter, but manages to snap me out of my paralysis and sends me into action.

Slamming the door shut, I stand there for a moment to process what I just witnessed. My heart crawls up into my throat and my stomach turns into a churning cauldron of bile. My body knows there's something wrong before my brain can catch up.

Long tan muscles. A dolphin tattoo on the outside of his calf. Brown hair.

That's why I haven't seen him all night. He was celebrating the victory at a private party of three. Or drowning his sorrows. Either way he was having a great time while I was worrying about him.

I'm stuck again, unable to move, shock and disappointment serving as lead weights strapped to my ankles. And even though I know I have no right to be upset, I'm devastated. Accomplished athlete usually equals a string of bed buddies. Hot, accomplished athlete means lower your expectations into a grave and throw dirt on top. But for whatever reason I wanted to believe he was different. That's on me—my fault.

Weak-kneed, I lumber down two more doors. Guys like Reagan Reynolds don't do girlfriends because they don't need to, I remind myself. Not when he has so much being offered to him on a silver platter. Why would anyone choose to eat hamburgers and French fries every day, no matter how much they love hamburger and French fries, when they have a veritable smorgasbord of delights to choose from? They wouldn't. And do I blame him? Hell no. I wish I could *be* him.

All the same, it's time to stow this festering attraction someplace where it will never see the light of day again.

The urge to leave is a strong one. Mood bruised, I contemplate walking out the door and springing for an Uber with money I can't spare. I can text the girls once I'm in the car. They'll understand. First, I need to find a bathroom.

Grabbing the last knob on the right, I send up a prayer to the Lord to cut me a break and let this be it. Unlocked, the door swings open.

"Uhhh...sorry," I mumble.

Lying on a bed with one hand tucked under his head and another clutching a beer bottle, Reagan tears his gaze away from whatever's got his attention on the television and aims those go-green eyes at me.

No random girl is riding his dick, or his face. Blessed be the Lord.

"Bailey?" I don't answer right away because I'm much too busy doing a full-on Alvin Ailey modern dance routine in my head.

My eyes fall on the tattoo on the outside of his calf. They slow-climb up his tanned legs, get past the long gray basketball shorts, skim over the black t-shirt, and reach his messy brown hair.

"Bailey," he repeats more forcefully and this time my gaze snaps back to his face. His brow quirks and his mouth lifts into a weak smile.

"I was justlookingforthebathroom," comes out a hot freaking mess.

This night is quickly descending into black comedy

territory. I sound like a breathless twelve-year-old speaking to her first crush and he's looking at me like I just grew a dildo in the middle of my forehead—familiar but at the same time out of context and confusing.

Reagan points to a door within his room. "You can use mine."

Only now do I note where I am. And his bedroom is swank. Dark contemporary designer furniture instead of Ikea and hand-me-downs. Silky gray linens. Trophies lined up on top of a built-in bookcase...a bookcase. Wow. I don't know anyone who lives this well, let alone a college student. "You live here?"

"Seems I do," he replies flatly, his expression missing the carefree teasing smirk he usually wears. I should leave, turn around and excuse myself. That's the smart thing to do. "Are you going to stand there acting weird all night, or are you coming in?"

I hop inside and gently shut the door behind me because, you know, I like to torture myself for a good time. "I'm not *acting weird*," I say, hiding behind an annoyed tone. This profoundly witty comeback is followed by a sixty-second stare-off, which I end by hopping as quickly as I can to the bathroom.

I'm acting weird.

The bathroom is about as big as my entire dorm room. Maybe even bigger. And tidier—I'm ashamed to admit. I do my business, and afterward, simply because I cannot help myself, I trample his privacy by conducting a thorough examination of his personal items.

The cologne he uses is French and expensive. I take the top

off, sniff. It smells like cedarwood and musk. The perfect blend designed to transform the entire female population into a pack of panting sex zombies.

His toothpaste is the whitening kind. *Hey! Same one I use*, I think to myself and officially flirt with rock bottom on the pathetic scale.

The designer shampoo is a brand you can only get at a department store. And last but not least, a pack of magnum condoms—ribbed for her pleasure. I shake the box and determine it's still full.

Thy name is shameless.

After running the faucet to cover my tracks, I step out of the bathroom and find him sitting up against the padded headboard.

"Did you look through my stuff?" His smile is lazy and one-sided

"Hate to be the one to let the air out of your ego bag, but you're not that interesting, Reynolds." What's left of my conscience tells me I'm going to pay for this disgusting lie at a later date.

My attention follows Reagan's back to the television screen and any lingering amusement I was feeling over my snooping dies a sudden death when I see what's playing. A home movie with the sound muted. Two young and very tan boys shove each other playfully as they stand at the edge of a backyard pool. They dive in and race head-to-head in an American crawl.

"My brother…" he tells me in a low husky voice. He has eyes only for the television. "Brian was eleven and I was eight." Raising the longneck beer bottle to his lips, he drinks.

"Want one?"

"No, thanks."

"Have a seat."

I slow-hop to his enormous bed and sit on the foot of it, back erect. The crutch falls to the floor and a hiss of satisfaction leaves my lips as I rub my aching armpit, the left one still bruised.

I can feel him watching me. The back of my head burns as if I've developed supernatural sensors for him.

Glancing over my shoulder, I find his head tipped back against the navy blue padded headboard and his blank stare moves from my ass, which is directly in his line of sight, up to my face.

"You're not in danger, Bailey. Take a load off that ankle." He pats the spot next to him on the bed with a gleam of mischief in his eyes.

"Only because you're not driving." He winces and I immediately regret my shitty joke.

I feel stupid declining. I'm the one that barged in and intruded in his sacred space, his bedroom. Playing the role of the virgin ingénue seems kind of dumb. So after a moment of indecisiveness, I scoot up and stretch out my legs, mirroring his position against the headboard. I'll be twenty-one in a month. I'm a college junior. I can vote, for Pete's sake. I can be cool about this.

The white denim miniskirt I borrowed from Zoe rides up. It becomes practically nonexistent once I'm fully on the bed. Trying not to draw too much attention to it, I fight with the hem.

"Having trouble with your skirt?"

If I can leave with just a little piece of my dignity intact tonight, it'll be a miracle. "It's not mine," says the part of me that has no problem throwing Zoe under the bus to preserve even a smidge of it. And I am *this* close to adding, "I don't know how it got on me."

He takes another sip of his beer as he studies me. "How is it?"

"Too short."

"I mean the ankle."

"Oh. Better. Not as swollen." I wiggle my bare toes that are poking out from the ACE bandage. "That doesn't hurt anymore." Female laughter drifts in, the sound of footsteps walking past his door.

"I thought the room before yours was the bathroom." An involuntary smile spreads across my face.

"It's Cole's bedroom," he casually informs me, not at all aware of where I'm going with it.

"Mmmyeah." My face gets warm.

He eyeballs my profile and a crooked grin comes and goes. "Did Cole have company?"

"Mmmyeah."

"More than one?"

I nod slowly. "An image that will stay with me forever."

He chuckles and I flush to the roots of my hair. His amusement fades. It blends into a tension-filled silence. I've never felt at a disadvantage around him before.

Annoyed? Definitely. Amused? A lot. Vulnerable? Not till now.

Unable to bear it for very long, I find myself bridging the silence by babbling. "Why do you guys have the same dolphin tattoo?"

He makes a face. His mouth puckers. "It's a shark...a shark, Bailey. As in Malibu Sharks water polo."

Laughter builds in my chest, dying to come out. "But it's got a cute little bottle nose."

"It's a man eater with razor-sharp teeth." He fake chomps the air.

"The game was a lot of fun today. It was very..." What's the word that won't get me in trouble? "Dynamic."

"Yeah?" He chuckles. At me, it sounds like.

"It's exhausting just watching. You must be in great shape. I mean, you are in great shape, obviously. What I meant was aerobically. Like...you must have good lungs."

Good lungs? Wtf, Bailey?? Just shut up.

"Was this your first sporting event?"

I swear there's laughter in that question. Hidden, but it's there. "Give me a little cred, would you. I went to a football game once."

A coy smile appears. "I'm flattered."

"I didn't say I went to watch you."

"But we both know you did," he responds without missing a beat.

Shaking my head, I chew on my lower lip to impede the grin parting my lips. My attention returns to the screen, where more of the home movie plays.

"That was your brother today...at the game?" He nods. "I'm sorry," I murmur.

He exhales audibly. "Yeah. Me too."

The importance of the moment is not lost on me. He's trusting me and I need to tread carefully. I don't want my sympathy to be misconstrued for pity. I'm fairly certain he wouldn't appreciate it. Hence, I carefully contemplate my words before speaking, clear my throat, and start.

"How long has he—"

"Since high school—" he says beating me to the finish line, his gaze far away as the movie ends and the screen goes dark. "A long time."

"Your parents must be worried sick." Which is entirely true. Whose parents wouldn't be anxiety ridden over a son being a drug addict and, judging by Reagan's brother's appearance, living on the streets.

Reagan snickers. There's no real humor in it, though. It's dark and cynical and makes me dread whatever else he's about to say. "They *were* worried. For about a minute. They tried to fix the problem and when their best efforts failed they gave up on him."

"They gave up on him? What do you mean?"

Releasing a heavy sigh, he looks out the large window. It makes me wonder what he's looking for. Relief? Answers? A moment's respite from all the heavy feelings? I don't know, can't say for sure, but when his attention returns to me he looks tired.

"They forced him into rehab three times. It was easy while he was still a minor. But then he turned eighteen and they, uh...they gave up." Lost in thought, he shakes his head. "Stopped trying to get through to him. They threatened to have him arrested if he came by the house...cut him out of the family like he was already dead to them."

My hand automatically moves to cover my mouth. "That's..." I eat my words, not sure what's okay to say or not say. I'm appalled that anyone would do that to their own son. But does he want to hear that I think his parents are monsters? Probably not.

"Fucked up," he finishes for me. "Yeah. It is."

"You're close? With your brother?"

"Used to be."

A commiserative silence falls between us.

"I don't remember my mother," dribbles out of me. "She died when I was five...cancer," I add before he can ask. Because inevitably everyone asks.

His head turns, he holds my startled gaze. Startled because I don't talk about my mother. Not to anyone. Mostly because of what I just confessed to a basic stranger. "I can't remember anything about her." I shrug. "Except that I liked the sound of her voice and she would snuggle with me and watch movies." I brush my damp palms on my denim miniskirt and shift uncomfortably. "It makes me feel guilty that I can't remember her. That I can't...miss her."

"You were five—" I nod. "A baby. Why would you expect to remember her?"

Guilt is a strange thing, a self-inflicted wound that's hard to heal because your own mind keeps opening it up.

"I don't know, I just do. You can't reason with guilt."

His brow furrows. "Yeah, maybe you're right."

His gaze cuts to my lips and the silence thickens again, buzzing with pent-up sexual tension. I can't be the only one feeling it. The air around us pulses with it, my body becoming increasingly aware of the lack of space between us. Heat travels south of my waist and north to my face.

Not a moment later reality intrudes in the form of a sharp

knock. "Reagan?" a girl's voice calls out. It puts a quick end to the heat.

Reagan places his index finger to his mouth gesturing for me to stay quiet while some heavy eyes-to-lips contact happens.

On the other side of his door, the girls speak in hushed voices. More is said that we can't make out. Then we both hear a distinguishable, "Whatever. He's not in his bedroom. Come on, Kaitlyn. Let's check the beach."

At the sound of footsteps moving away, he gets up and retrieves a water bottle out of a small refrigerator. "Want one?"

"No. I'm good." But I'm not good. I'm irked. He doesn't even have to go out for it. The "smorgasbord" has legs, probably long tan ones, and it comes to him.

He drains the entire bottle in a few long gulps, chucks it into a bin, and lies back down. Closer this time—a lot closer. Every nerve ending in my body starts calculating exactly how close.

"You missed the party," he says, voice low and raspy.

"I'm not much of a party girl."

I've always been more of a one-on-one person. Parties force me to seek out conversation and that's not my jam. I'm more of a hang-back-and-observe kinda girl. "I always end up hanging in a corner, wondering why I'm at a party in the first place." More heated glances get exchanged, making me increasingly more uncomfortable. "Anyway, my friends are probably looking for me. I should, umm...get going."

"Do you guys need a ride back? I only had the one beer. I can drive."

"No. That's alright. Dora's the designated driver." A

question crosses his face. "A friend," I answer. "We live in the same dorm suite."

He gets off the bed and I throw my legs over the side, reach for my crutch. He beats me to it, props it up for me, and holds out his other hand, palm up.

I stare at it the same way I stared at it the first time he offered it to me. At the ridge of calluses, the pale skin of his long thick fingers. What would it feel like to have those hands all over my body? This time I don't want to refuse.

I place my hand in his and his fingers, warm and strong, close around it. He pulls me up and doesn't let go until I'm safely balanced on my one crutch. Our bodies are only inches apart. And while his eyes say go, the rest of his face holds a fair bit of reluctance.

"Bailey…"

"Yeah…"

He sighs deeply, gaze flickering over my features. "I can't do relationships. I can't. I have medical school next year and…" His voice fades, lips fall shut. His gaze stays on me shuttered, reserved.

Even though I am painfully aware that I am not the type of girl he dates, it's hard to hear it said out loud. I turn redder than hot sauce. Regardless, he's right. We both have goals to accomplish and lives leading in separate directions. I can't lose sight of that. I only have so much time and money.

"Hey, don't beat yourself up. A lot of guys your age struggle with it. Just keep working on it and you'll be fine. There are a lot of books on the subject. Maybe there's even a TED talk you could watch on YouTube."

A wide grin splits his face in two. The first true carefree

grin all night. "I guess I deserve that."

"We're good, Flipper. I'm not looking for one, either." Which is mostly the truth. I'm not looking, but if one finds me I'd go with it.

A faint smile remains. "Thanks for keeping me company. I really wasn't in the mood to be out there"—he tips his chiseled chin at the door—"tonight."

Despite all the inconvenient heat between us, I can be his friend…and I can let him be mine. "Thanks for giving me your corner to hang in."

"It's yours, Bailey. Anytime."

"Only friends, then." Because sorry not sorry—I am not about to become part of his walking buffet.

He goes to speak and pauses. Nods. "Friends."

TWELVE

REAGAN

I walk into the aquatics center ten minutes before practice is due to start. Our head coach practically built this house. Five of the seven NCAA championship banners draped along the walls are a testament to not only his skill as a coach, but also as a motivator.

The guys are already either undressing by the bench or stretching. Armed with a heavy dose of resolve, I approach Coach Becker as he's nearing the pool. I figure if I got him in public he'd have less of a chance to think through what I'm about to ask of him.

"Coach, can I talk to you?" I murmur. No way do I want the guys sticking their noses in this. Coach eyeballs my neutral expression. I'm not giving anything away until I'm good and ready.

"Gimme a minute, Reynolds," he tells me, then scans the crowd milling around the edge of the pool. "Van Zant?" he shouts. "Where the fuck's Van Zant?" Coach searches us one by one. "Moss?"

Warner stops stretching. "Yeah, Coach?"

"You seen him?"

"No, sir," Moss returns immediately.

"Reynolds?"

"No, sir."

Coach grimaces. The guys glance around the group. Mostly because they all know the drill—if one of us is in the doghouse, we all are.

The name Terry Becker is synonymous with legend in men's water polo and it's well-earned. He's won everything there is to win. An Olympic medal. The coveted Peter J. Cutino award as the nation's best player while he was at Cal. Five championships as a head coach.

He doesn't suffer fools and he has even less tolerance for guys that aren't serious about this sport. Which is why he flushes deep red all the way to his graying blond hairline when he sees Dallas stroll through the double doors without a care in the world.

"Here," Dallas shouts. He does not have the look of a guy that's five minutes late to practice and on the verge of being eaten alive by Coach Becker. "Sorry, Coach. Late getting back from an appointment in Beverly Hills." He shucks off his t-shirt and shorts.

Coach plants his hands on his hips, a twitch pulling at the corner of his left eye. "Getting your hair highlighted?"

"No, sir. These are natural," Dallas answers flatly and points to his head. "Thanks to Brenda Van Zant." Then he cannonballs into the water and the rest of us groan because we know what's coming next.

Guys come from Hungary, Montenegro, even as far away as Australia to make this team. There's a string of them sitting on the bench ready to take Dall's place at a moment's notice. And yet, despite all the stunts he pulls, Coach has yet to bench him because Dallas is by far the best driver we have. Quick as lightning and just as deadly.

So he'll make the rest of us suffer instead.

Coach nods slowly. "In honor of Van Zant's oversized testicles the rest of you ladies will now do an extra fifteen minutes of eggbeater intervals. I want you crossing the length of the pool and outta the water waist high."

More groans.

Heads swivel in Dall's direction and everybody issues death warrants with their eyeballs. Unfazed, Dallas shakes out his hair and flips them off, double-handed.

"You, Van Zant, will be benched for the first quarter of the game this weekend."

I never thought I'd see the day. And by the sound of the quiet gasps and muted murmurs, neither did any of the other guys.

"What?!" Dallas shouts, all trace of amusement dropping from his face.

"You heard me, princess. Everybody in the water while I speak to Reynolds." He waves me over. "Let's hear it, son."

* * *

After practice we all meet up at the quad near the cafeteria.

"What are you smiling at?" Dallas says, sitting next to me on the stone bench. Across the way, my eyes find Jersey girl the instant she makes it up the steps.

"Nothing," I answer absently, incapable of peeling my

eyes off of her.

I was a wreck Saturday night, the lowest I've been in a long time and she was…well…amazing. A surprise, a comfort, everything I needed.

On crutches, she slowly makes her way to the cafeteria entrance and pauses to take in the view. From this vantage point, the scenery looks unreal, worthy of a screen saver, and I grew up here. I wonder what she's thinking.

"That's the chick you ran over?"

Glancing sideways, I catch Dall's eyes all over her. He runs a hand through his wild hair and smirks, causing an uncomfortable twist of my gut.

"Almost ran over."

"Not much of a rack but her ass and legs are a ten. Now I know why you mobilized the entire team to get her info."

Head shaking, I'm quick to correct him. "It's not like that."

Most days I already feel like Atlas carrying the weight of the world on my shoulders. Between keeping up my grades, getting into medical school, and leading this team to another national title, there's no room for anything else. Most of all for a girlfriend. And this is definitely the type of girl that requires commitment and promises I don't have it in me to give. Despite what she said the other night.

"You guys grab food yet?" Cole asks, walking up with Brock, a couple of the younger guys, Warner, Shane, and Quinn.

"Waiting for your lazy ass," Dallas tells Cole.

"We're all a little spent from your bullshit. You happy about being benched this weekend?"

Dallas shrugs. Though it doesn't hide his thoughts. Or the

way his amusement dims. Typical Dallas. He'd rather cut his arm off than admit he's upset.

His attention returns to Alice. "You didn't tell us she's hot, Rea. I'd do her."

I knew it was too much to ask that he drop it. "Keep your voice down, dickhead." All the guys turn to stare at her and a feeling of hyper-awareness creeps up my neck. "And you'd do anyone," I point out the obvious.

"Erroneous," Dallas fires back, pretending to be offended. "Erroneous fucking assumption. Did I do that UCLA Kappa chick that was all over me last year? No, I did not."

"Only because Calvert warned you she'd gone fatal attraction on him," Brock rebuts.

"This one definitely kicks it old school which means she's off-limits to you savages. Mitts. Off—you feel me?" I warn and mean it. The thought of any of these guys touching Bailey makes my blood curdle.

"What about you, Rea?" Dallas chimes in. "She off-limits to you too?"

I shrug, not giving him the satisfaction. "I'm not in the market for a girlfriend." And that's the absolute truth. No matter how cute she is when she laughs and that she gets all my movie references. This year is about some well-earned fun, and a girlfriend doesn't belong anywhere near that equation.

"I kick it old school." Brock's deep voice slices into the conversation like a hot knife into butter. Every head on the team swivels in the big guy's direction. To call him quiet is a serious understatement. So when he does speak, people tend to pay attention. "Does that mean she's not off-limits to me?"

"Ho-ly shit. Could this be the angel sent from heaven to

finally steal your cherry, B?" Dallas stands on the bench with a hand over his heart. "Because if you've got your sweet feelings set on her, who am I to stand in the way of a brother entering into manhood."

Brock's mouth tilts in a wry smile. That's all the reaction Dallas's ball busting gets. Brock's one of those rare individuals who's immune to other people's opinions. "Fucking doesn't make me a man, bro. If that were the case, you'd be ten times the man you are."

"Oooo...Dayum...Dallie, he murdered your ass," the chorus shouts, one over the other.

Grinning, Dallas opens his arms wide and advances on Brock. "I hate it when we fight, sugar bear. Let's kiss and make up." Brock pushes him off as Dallas attempts to throw his arms around his neck.

"I'll give ya a kiss, Dallie." Quinn leans back in his seat on the bench, arms crossed. He's wearing the same sly look I've seen on him when he's baiting an opposing team's player. This usually precedes one, or more of us, getting thrown out of the pool for a foul.

"Smith—" I shake my head. "Give it a rest, man," I beg before it goes any further. I swear he loves to get under D's skin.

Dallas flips him off and returns a similar smirk. "Fuck you, Quinn, you fucking slut. If I was bent, you wouldn't be my type."

Quinn snickers. It's common knowledge that he burned through the West Hollywood scene as soon as he stepped foot in Southern California—something he openly brags about.

And since Quinn literally fought his way out of the slums

of Liverpool, having his nose broken three times and losing a spleen before his fourteenth birthday because it "didn't feel right" to hide his sexuality, he now does whatever the hell he wants, with whomever he wants, whenever he wants. And don't get in his way, or pay the consequences in blood.

He's also ranked best goalie in the league so none of us give a single shit what he does in his spare time. Or how many.

"Pot, meet kettle, wanker," is his quick response to that.

While that goes on, Brock's attention returns to me as if to say, *well?* A flare of heat shoots up my neck. Shit. Am I attracted to her? She's got curves in all the right places. That heart-shaped ass would make a man a nice soft place to land. I'd have to be gay not to notice. But is it more than that?

It can't be.

B watches me intently. As much as I want to deny it, I just can't seem to form the words. A slow cat-that-ate-the-canary smile grows on his face. "Thought so."

I get up, rake my fingers through my hair, stretch out my back.

"Rea! Where are you going?" Dallas shouts from somewhere behind me.

My feet carry me away before I even know how to answer.

* * *

ALICE

"Jersey," I hear while I'm in line to pay for my turkey sandwich.

I'm starving. Having both crutches tucked under one arm and the food tray in the other is a gamble. Considering the hole in my gut, however, it's one I'm willing to take.

Reagan walks up to me wearing a lopsided grin, the plate tectonics of his face shifting to render him even more tediously handsome. All over the cafeteria, heads lift. Gazes sharpen. It's a given that wherever Reagan Reynolds goes so do eyeballs. Case in point, most of the people in this joint are watching us. Which makes my skin crawl.

There's a good reason I live behind the camera: I'm a natural-born observer. All my instincts rebel at the notion of being on the receiving end of any attention and this is *a lot* of attention.

"Well if it isn't *the* Reagan Reynolds."

The flash in his eyes has an involuntary smile sneaking up on me. There's something innately smile-inducing about Reagan. Gorgeous face not included.

He takes inventory of my situation—the tray I'm holding, the crutches—and frowns. Then, ever the gentleman, he reaches out for my food tray and practically knocks me to the ground in the process.

The crutches clatter loudly. I wobble, on the verge of face-planting. But right before that can happen, a muscular arm wraps around my waist and saves me.

"Is someone paying you to maim me? Or are you really this sloppy out of the water?" While the people in line behind me graciously pick up my crutches and hand them to me, he pulls me closer. A smirk already in place.

"Trust me, I've got rhythm where it counts," he murmurs quietly for my ears only. His eyes move over my face and pause on my lips.

He's an unapologetic flirt, that's for sure. "You did not just say that."

"I think I did—"

"What a cheeseball you turned out to be."

On a deep inhale, I catch a whiff of him. The subtle scent of laundry detergent, a trace of chlorine, and a hint of eau de stud muffin. I waste no time sucking in more of it.

He pulls away, helps me find my balance on the crutches, and gently lets go. I feel strangely bereft without the hard, steady presence of his body anchoring me down. This friends-only thing sucks.

And to add insult to injury I haven't been on a date in forever. And when I say *been on a date,* I mean I haven't had sex since senior year in high school. That's embarrassing! But I won't apologize for being choosy about my sexual partners. The sizzle hardly ever happens to me and I need sizzle to sleep with someone. Otherwise, what's the point? I'll satisfy my own needs. Problem is, I'm currently experiencing sizzle with the wrong person. One that's not interested in anything sizzle related with me. Like I said, this friends-only thing sucks.

"Mind if I eat with you? I have an hour before my next class."

I peek around his shoulder, and through the glass-paned wall that overlooks the quad, I spot his teammates still out there. Every single one of them is tall, tan, armed with a thousand-watt smile and the confidence to flaunt it. It's not fair. And a hazard to the general public. Traveling in a pack of guys that smoking hot should be criminalized. People could injure themselves rubbernecking to stare.

The reckless blond, Dallas, catches sight of us and alarm bells ring. It's only a matter of time before they all migrate over here and if one likes to fly under the radar like I do it's enough to make one want to run.

"Aren't your friends waiting for you?" Fingers crossed he gets the hint that I don't want to be around when they do.

He follows my gaze over his shoulder and pauses at the sight of his friends. When his attention returns to me, he's wearing a teasing smile. "They know how to feed themselves. Come on, let's grab a table and I'll get our food."

Without waiting for a reply, he escorts me to an empty one and leaves. Ten minutes later he's placing a tray in front of me with the same turkey sandwich, Terra chips, and bottle of water I was about to buy before he crashed into me.

"Did you find a new job yet?" he says as he bites into the first of his turkey sandwich. There's two of them on his tray. Plus a large bag of chips, yogurt, and an apple. Can one human actually consume this much food? I'm about to find out.

"Bailey? I said, did you find another job yet?"

My eyes widen, the question catching me off guard. I spent hours last night scouring the campus job listings for something office related that wouldn't require me to stand and once again I came up with zilch.

"No." I shake my head and take a big bite of my sandwich to hide my rising anxiety. If I don't find something soon, I won't have any choice other than to do the unthinkable.

"If I can't find anything by the end of the week, I'll have to put my camera up for sale."

I don't know what to make of his expression. Contemplative maybe? Yeah, that's it. He nods slowly as he chews his food.

"Hey, Reagan," a small, curvy girl with shiny black hair says as she walks up to the table. Her face and all the perfect makeup she's wearing look like they both stepped out of a YouTube beauty channel. She checks me out—dismisses me just as quickly. Heat ramps up my neck and paints my cheeks.

"Hi, Layla." Reagan smiles. One of his well-oiled ones. The one he uses for cover. I don't know who he's fooling with that smile.

Layla's dark almond-shaped eyes dart between me and him. She's late to realize he doesn't intend to say more. "I guess I'll see you in class."

"Yeah, see you later."

Layla reluctantly leaves and a few taut minutes of silence happen. I'm about to speak when he beats me to it.

"I think I have something for you."

I'm immediately suspicious. And although I'm endeavoring not to jump to the wrong conclusion, we've already established that it's not so easy for me. That said, I trust Reagan. He's proven himself worthy.

Saturday night was...heavy. A turning point for us, I think.

He shared very personal information with me. I did the same with him. I still can't believe I did that. It's way out of character for me to speak about myself. And yet with Reagan it felt natural. Unforced. The definition of which completely escaped Jack, my one and only relationship.

"Umm, okay...like a job?" I get out between sips of water.

"No. A puppy."

At my blank stare, he grins. "Yes, a job. Jesus, don't look so suspicious. I'm not going to ask you to blow the entire water polo team."

Water comes shooting out of my nose. I nearly cough up a lung. He gets up, his chair scraping back loudly, and starts pounding on my back.

Once my coughing fit ends he sits back down and explains. "Coach is looking for someone to take pictures and some video...maybe even tape an interview or two for a recruiting campaign."

I take a gulp of water and exhale. Work? Work that has me filming? Holy crap, I really did fall down a rabbit hole.

"Really?"

"Really," he says, clear-eyed, earnest.

The heavens part. I'm on the verge of happy tears. But then old instincts die hard. Grim-faced, I ask, "What do I owe you?"

"Nothing—except your eternal gratitude."

My smile is back. I want to launch myself at him, hug his beautiful face. I really wish I could. But...friends only. Which is why I say, "Deal."

THIRTEEN

ALICE

"So what does this new job pay?" Even Nance can't contain her excitement. A day later and I'm still doing backflips in my mind.

After Reagan got done with his last class, he picked me up in front of the library and drove me to meet his coach, a stern man who closely resembles an elderly Viking.

Coach Becker explained what his needs are, what he requires of me, and what he considers is the best time for me to film the team. Which is when I explained to him that light would be a critical factor as far as best time of day to film was concerned.

He cracked a small, painful-looking smile—this man does not look like he smiles a whole lot—turned to Reagan and said, "I'm satisfied." And that was that.

"Two grand! Two freaking grand to film and take pictures. Isn't that amazing!"

I'm officially the new videographer and photographer of the Malibu University men's water polo team. Well, according to his coach, I am until I have enough footage for the athletics department to produce a recruiting video for high school prospects.

For now, they're paying me for the raw footage. A professional production company is supposed to put together the finished product. But I figure this is my big chance, dropped from the heavens into my lap, and I'm not about to squander it.

I have the software on my Mac to produce it myself. If Coach Becker likes it, the athletics department might pay me for the finished product instead of outsourcing it. And if they don't I can use it as my sample submission for the internship. Either way, it's a win. I have a source of income—and Reagan to thank for it.

"It's so exciting. And you said a boy got you the job?"

Boy? Yeah, no. There's nothing boyish about Reagan. Except for the occasional regrettable *Anchorman* reference. Notice how I also don't mention that the *boy* who got me the job is also the one who played a part in my ankle being injured.

Speaking of the man/boy, I step outside my dorm to find him waiting for me in the Jeep, crooked smile already in place. It's Thursday night and I'm headed to study group, the one he insisted he drive me to.

He jumps out and opens the passenger side door for me. I wasn't aware that men still did that sort of stuff, and I gotta say, I love it.

I mean, I'm all for women's lib. Hell, I'm as liberated as they come, but chivalry should never ever die. Let's go ahead and put that in the Constitution. Only a monster would object.

"I gotta go, Mom," I say to her while he looks down at me

with smiling green eyes. "My ride is here."

"All right. Call me tomorrow. Love you!"

"Love you too."

I get in, slip my cracked iPhone into my messenger bag. The crutches go in the back and the Jeep pulls away from the curb.

"My stepmom," I say because after our talk on Saturday I know he's wondering.

"Do you speak to her every day?"

"Sometimes." Knowing what a delicate subject this is I don't chase any of the questions I'm dying to ask him.

He nods, looking pensive and a little forlorn. My heart knots, a painful reminder that things are rarely what they seem. That even the ones we assume are living the life we covet, without a care in the world, are dealing with their own little shopping cart full of issues.

I'm ashamed to say I'm one of those people falsely assuming his life was perfect because he's beautiful and privileged. Because his parents are still together. Knowing what I know now I wouldn't trade places with him for anything.

"You're close, huh?"

"She raised me." A smile stretches my face every time I recall the story of how they met. "When I was seven I got the flu. It was really bad—my temperature was close to 104. Dad took me to the ER and Nancy was the emergency room nurse that night. She took care of me."

Reagan's attention shifts between me and the road. "After I was sent home, once the fever broke, Nancy showed up at the house and unleashed hell on my father, shouting about how irresponsible it was for him to wait till my fever was out of control to seek help. He said he fell in love with her that second. Two years later they were married."

A strong gust of hot air invades the car and Reagan's hair gets ruffled. It's been like this the last few weeks. Crazy hot winds picking up now and then. Mine is literally standing on end. I'm forced to hold it down with both hands.

"The Santa Anas," he says as if reading my mind. I look over and find him smiling at me. "The hot wind." He swirls his index finger.

I let go of my hair, close my eyes, and let it have its way with me. It stands instantly upright, like I stuck my finger in a socket. I'm sure I look like an idiot but it makes me laugh, a burst of pure joy emanating from my chest that can't be contained any more than the wind can.

"Nice hair," he mocks with a teasing smile.

"Thanks, Flipper."

"I thought we established that it's not a dolphin."

"You're not going to like me saying this, but you're more dolphin than shark," I happily point out. He's always perky and upbeat, likes to socialize, loves all the attention. He's a dolphin—whether he likes it or not.

He levels narrowed green vengeance on me, offset by a sly smile. "I'm the top of the food chain, babe. I'm all shark."

"That's adorable. Especially coming from someone that wears a swim cap similar to the one my nana used to wear. Except yours has those darling Princess Leia cinnamon buns over the ears."

He fights his amusement. "Those cinnamon buns are meant to protect my ears from all the rough, manly activity.

And I'm tellin' on you. I'm tellin' all the guys you said that."

The Jeep comes to an abrupt stop. Only then do I realize we're parked in front of the apartment building where my study group is being held. Scanning the parking lot, I see people I recognize from class pouring out of a car.

My attention returns to Reagan and I find him watching me. His smile melts. His expression grows serious like he rarely ever is. I rake my hair down and get my fingers snagged on a few knots. Unfortunately I'm not the comb-carrying type.

Mental note: purchase comb. Crazy winds are afoot.

"Thank you for driving me." I look for some sign of what's going on in his mind and finding the door shut.

"What time should I pick you up?" He reaches out and I lean away, staring at his hand. "Chill, Bailey. You have a piece sticking up."

"Oh...okay." He's trying to be helpful and I treat him like he's a festering case of the bubonic plague. How embarrassing.

I lean in and he sets about gently brushing down each and every one of my stray hairs, so gently I can barely feel him picking apart the knots. I can feel his breath on my skin. Fresh from a shower, I can smell his shampoo. My scalp tingles and goose bumps break out on my forearms. Lord grant me strength.

"Don't worry about it. I can catch a ride home."

Finished, he leans back. Simon walks past the Jeep then, squinting into the headlights that are aimed right at him before he enters the building. I glance over and find Reagan staring after him, expression flinty.

A little odd but I cast it aside until he says, "From *that* guy?" He tips his head at the closed door behind which Simon disappeared, his voice sharp.

"Who, Simon?" I say, thoroughly confused as to why he looks pissed all of a sudden. Between the question and the expression he's wearing, we've passed the *little* odd threshold and are well into *a lot* odd territory.

"Is that his name? Skinny-pants guy? He looks like he uses rock crystal deodorant and writes lyrics in his spare time just to impress chicks."

Uhh…

My brows jack up to my hairline. This conversation has gone way off course, like…made a sharp left into funky town.

"Okay…oookay…" I don't know what else to say. I'm a little taken aback. I open the door, get out, get my crutch situated. "Thanks for the ride, Reagan. I mean it, really."

* * *

REAGAN

Am I going anywhere? Hell no. And the shady dude is not driving Alice home. Luckily for me, I have my advanced chem textbook with me, my iPad, and notes. I spend the next hour and a half holed up in the quiet comfort of my car, studying for an upcoming exam and get more done than if I were doing it at home.

By 9 p.m., bodies start pouring out of the building. I spot Alice walking between a pixie with light pink hair, a collection of tats, and a few piercing—and Shady Sean. Their feet stop when they spot the Jeep. Two curious stares directed at me. His more aggressive than curious.

Nah, bro. Not on my watch.

I'm not going to make a scene. That wouldn't be cool and

Bailey would get the wrong idea. And I like her. We're friends. Good friends, I'd say after Saturday night. I don't want to do anything to screw that up. Shady dude, however, is now on notice.

She looked so low-key sexy laughing at the Santa Ana winds blowing her hair up that I almost leaned over and kissed her. It took everything I had to stop myself. Talk about a gut check. Yeah, that would've gone over real well.

And this only days after we agreed to be friends. And it had to be done. She had that look in her eye and I was seconds from pushing her down on my bed and fucking her till we both fell into a coma, consequences be damned. And there would've been a whole bunch of them. It did surprise me, though. How readily she agreed. My first impression of her that night was that she was into me. Though in hindsight it may have been wishful thinking.

An image of Alice laughing, little white teeth showing, floods my brain and I get a semi. Damn. This is the wrong time and place for this to be happening. With no other way to remedy the problem, all I can do is shift and adjust my sweatpants. Lesson learned—I need to get laid and soon.

Alice turns to the other two, says something I can't hear, and they move in opposite directions: Pink-haired girl to her Prius in the parking lot, shady dude down the sidewalk in the opposite direction. He eyeballs me as he walks past the Jeep.

Atta boy. Keep walking, shithead.

"You're still here?"

She looks confused, cute and confused. "Bailey, you look confused. When I give someone a ride I don't dump them off in front of a strange building and burn rubber out of the parking lot." Those big brown eyes of hers blink. I sigh. "You might find this hard to believe but I don't like to see my friends wind up on the side of a milk carton."

"Have you been here the entire time?"

I hold up my iPad. "Most productive hour and a half of studying in a long time. I'm nailing this chem test. Get in."

The confused look hasn't left her face yet. Nonetheless she gets in the car.

"You hungry?" I bite down on the inside of my cheek to school a grin that I don't think she'd appreciate. "'Cause I'm starving."

She shrugs. "I could eat."

* * *

ALICE

"Hope you like seafood," Reagan mentions as we get out of the Jeep in front of a restaurant called Neptune's, a cute open-air restaurant made to look like a shack with picnic tables and a very long line of people waiting to order.

"I do. But I'll try anything," I tell him as we take our place in line.

Skepticism crosses his face, closely trailed by bewilderment. "You'll try anything?" he repeats. "I don't think I've ever heard a girl say that."

The arched, disapproving brow cannot be helped. It's an automatic reaction when men get stupid. "Welcome to the twenty-first century where shit like that no longer flies. I didn't peg you for a meathead."

He rolls his eyes. "I'm not, believe me. Nothing's hotter than a woman that knows what she wants and goes after it.

But I honestly have never heard a woman say she'll *try* *anything*, especially when it comes to food."

I shrug, satisfied with his answer. "Why not, right?"

"Why not?" he repeats. He's back to disbelief. "That's another thing girls never say. You're full of surprises, Jersey girl."

"What's the harm in trying? I mean…you may never get another chance. Carpe diem and all that stuff."

He shoots me a strange look. I'm about to ask him what it means when the person in front of us steps aside. It's our turn to order and we both go for the fish tacos, Reagan's meal three times the size of mine. He hands the guy behind the counter a fifty-dollar bill and when I argue and try to hand him money, he body-blocks me and murmurs, "I don't like eating alone. You're doing me a favor."

I highly doubt it, but I'm too tired to argue.

Carrying our food, he leads me to a table on the outer edge of the lot and sits on the tabletop. "Up here. You'll see why." When I'm slow to move, he smiles down at me and pats the spot next to him.

I get up on the table next to him, park my crutch against the side, and what I see next takes my breath away. A galaxy of flickering lights spilled against a patchwork of midnight blue and gunmetal gray. From our modest perch, we have a perfect view of the darkened coastline.

"Wow."

"I know. Almost as awesome as it is during the day."

"I'll have to come back with my camera," I say and bite into my fish taco. Eyes rolling to the back of my head, I moan. "Almost better than sex," I mumble with a mouthful and wipe the sauce that drips out the corner of my mouth with my napkin.

"If food is almost better than the sex you've had, then you've been having it with the wrong people."

Uhhh...Am I discussing my sex life with him? No. Not happening. Should I tell him I haven't been having any other than with myself? Definitely not. I let his comment slide away nice and easy. Silence is my friend and I embrace it. The inevitable strange awkwardness happens for a while, but I ride it out until he ends it.

"Why did you say *you may never get another chance* earlier? That was kind of dark."

I shrug casually. Little does he know there's nothing casual about this topic for me. "We all assume we have a long life ahead of us, but you never know."

His face twists, so I elaborate.

"My mother died at twenty-nine of ovarian cancer." His face falls, his taco suspended in mid-air and all but forgotten in his hand. "My grandmother died of the same thing at forty..." I made peace with the knowledge that life is fragile and temporary long ago. It hardly fazes me to discuss it. "Time is a gift, not an entitlement."

He puts down his taco and swallows, face wrecked by sympathy for me. Sympathy's the one thing I have no use for.

"I'm sorry," he says in a low raspy voice.

At fifteen, Nancy sat me down and explained that it could very well be hereditary and I would have to get regular checkups. It's then I decided that I wasn't going to waste one precious minute—whether there were a million of them or less. That I wouldn't let an expiration date hanging over my head rule my life.

"It's why I live my life without shame or regret. As long as I'm not willingly hurting someone else, I do what pleases me." I take another huge bite of my taco. "Eat what pleases me." And smile around it. I'd like to add *fuck who pleases me* but that would be a lie.

Staring at my mouth, Reagan reaches out, and before I have a chance to move away, he wipes a spot of sauce from the corner with his index finger. Then he sticks the same finger in his mouth and sucks it clean.

"You're my hero, Jersey."

I just about die.

FOURTEEN

ALICE

"Am I picking you up tomorrow from the library or your dorm?" Reagan asks without even bothering to glance up, his attention fully on my camera bag. He's already diving into it, investigating its contents, before I can answer.

We're parked on the bleachers by the indoor pool, practice having finished only twenty minutes ago. I shift in my seat, raise my Leica, and look through the viewfinder.

Life is stranger than fiction. It really is. Five weeks ago I was alone in an unfamiliar place. The less than proud owner of a junker that was more trouble than it was worth, and a sprained ankle. Now I'm the official videographer for the men's water polo team—a dream come true. I have a posse of girlfriends. The ankle's almost completely healed. And then there's Reagan...my chauffeur...my dilemma...the object of my dirty fantasies. The guy I spend all my spare time with, which makes the prior statement a problem. Immediately following our first taco night—what he's calling Thursdays—the texts started coming in and most of them look like this...

Big Deal: jumping out of an airplane?
Me: Uhhh what?
Big Deal: you said you'd try anything.
Me: With a parachute?
Big Deal: yes bailey.
Me: Yes, then. But only after a thoroughly accredited instructor teaches me how. I don't have a death wish.
Big Deal: yeah. you haven't even had sex that's better than food yet. might want to put that on the list before jumping out of a plane.
Me: Go away.

It hasn't been dull.

"You don't have to pick me up. The ankle's almost as good as new."

"I'll pick you up from the library."

We've had this conversation multiple times. It started with him insisting he drive me to each practice I filmed because I needed someone to "carry my precious camera equipment." According to him, taking the shuttle would've "placed it in grave danger." I couldn't very well thwart all the effort he put into this harebrained explanation so I agreed.

After having spent every spare minute together for the past few weeks I can say without a shadow of a doubt that Reagan is one of the good guys. He's not just a pretty face and a hot body. The man/boy is all heart. He's sweet and understanding, and despite the fact that he sees me as an asexual amoeba with a dry sense of humor, I like him. I like his company. I like his shitty film quotes and his curious nature. I like his upbeat attitude. But most of all, I like that Reagan doesn't have a single mean bone in his body. Basically, he makes it impossible not to like him.

He said he's not looking for a relationship. Translation: he wants to play the field. Got it. Message received. No judgment. He was warning me off. Except every hot stare I get from him says otherwise and the more time we spend together the harder it's getting to ignore them. Thus, the dilemma. Which is not really a dilemma for him. Only for me, the one in this "friends only" agreement who can't seem to remember that.

"Can I see the camera?"

"No." I stick my leg out, stretch out the ankle. I've been doing a lot of rotational stretching exercises. It's close to completely healed but I'm still being extremely careful with it.

The boys had a late practice today. A scrimmage. Four on four. I got tons of usable footage with my cinecamera and finished with stills. I finally understand how physically and mentally taxing his practices are. This is only the third time I've filmed them and I'm still in awe. All that explosive energy being expended—I won't mince words; it's a major turn-on. Watching them do sprints alone makes me want to take a long nap...naked...with a friend.

Speaking of friends. The camera definitely loves his face. Slanted brows pulled low over focused emerald eyes. Mouth fixed in a pensive pout. Jaw scruffy. Reagan usually shaves so this is new, worth investigating. I take a picture.

"Are you taking pictures of me while denying me access to your toys?" I ignore his question, keep shooting. "C'mon, can I?" he persists.

He's talking about my prized baby. "That's like asking a mother if you can hold her newborn. It's my Blackmagic—my precious. I have five grand invested in that camera. More with all the attachments."

Reagan's gaze meets mine. He's seated two rows down

from me, which puts us eye to eye. "I'll be gentle." His voice dips low, curves around me, and gets inside.

And so it goes. This constant flirtation. The heavily veiled innuendos that coming from anyone else would mean zilch. But they're *not* coming from anyone else. They're coming from him. And, no, I really don't think I'm reading too much into it.

His sensual lips are pried apart by the mother of all sexy grins. This is exactly what I'm talking about. He shouldn't be smiling at me like that. It's just plain wrong. You know what else is wrong? Lusting after the one person I am forbidden to lust after.

I take another picture. He narrows his eyes and I take two more. "You're a proven klutz," I remind him.

"I'm good for it."

"I'm sure you are."

"I'll feed you if you let me hold it."

I snort. "Does that line usually work for you?" Pressing down a smile, I refocus the lens for a closeup of his eyes. Take a few more.

"I don't have to bribe them with food, babe."

We're talking about his women. The smorgasbord. I can't imagine he's been able to do much "dating." Between practice, games, and me all his time is accounted for. And he hasn't mentioned seeing anyone.

Unless he's having them come over late at night.

Shit. I shouldn't have done that. Contemplating it makes my stomach sour. My head knows we're only friends. My heart and the rest of my body strongly object to this arrangement.

My eyes trace down the line of his pec where it leads to the groove between his cobbled abs, to the fine brown hair that thickens below his belly button. Zoe wasn't wrong. His body is a work of art. Photographing him naked would be amazing but I'm too chicken shit to ask him.

His eyes slide up from the camera bag, two heat-seeking missiles that lock onto mine.

"Your bedroom eyes don't work on me, Flipper. Save it for the Speedo chasers." He keeps staring, eyelids heavy. I hate him. "Fine. Go ahead, *babe*."

He takes the cinecamera out of the foam protective case, holds it in his big hands with reverence.

"And you'll feed me anyway." Since the first night he drove me to study class two weeks ago, we've eaten one meal together at least every other day. It's like I no longer need a food budget because he usually sends me back to the dorm with extra. "It's mind boggling how much food you consume."

"Imma growing boy."

He's six foot two inches. "I hope not. That'd be scary."

"I need to eat around 7,000 calories a day during the season. *That's* scary. You know how much food it takes in the right balance of sixty-twenty-twenty of carbs, proteins, and fats?"

"Yes, I do. I watch you do it all the time." The man is constantly eating and I'm getting an increasingly alarming amount of texts that look like this…

Big Deal: u hungry?

Never any capitals. Never. He never capitalizes. What's that about? Is this a new thing? Everyone too lazy to capitalize now? What's next, are we going to do away with commas altogether and just use periods?

He looks through the viewfinder of my camera, points it at me. "You really love it, huh? Filming, making movies?"

There's no need to even consider the answer. It trips from my tongue effortlessly. "Nothing I love more outside of my family." Playing with the camera, he nods. "What about you, Rea. What do you love?"

He looks up, looks off. "I don't know yet...But if I could choose anything, I'd choose to see the world."

Of all the things he could've said, this one surprises me. "Haven't you seen a lot of it already? Surely the family Reynolds summers in Europe?"

He shakes his head. "When Brian and I were kids, my parents worked nonstop. We sometimes went to Mexico for Christmas. That was about it. Once my parents started working less, Brian had already started using. We couldn't go anywhere—not with him. So we never traveled as a family after that." He shrugs. "Water polo was taking up most of my time by then anyway."

How ironic. All that money and still denied the one thing he wanted. "Where would you go first?"

His head lifts, eyes focus, searching my face for God knows what. It dawns on me then that he's searching for an answer. "Has no one ever asked you?"

He shakes his head, loses himself in thought for a bit. "Patagonia...The Great Wall of China. Iceland. Kenya..." He smiles, warming up to the subject. But that smile slowly creeping up? It's nothing but trouble.

"New Jersey."

"Jerk," I grumble and he laughs. "Go ahead and laugh it

up, asshole. New Jersey is not known as the Garden State for nothing, I'll have you know." I take more pictures while he wipes his eyes, the laughter slowly dying.

Entering the arena through the locker room door, Brock approaches. He's a big, intimidating guy on any given day. Wearing sweats with a hoody up and a black backpack slung over a shoulder like he is now, however, makes him look a little murdery.

Seeing us, he smiles knowingly. Whatever he's assuming, he's wrong.

"I'm going to the store. You need anything?" he asks Reagan, stops at the bleachers where we're hanging out.

"I'm good. Bailey and I are going out to eat."

"Yeah? Where?"

"Neptune's."

"Cool. Mind if I come along?"

"Sorry, man. Just us."

Totally awkward silence ensues. During which a flush starts at my collarbone and covers my entire face faster than you can ask *what just happened*.

From behind the viewfinder, my eyes slowly lift. Feeling awful and complicit in this rudeness, they meet Brock's with a silent apology in them. Meanwhile, Reagan continues to fiddle with my camera.

"Guess I'll see you at home, then. Bye, Alice."

"Yeah, bro. See you later."

"Bye, Brock."

While Brock walks away, Reagan gently tucks the camera back in its protective case inside my camera bag. "Ready?" he says, doing everything in his power to avoid eye contact.

"Ready."

* * *

REAGAN

It's midnight by the time I roll in. My stomach's full and my mind's at peace. Spending time with Bailey always leaves me feeling better. She's a shot of serotonin to my restlessness. Even after she chewed my ass out about being rude to Brock. Not a lot of people I can say that about. As a matter of fact none, now that I really think about it.

I enter the dark kitchen and find the man in question in his underwear, standing in front of the open refrigerator door with the light illuminating his face. He frowns when he sees me, grabs a quart of milk, and shuts the door. Okay, maybe I was a douchebag, but he was stepping on my time with Alice and I didn't much appreciate it.

"Hey," I throw out as I drop my backpack. I get nothing in return, only the silent treatment as payback.

I grab a water bottle out of the fridge while Brock opens the milk and takes a long drink, his stare never wandering from the side of my face.

"Listen, dude—"

"Uh huh—" he interrupts, shaking his head. "No, you don't." He wipes his mouth with the back of his hand and pushes off the counter, walks past me. "Next time you want to spend alone time with your girl, just say so. No need to be a dick about it."

He's halfway down the hall, headed to his bedroom, when I remember to speak. "She's not my girl."

His door bangs shut.

FIFTEEN

ALICE

"So you guys aren't fucking?" Zoe says—loudly, to my great misfortune.

"Shhh, keep your voice down." I look around the library and find some curious glances being thrown in our direction.

"No…" I whisper, slouching lower down in my chair. I take another furtive glance about the room for anyone I may know. That or the man in question. Nobody catches my eye, so I lean over the table. "I've been friend-zoned."

After spending all our free time together for the last two weeks, I can say that I've been zoned beyond a shadow of a doubt.

I don't know what exactly happened the night that he was rude to Brock. Since then, however, he's been completely hands-off. The texts haven't stopped. We still spend way too much time together—that hasn't changed. The difference is that he hasn't come within an arm's length of touching me. As if I'm contagious.

I'll never understand men.

"I h-hate that. I'm always f-friend-zoned," Dora

commiserates.

Zoe's flinty hazel eyes bounce back and forth between me and Dora. "That's because you two losers allow them to friend-zone you." She shakes her head. "Who does that?"

I'm pretty sure that was rhetorical but I tuck my hair behind my ear and raise my hand anyway. "Umm, I do."

Dora's hand shoots up. "Me too."

Zoe exhales tiredly, sucks in a deep breath. "We're going to have to fight fire with fire to fix this."

I chuckle. "This isn't a fight."

"Isn't it?"

Wearing a vintage David Bowie t-shit, shredded skinny jeans, and lemon yellow sandals, Blake walks up to the table and sits. She's so cool she makes everything I deemed cool before her look uncool. Out of her Louis Vuitton messenger bag, she pulls out a Mac Air and a textbook. "What did I miss?"

"Alice is *not* fucking Reagan Reynolds."

"Oh my God, use a library voice!" I hiss very, very quietly.

Blake looks shocked. She aims her shock at me. "Really?"

"She's been friend-zoned," Dora explains, sad face on.

More heads turn in our direction and my neck gets hot, my shoulders bend inward. "Yes. Now will both of you shut up before we get kicked out."

"Do you want to be?" Blake asks, genuinely concerned. "Sexing him up, I mean. Not friend-zoned."

I look around, stall for as long as I can. The one thing I cannot do is lie. Zoe will know. She's scary perceptive. "Kinda?" I cringe.

"That's a yes," Zoe responds, jumping right back in. "So…

enough." She slams her palms on the table and draws everyone's attention. "Stop spending so much time with him. He's got it too good right now. It's in the book I'm reading. I should lend it to you. There's a whole chapter on this. It's all on his terms. You need to let him know *he's* the one that's been friend-zoned."

She's onto something. He calls and I'm available. He texts and I'm there. A handful of hours ago this happened...

Big Deal: what are you doing?

I was about to walk into a free yoga class they offer at the campus health center only I got stuck outside, answering his text.

Me: Walking into a yoga class.
Big Deal: ants?
Me: What about ants?
Big Deal: you said you would try anything.
would you eat them?
Me: Seriously?
Big Deal: why not, you said. that's what you said.
what if they were chocolate covered?
Me: Then yes. I would. Because why not? One try won't kill me.
Big Deal: admirable bailey. i like a girl with conviction.
Me: Go away.

I never did make it to that class.

"I don't play games. I can't do that to him," I tell Zoe. Or anyone else for that matter. "He's my friend. He trusts me. And I wouldn't appreciate someone doing it to me."

Zoe tilts her head, her pale blonde ponytail swaying with it. "Then get ready to see him with another girl, because there's one universal truth about men—"

"They're clueless?" Dora startles us all by saying. We all stare at her, pausing for a moment to absorb this.

"No. But I like where your head's at, Red. What I was about to say is…if he's not gettin' sum from you, he's gettin' it somewhere else."

* * *

REAGAN

Tuesday night at the Cantina is a bust. Or maybe I'm just in a crappy mood. Tipping my chair back, I let it slam back down and reach for my third beer of the night because I need to either get trashed, or get laid. What I can *not* do is go home and jerk off to thoughts of Bailey one more time. My dick won't allow it. It's probably too chaffed for sex, but I'll risk it for some seriously needed body-to-body contact.

"So what's the real story with phone-tree girl? Is she available?"

I don't like the smirk Cole's wearing. I don't like it at all.

"Why?" I ask, suspicion riding high. Why would he bring her up now? I scan around and find nothing to explain his sudden interest.

Most of the guys have moved to the bar. The only ones left at our table are Dallas, Brock, and Cole who's usually off hunting for a new hookup but for some reason decided to stick around tonight just to fuck with me.

"Why?" he repeats, half chuckling. "Because I'm a hetero dude and she's cute."

She is cute. And sexy. And funny. And fun to be around. And easy to be with…damn, this is turning into a problem.

I've been trying to give her more space lately, not spend so much time with her, but that has not worked out well. In her defense, it's not her fault that she's the first person I want to speak to when I wake up, and the last before I hit the sack.

"No story. We're friends." The words do not come easily. They feel like a lie.

He crosses his arms over his chest and nods. My attention moves over to Dallas, to see if I'm the only one finding this line of questioning odd, but he's staring at the television screen over the bar behind me. Whatever.

"Friends?" Cole repeats. Like a dick.

"Yeah."

"So she's available?" He smiles wider. "For dates and such?"

The hair on the back of my neck stands up straight. Eyeballing him, I take a sip of my beer. "Nah, man. She's not available. I don't even think she dates *and such*."

"Really? Why not? Is she a Bible banger?"

He's really starting to get under my skin. "Because she's got a full course load and a scholarship to hold on to. She's not your type anyway."

He nods again. His mouth pressed tight. I swear, laughing at my expense is his favorite hobby after hooking up and polo. Shrugging, he says, "What's her type?"

I glance at Dallas and note he's trying not to smile. "What are you two assholes up to? What's going on?"

"I'll tell you what her type is—" Cole starts. "About, mmm"—he looks off, squinting—"six feet." He glances at Dallas. "Six feet, right?"

"'Bout six feet," Dallas answers with a quick nod.

I know something's up when the chuckles start.

"Blond, surfer type," Cole chokes out.

"The hell is going on?"

Cole points to a spot over my shoulder. "Your girl's at the bar."

My head rips around and the two idiots I call friends break out in laughter.

* * *

ALICE

The Cantina is packed tonight. It took fifteen minutes of intense stalking and searching to finally earn me an open seat at the bar. I look around. Zoe's busy gettin' her flirt on with the bartender. Blake is talking to a guy I don't recognize, and Dora has yet to return from the restroom. In the meantime, I'm getting to know my barstool next-door neighbor. He's kind of cute.

"What's your major?" Ken says in a slow voice.

Seriously, Ken? You can do better than that. Cute, but not my type. Too blond, too surfery, and way too baked. His eyes are so bloodshot they make his red t-shirt look orange.

"Film. What about you?"

"It was business, but I'm taking a year off to reassess. Maybe go to Australia and catch some waves."

Ken does not strike me as the type to inhabit an office. He also must not have bills to pay.

"Living the dream, eh?"

He gives me a crooked grin and points to my half empty beer bottle. "Can I get you another?" Then his big brown eyes descend to my boobs.

Here's someone not interested in friend-zoning me.

That's when I spot him, a wall of testosterone and determination headed my way. He's wearing his usual: white t-shirt, gray basketball shorts, flip-flops. It shouldn't trigger sizzle. It really shouldn't. And yet it does. Sizzle in my tummy, sizzle between my legs. This is really inconvenient sizzle.

As he reaches the bar, I get a load of the scowl he's wearing.

"Bailey? What are you doing here?"

"What am *I* doing here?" I can't keep the confusion out of my voice. I look around to see if maybe I missed something. Is this place closed for a private party tonight? Nope, doesn't look like it.

"Yes. What are you doing here?" he reiterates, and awaits my answer with one hand planted on the bar, his arm serving as a security partition between me and Ken who looks more confused than ever. Though in his defense, he's high as a kite.

"Partaking in the age-old college tradition of fun? What are *you* doing here?"

He squeezes his extra large body between me and Ken, boxing him out.

"Hey, dude—" Ken finds the wherewithal to say.

Reagan glances behind him. "Yeah, thanks for saving my spot." He turns back around to face me. Only inches separate us. I have to squeeze my legs under the bar or risk having him step between them.

"But I wasn't..." I hear Ken attempt to say. His voice fades. I assume anything more would've taken too much effort.

"You realize Tuesday nights are pick-up nights?" he says,

skipping right over my question.

"So I'm here on a good night? Is that what you're saying?"

He grabs one of the French fries out of the large basket I ordered. "No, don't—"

Too late. Gagging, he immediately spits it back up into his hand and dumps the remains in a cocktail napkin. Then he guzzles the rest of my beer and glares.

"The hell?"

"I was going to tell you"—a burst of laughter escapes me—"that I poured salt on them. It was a huge portion, and I was going to eat them all, so I ate half and ruined the rest."

Grimacing, he shakes his head. "Women."

My amusement won't die. Which causes Reagan to smile. Our eyes lock. He's so close I can smell him and it's like a spell is cast, my body going hot and soft and amenable to being tampered with. "You didn't answer me," I ask to hide the fact I'm getting turned on by his mere presence, my voice sounding strangely seductive even though I don't mean it to. "What are you doing here?"

He looks down on me with a searching glance, his eyes so bright against the fresh spot of color from outdoor practice today. "I was about to head home, but I think I'll stay now."

"Why?" I press. This back and forth needs to stop. I know I'm not the only one feeling this magnetism between us—this *attraction*. Let's call it what it really is.

"Because..." He huffs, a mix of confusion and irritation written in the v between his brows, in the way his full lips press together. I want to kiss those lips until they soften and kiss me back.

"What are you, four? Because why, Reagan?"

"Because you need someone to watch over you."

"I'm here with the girls." I motion to Zoe and Blake. Zoe pauses her conversation to glower at him. "I don't need protecting. As a matter of fact I was having a nice conversation with Ken before you showed up and interrupted."

"Rea, we're heading home. You coming?" Cole Peterman walks up saying. He levels his dark blue eyes on me and runs them up and down my body with intent. Okay, that's weird.

The air around Rea changes, his entire being stiffens. "I'm staying. Alice will give me a ride," he casually throws out.

I will? This is news to me. He inches closer and the tops of his thighs press into my knees and every bit of my attention goes there, held hostage by that small spot where we touch. Jesus, this is bad.

Cole's eyebrow hikes up. "See you later."

We both watch Cole walk away. Then his attention returns to me and anticipation thickens the air between us. My insides somersault. "Do you think that maybe you could…umm, back up a little."

"Why?" His face puckers as if this is the most absurd request he's ever heard.

"Because I'm here to meet people and you're in the way."

"Like who, Ken?" He hooks a thumb behind him. "That dude got caught dealing weed on campus and got tossed out of school."

"Oh." I chew on my bottom lip to stop from giggling. "He said he was a business major."

"Yeah, he's a real entrepreneur."

"Fine then. Who should I go out with? Let's hear some suggestions."

He frowns. "Somebody who's responsible. Somebody loyal, who will be there for you."

"I'm looking for a fling, Rea. Not a dog."

"Hey. Are you ready to go? Blake has an early class tomorrow," Zoe says while staring a hole in Reagan's head.

"Yeah, let me just go to the bathroom first." I hop off the stool and my breasts brush against his chest. We both freeze. His body turns to stone and mine is ready to make a run for it lest he notice that my nipples are just as hard.

Without looking into his face, I dart away and make it as far as the dim, narrow hallway that leads to the ladies' room.

A hand cinches around my wrist, stopping me. "What do you mean a fling?"

I turn and face him, mustering all the courage I possess. "I'm pretty sure you can find the definition of *fling* in Urban Dictionary."

A guy coming out of the men's room walks past us and Rea pins me up against the wall. "You're looking for a fling?" If I didn't know any better, I'd say he looks genuinely hurt and unpleasantly surprised.

"Maybe." I squirm.

He continues to stare at me like I'm the last clue in the Sunday crossword puzzle—unsolvable and annoying. Then I recall Zoe's advice and plant a hand on his chest, push him back. "We have to go. The girls are waiting for us."

Ten minutes later, standing by Zoe's G wagon, the lack of space becomes evident. Without waiting for direction, Reagan gets into the passenger side and pats his lap for me to get on. Whatever is going on in his head is well hidden behind a blank expression. With my heart in my throat, I climb on. And as soon as I do, I'm immediately overwhelmed by every detail of him. Not a single one escapes me. His scent, his heat, his erection under my ass—the absolute sweet torture of it. There's nowhere for me to put my arm so I'm forced to drape it around his neck.

"Is this okay?" I murmur.

"Fine." He exhales and I feel the puffs of breath hit the sensitive skin on my throat. Then he arranges my legs and curls his hand around my thigh, leaving it there for the full ten-minute ride back to his house.

Being held by him, like this, feels so good, comfortable, familiar. He feels like he's mine. Except he's not. Zoe studies us out of the corner of her eye, stealing furtive glances, but doesn't say a word. No one does. We ride the entire way in silence.

SIXTEEN

ALICE

"How's your submission coming along?" Simon asks as Marshall's class lets out.

"Really well. I told you I'm filming the men's water polo team for a recruiting video, right?"

I'm filming today. Which means I'll be spending time with Reagan. I'd be lying if I didn't admit that what Zoe said the other day didn't affect me. It did. Mostly because I agree with her. I've seen the evidence with my own eyes. The girls hanging out on the bleachers during practice. The ones on campus constantly vying for his attention. I can't even blame them. I'm attracted to him too.

I've been gently ignoring his invitations to hang. Instead of switching stuff around to accommodate our time together, I've been declining. And even that's been hard. Twice I caved when I got the disappointed pout. It's an Alice slayer—that disappointed pout.

"Yeah. Great gig. How'd you land that?" I don't think I like the flash in his wily dark eyes. Nor the inflection in his voice. It feels like condescension and sounds like he's insinuating something creepy. I really hope I'm reading too much into it.

The submission sample is coming along better than I had anticipated. It doesn't hurt that the content is dynamic, the subject matter exciting. All that grace and raw beauty makes for an extremely powerful visual presentation.

We file out of the stadium seating and slowly move down the steps toward the exit.

"A friend helped me get it." I go with the truth, which is nothing to be ashamed about. I know Simon has seen me with Reagan—getting dropped off and picked up at study group, eating lunch in the quad.

Simon runs his hand over his dark, curly hair, the action pulling his gray henley tight against his sinuous torso. My eyes run over his chest, his biceps, study the leather bracelets accenting his wrists, inspect the skinny black jeans. His lean thighs. It's an automatic, unintentional reaction. He really is hot. He's got that tortured artist, too-cool-for-school look down pat. One that I am personally a big fan of.

For a half second Reagan's voice whispers in my ear and it makes me wonder if he uses rock crystal deodorant (which doesn't work) or writes lyrics in his spare time. Not my proudest moment. And the fact remains that Simon is definitely more my specie than Reagan. Even if he was interested in me—which he isn't. I mean, Thoroughbred horses don't mate with zebras. I need to stick with the other zebras.

"Alice?" Simon says, his expression quizzical, his slanted eyebrows pulled together in one of those moody made-for-TV expressions. It dawns on me that we've already made it outside the film and television building and are standing near the curb.

"Yeah?"

He stuffs his hands in the back pockets of his jeans, for once looking unsure of himself. "I asked you if you maybe wanted to go out sometime...there's a Scorsese retrospective at the Nuart Theater."

* * *

REAGAN

I park the Jeep at the curb in front of the film and television building and stand in my seat. I'm watching Alice smile up at the shady guy as if he's something special. Christ, she's making heart eyes at the guy.

A *fling,* she said. She's looking for a fling. My insides roil at the idea. And the ride home last night—what lasted maybe ten minutes—felt like a damn eternity with her ass pressed up against my hard-on. Thing is, despite the worst case of blue balls ever, it felt good to hold her, to have her there. It felt right.

Shady smiles back and a feeling of possessiveness so powerful comes over me, I'm ready to blow like a goddamn geyser in Yellowstone. *Wtf?* Unless I'm playing sports I'm pretty easygoing. And I'm definitely not proprietary. Which is why I'm surprised at my own response. Jumping out of the Jeep, I'm bearing down on the two of them before I've decided what to say, or why I'm saying it. Somewhere in the back of my mind I know this is bad, that it won't end well because control feels like an abstract concept right now and that never bodes well.

"Hey, Reagan. Have you..." Alice's voice fades when she

gets a good look at my face, her big eyes narrowing on me.

I adopt an air of indifference, give her a lazy smile. She can't know that it bothers me. That it makes me anxious and sick to my stomach. Because that would make me a hypocrite seeing as I'm the one that insisted on us being friends.

"The hell is this?" is my opening shot.

My forced smile isn't fooling anyone. Shady scowls at me. However tempted I am to knock it off his face, I manage to curb the impulse. Except I just can't seem to get a handle on this feeling that there's a fox in the hen house and it's my job to rip out the throat of the fox.

Alice eyeballs me warily. "Umm, what do you mean?"

She's going to pretend nothing's going on here, really? The fake smile drops and a scowl replaces it.

"I have practice. You're filming today. But apparently we're both going to be late because you're too busy flirting." I hook a thumb at the guy. Aside from that, I pretend he's not still standing there and dump all my irritation on Alice.

Her eyes go wide. She blinks. Then she turns to him. "Simon, I have to go but I do want to see the Scorsese retrospective."

Simon/Sean, whatever the fuck his name is, loses the attitude and smiles back at Alice like he just caught himself a nice fat chicken…my chicken. I don't like the look or sound of this—at all.

"Can we go? Or would you rather stay here and continue to make eyes at each other."

I don't think I've ever seen someone turn a flaming shade of red so fast. Alice looks like a burn victim.

"Hey, dude." Shady decides now is the time to get really

stupid. "Maybe you should—"

"Maybe you should run along, Simon," I cut in, taking care to pronounce his name extra carefully.

Alice walks away, heading for the Jeep, and I follow. She gets in, buckles up. I do the same.

"Alice—"

"Don't." Her throat works. She refuses to look at me. Not a word is spoken on our way to the aquatics building, and a sinking feeling tells me the fallout is just beginning.

* * *

ALICE

Big Deal: i'm hungry. wanna grab something to eat with me?

I read the text that comes in with a scowl puckering my face. The lack of capitals is especially nauseating tonight. I even tried it on my phone and now know for a fact that he has to actively make an effort to not capitalize. Which licks at my raw nerves even more.

The truth is I'm still furious at him for the scene he caused yesterday. Humiliating me like that in front of Simon was total BS and I need to see some serious remorse before we're back to normal.

Me: No.

A good sixty seconds pass before the text alert rings again.

Big Deal: i'm traveling to palo alto for a game tomorrow.
i guess i'll see you when i get back.

I don't bother answering. If he thinks he's going to pretend everything is hunky dory after his tantrum, he's got another thing coming.

* * *

REAGAN

"I screwed up again," I walk onto the patio scratching my head and muttering.

For someone who never used to screw up, I'm really making up for lost time.

I fall into the chair next to Dallas and glance at my phone. Alice hasn't returned any of my texts since I dropped her off at her dorm after practice yesterday. She even refused fish tacos. It's official—she's mad at me.

"You're in the right place. We specialize in screwups here." He reaches into the cooler next to his chair, pulls out a can of Hazy IPA, and hands it over. Staring out at the Technicolor horizon, I crack open my beer and drink.

Two surfers bob on the water waiting to catch a wave. With the Santa Monica Bay as still as a hockey rink, they'll be waiting a while.

"Where were you this morning?" I looked for him before heading off to class and found him gone and D isn't a natural early riser unless he's catching waves.

"Beverly Hills."

That puts a confused frown on my face. "Why?"

"New shrink."

I breathe out a sigh of relief. He's been in danger of going off the rails lately—more so than usual—and the fact that he's willing to talk to someone about it makes me feel immensely better. "You like this one?"

He shrugs, sips his beer. "We'll see."

I check out the wet suit pulled down to his waist. "You went surfing without me."

"Had to clear my head."

I stretch out my legs, heels kicked up on the brick wall that separates the patio from the beach.

He side-eyes me briefly. "So...what happened?"

"I got in a fight with Alice." I'm still in shock over my reaction, the feelings that slammed into me when I saw her making heart eyes at the shady guy.

Ownership, that's what it was. Raw and primal.

The image of her beaming up at the guy flashes in my mind and I shift in my seat. My skin feels shrink-wrapped. My mood wilts. It's taking a lot to keep it up lately. Unless I'm with Bailey.

How could she really be into that guy? Maybe I misinterpreted. Maybe I didn't. "She was talking to some dude and I lost my shit on her."

Dallas chuckles. "Been there." Pushing off the wall, he tips his chair back and lets it drop. "You know what possessiveness is?"

My feelers go up. This sounds like a trap. I glance sideways, to get a better read on the exact level of bullshit I'm dealing with and find nothing noteworthy. "Toxic?"

"Nah, man. It's the soul's recognition that the object of your affection is so precious and singular you know you'll never find another."

Despite D's uncanny ability to read people, I wouldn't call

him particularly deep. His words do strike a chord, though. Alice *is* singular. I've never met anyone like her. She's smart and fun to be around, talented and passionate. And she gets me. I can't even articulate all the ways she gets me. She's the most precious thing in my life by far. "Are you fucking with me, or do you really believe that?"

Dallas's gaze cuts sideways, his expression contemplative. "Yeah. I'm dead serious. Read it in an Insta meme a while back and it stuck with me."

I knew the bullshit was waiting to make an appearance. "That's just great," I say, head shaking. "I should've known."

"Who cares where I got it. Don't throw out the message with the messenger."

Maybe he's right. "What would you do in my place?"

"Apologize and get on with the make-up sex. Best kind there is, bro."

"We've never had sex. We're only friends."

He finally turns to get a good look at me, confusion all over his face. "You're serious? I thought you were just trying to keep it low-key. Why not?"

"Because we're friends," I annunciate clearly, my frustration with the entire situation coming to the surface again.

"So you're saying you don't get a boner for her."

All I get is boners for her. I wish that wasn't the case, but it is. We agreed to be friends and only friends. That was the plan. Until one night I'm grabbing my dick and her flashing dark eyes appeared, next it was her heart-shaped ass, then her lips. And it didn't stop there. It *never* stops.

Even worse, I feel less than zero motivation to stick my

dick elsewhere. The dick wants what it wants. You can't reason or argue with it. But I also know you're also not supposed to want to bury it inside your friend.

"Man, c'mon," I say. It makes me irritable as hell to hear him speak that way about her.

"C'mon, what? Since when are we not allowed to mention boners?"

"Not about Alice." I crush the empty can and chuck it into the trash bin, rub my face. "Yeah, boners aren't the problem. Or maybe they are the problem. I dunno…"

"What *is* the problem, then?"

"I can't deal with any more responsibility, or expectations. I can't be in a relationship…I'd fuck it up anyway."

Problem is, I don't want her seeing anyone else. The mere thought of her dating whatever-the-fuck-his-name-is makes my heart jackhammer and my palms sweat. Thus, the possessiveness. I feel helpless and it's not a feeling I'm a fan of. I get enough of that dealing with Brian already.

We watch the sun take its last breath before it sinks into the Pacific. I check my phone to see if Alice has texted me back. Nothing.

"Bro—" D chuckles. "You spend all your free time with her. You never go more than two sentences without bringing up her name. And you won't let any of us near her. You already *are* in a relationship. The only thing you're not getting is the convenient sex."

Dallas stands, slaps my shoulder, walks back inside.

SEVENTEEN

REAGAN

I text Alice for the fifth time in two days.

> **Me:** on the bus and cole is entertaining everyone with stories of his sexual escapades. save me.

Half an hour later and still no response. We've been driving for an hour and it already feels like forever. Being trapped in this tin can, helpless to do anything other than wait Alice out, is making me antsy. I'm no expert on women, but I'm pretty sure that waiting is not the winning strategy here. Time is not on my side. The longer she has to be mad at me the worse this is going to get. And with each minute that passes without a text from her, fear that I may have permanently sunk this friendship gains traction.

> **Me:** what are you up to tonight? plans?

When that one goes ignored I start to sweat. I still owe her an apology and I didn't want to do it over the phone. I was going to take her out to dinner, do it properly, but she shot that plan down like it was target practice at the O.K. Corral. Before I check my phone again, I glance sideways to make sure I've got privacy. My co-captain is sound asleep in the seat next to mine. Brock's head is tipped back on the headrest, noise-canceling headphones on.

"Rea—where you at? We need one more for the card game," Shane says loud enough to get everyone's attention.

"Nah, man. Not in the mood."

"Lady problems," Dallas mutters from the seat across the aisle.

My head snaps up from the phone to find all eyes trained on me. I shoot Dallas a *knock it off* glare, and make a mental note to beat the life out of him later.

"Yeah? Let's hear it," Cole adds.

"How about you gossip girls mind your own business," I throw out casually. If Cole gets wind that I'm genuinely twisted up over a girl he'll never stop. He's the most anti-relationship guy I know and I really don't need him projecting his shit onto me. I got my own bag to deal with.

"That wouldn't be any fun now, would it," Cole tosses back with a cocky grin. "We have an eight-hour bus ride, and plenty of wisdom amongst us to dispense."

"Circle of trust, bro." Shane gestures with his index finger.

"Hard pass." I gesture with my middle finger.

"Phone-tree girl is messing with your head," Cole taunts. "Let us help you out of the darkness and into the light."

My irritation peaks. I don't have the fortitude to fend him off tonight. "Suck my dick, Cole."

"I'll suck your dick," Quinn shouts from three rows up and all the guys react at once, laughing, commenting, generally pissing me off.

"Jesus, Smith."

"Awww, c'mon."

"Bwahahaha."

"That's your captain, dude. A little respect."

"Love is love, you cunts!" Quinn shouts back, laughing like a madman.

It's on me to settle the troops, or none of us are going to get any sleep on this bus ride from hell. "Enough! Not a single one of you has a girlfriend with the exception of Rhodes and Finley, and fuck if I'll take advice from a couple of freshmen— no offense, guys."

"None taken, Cap," comes from the head of the bus where those two are probably FaceTiming their GFs.

Cole chuckles. "I've had relationships."

"Those are called hookups. I take naps that last longer," I'm quick to correct, drawing snickers from the audience.

"Your loss, bro. Just make sure the sorry-ass moping doesn't interfere with the game tomorrow."

A moment later, thankfully everyone goes back to doing whatever they were doing before the spotlight fell on me.

"You said she wasn't your girl," Brock murmurs on my left. Guess he's not asleep anymore. True to his nature, which is to be the most chill guy I know, his expression holds no condemnation. "You said the two of you were just friends."

"She's not and she is—at least, I hope we're still friends. I, uh, kinda messed it up."

"What'd you do?"

"Made a scene when I found her talking to some guy. I just...snapped—" My eyes skirt the edge of the window while my hand nervously runs through my hair. "And I think she likes him," I glumly admit, my face puckering in bitterness.

Brock nods slowly. "Did you apologize?"

"I tried but she's icing me out." My mood grows grimmer by the second as I recall the hurt on her face, the shock.

"My two cents?"

"Yeah."

"You're sending mixed messages, stringing her along. That's not cool, man."

Mixed messages? Is that what I've been doing? "You think I've been sending mixed messages?"

A wtf look pops up on Brock's face. "You honestly don't see it? You guys spend every minute together." Noting my blank expression, he continues. "You get nasty whenever anyone else tries to cut in on your time with her." The sinking sensation in my chest tells me there's truth to this. "Either make her your girl or cut her loose. It's not fair, what you're doing to her."

"You think she's into me?"

My heartbeat thunders as I await his answer with bated breath. "I know she's into you. Everybody knows she's into you—except for you."

Relief floods my chest. But then the feeling pivots, takes a nosedive. It sounds like I've been using her, and that couldn't be farther from the truth. And I'm not completely to blame here. Alice friend-zoned me too. I haven't been seeing other people on the side. As a matter of fact I haven't been able to see anybody else with the amount of time we spend together.

"I can't cut her loose."

He shrugs. "I guess it's option A, then."

"I'm not sure option A is the best thing for her, either. I've got too much bullshit to deal with as is. I can't add a girlfriend to the list of responsibilities I already have. I'll screw it up and then I'll lose her for good."

Brock stares at me for a beat before putting on his noise-canceling headphones. "Let me know how that works out for you."

* * *

ALICE

It's almost midnight when my phone rings and Reagan's name flashes onscreen. I haven't seen or spoken to him since we argued four days ago. The six missed calls on my **Recents** list and multiple text messages say not for lack of trying on his part.

Chewing on the end of my thumb, I debate whether to answer. I miss him. God, do I miss him. Amazing how three months ago I didn't even know he existed and now four days apart feel like an eternity. I better get used to it, though. Our current arrangement can't be sustained. Too many unrequited feelings. Too much physical chemistry. Only on my end, apparently. He's more than happy to continue as we were. Which depresses the shit out of me.

After bookmarking the article I'm reading on my laptop, I close the tab and power it off, setting it on the small desk that butts up against my even smaller bed.

The call goes to voice mail but it looks like he's hit his patience limit for being ignored because the phone starts ringing again only a minute later.

"What are you doing?" he says as soon as I answer.

"Talking to you apparently when I should be studying for my History of Italian Film exam tomorrow. Don't you know how to text like the rest of the civilized world?"

"But then I wouldn't be talking to you, would I?"

The deep breath he takes reaches through the phone and raises the hair on my arms. It also puts a reluctant grin on my face. No one has the ability to disarm me as effectively as Reagan can. I was all ready to be aloof and mysterious but no, I'm smiling like a goofball. It's kind of exasperating how easily he decimates every attempt I make to keep some distance between us with only a few sweet, well-timed words.

"You've been ignoring my calls."

I've missed him. I don't want to argue anymore and I'm even willing to forgo an apology to keep the peace. Ignoring his claim, I steer the conversation elsewhere. "Are you still on the bus?" The team traveled to Palo Alto for a game against Stanford yesterday, and I know they lost because I checked.

"No, just got home." He sounds down so I don't press for more about the game. From what I've been told the division is super competitive and Stanford is already two wins ahead of us. Us...I think of the team as us now.

"So I'm watching *Justice League* and I have to tell you, no contest, not even a shadow of a doubt, the best character is the Flash."

"Mmm. Bold assertion. And this very important business couldn't wait?"

"Friends don't let friends walk around clueless, Bailey. It's one of the pillars of friendship."

Friendship. Why does that word make me a smidge bitter. That's not really a question. Reclining in bed with my hand tucked behind my head, I take the olive branch he's offered. "Wonder Woman."

"Alice…"

"Reagan…"

He sighs loudly. "Fine. She's hot. I'll grant you that. And she's got a neat lasso. But she's not funny. She's not really, really fast. Which is awesome. And frankly she's sort of a stuck-up bitch."

That earns him a horrified gasp. "You did not just say what you said."

"Yeah, I did."

"I am so disappointed in you, Reagan Archibald Reynolds. She's so much more than a hot chick with a neat lasso. And she's not a bitch—she's regal. There's a very clear distinction."

"Archibald?" He snorts. "That's not my middle name."

"I know. But since you won't tell me what it is I'm going to keep guessing until I score." I get a whole bunch of tension-fraught silence in return, and the realization that I might've misspoken creeps up on me.

"You wanna score, Alice?" he murmurs, pitch low, whispering in my ear as if he were tucked up against me in bed. It's the sexiest sound I've ever heard, kick-starting a slow-moving heat that works up my neck, slides down through my limbs, and pools between my legs. I'm throbbing. "I may be able to help with that."

I'm sure he could. It's on the tip of my tongue to ask him to come over and do that. Except…only friends.

The skin from my toes to my hairline is on fire, feverish and sweaty. This taunt will not go unpunished, however. We've been dancing around this, whatever this is, for far too long and I'm tired of it. My patience with all the mixed signals he keeps sending is wearing real thin. I have goals and responsibilities just like he does. Unlike him, however, I'm willing to make room, to carve out a space for him because he's that important. That's the difference between us.

"Oh really? You'll set me up with one of your friends? How nice of you," I volley back because two can play this game.

"Uhhh, no, Bailey. Not even if it was on your Make-A-Wish list."

"Aww, that's okay, BD. Don't sweat it. I can find my own dates."

A deep slow chuckle filters through the phone. "Did you just call me big dick?"

"What? No. No, I called you BD as in Big Deal. Remember when we met and you said you were 'kind of a big deal'?"

"No."

"Forget it. Forget I said anything."

He laughs. "And when you say dates you mean the pasty, emo dude I caught you making big eyes at?"

In truth, Simon is exactly my type. At least he was before an annoying water polo player almost ran me over. "I do not make 'big eyes.'"

"He wears skinny jeans, Bailey," he continues right over me. "That's your type? A guy that models himself after a vampire book? Is he going to want a blood oath at some point in your relationship?"

I tap the phone to interrupt his rant. "First of all, Simon's a nice guy and we have a lot in common—" Like capital letters and sunscreen. "And yes, he is my type. Second of all, I like those vampire books and who cares what he wears. Why am I even arguing with you?" My patience is so gone. "Oh yeah, because I thought you were calling to apologize for being riiddiicuulous," I annunciate clearly with my mouth attached to the bottom of the phone. "I'm hanging up now."

"I thought I was your type."

"Negative. I like guys that are nice to me."

"Bailey—"

"Don't call again unless you have an apology ready."

"Al—"

Click. Whatever else he was about to say falls away as I power off my phone, punch the pillow, and pray sleep finds me quickly.

EIGHTEEN

ALICE

My bedroom door opens and Dora steps inside. She's wearing a smile so big and bold it could shatter a Guinness record. Meanwhile, I'm not smiling. I'm sprawled out on my bed, an open textbook before me, busy studying for a History of Television exam that is imperative I ace and not making much progress.

"Guess what?" She does a strange little dance and a wiggle of her curvy hips. Then, hand on a Bible, she attempts to moonwalk. I am so bummed I did not catch this on video.

I am, however, getting the feeling that whatever she's smiling about deserves my undivided attention so I close it.

"You're a really bad dancer?" I say, biting down on my quivering lips.

She stops and pouts. "That's not nice."

I admire her one piece at a time. Her pin-straight auburn hair is in a slick ponytail. Peach lip gloss that complements her coloring. Cropped faded boyfriend jeans, a tight white t-shirt, and bright red flip-flops with black toenail polish.

In other words, the Mayfield factor in full effect. She's

come a long way since the pleated khakis and oversized polos she was wearing when I met her.

"What is it, Dora? What's the news that has you dancing like a spaz and keeping me from studying for this godforsaken exam." I sit up, cross-legged.

A smile explodes across her face, full of white perfectly even teeth. "My dads got me a car for my twenty-first birthday! It's not for another week, but they couldn't wait to give it to me so they drove up from Del Mar to deliver it today!" There's no pause. Not even for a breath. She shimmies her shoulders. Does a little finger point to the sky.

On replay, my brain picks up a major plot point. "Dads?"

Her amusement drops. "Oh...yeah. Didn't I say?" She chews on her bottom lip.

I'm actually not that surprised. Dora's pretty reserved about her personal life, less likely to put it all out there than Zoe. Although Zoe, I suspect, has her own well of secrets too.

"Mnnno. I'm pretty sure I would've remembered that detail. You've called them 'the parents,' or sometimes 'the rents.' You've mentioned that your dad is a DEA agent. But that's about it."

She sighs. "My other dad's a high school art teacher." She stuffs her hands into the back pockets of her jeans to stop from fidgeting.

"Hey, I think that's really cool. It's not a big deal."

She shifts on her feet, her shoulders soften. "It was when I was g-growing up."

She's not exactly comfortable discussing it so I drop the subject. "And what about this birthday that you also *never mentioned*."

Her mood immediately brightens. "Yeah, well, 'cause, c'mon, can you imagine what'll happen when Zoe finds out? I'm going on the record now, Alice. No male strippers. I mean it. Please, please, please." She presses her palms together, a supplicating look on her face.

That elicits another grin. "Can't make any promises, but I'll do my best."

My door swings open. Zoe sticks her head in. "Coffee run. You hookers coming?"

"Oh, oh, oh!" Dora jumps up and down screaming. "I'm driving!"

Ten minutes later the four of us are standing in the parking lot, staring at Dora's brand-new mint green Fiat 500. I'm smiling. Dora's beaming, petting the hood. Blake is hiding her chuckles behind her hand, her gold medical bracelet glimmering in the sunlight. And Zoe just looks…bewildered.

"It's not a car, it's a Skittle on wheels," she mutters out of the side of her mouth.

"Isn't it effing awesome?!" Dora shouts.

Zoe rolls her eyes. "*Effing*? Oh, Lord."

"Shotgun," Blake calls out.

"I guess I'll ride on the hood," Zoe grumbles.

"You'll make a beautiful hood ornament," I tease.

Smirking, Zoe walks to the head of the car and sits on the end of the hood. Her hands go to her waist. She tucks her bent arms so the elbows point backwards and arches her back. "Let's go."

"Stop being so dramatic," Dora tells her.

"Some of us aren't the size of a garden gnome, Dora," Zoe fires back.

"I'm five feet three inches, thank you very much. Hardly a g-garden gnome. And size doesn't matter. Bernadette is beautiful."

Zoe's eyes snap open wide. "You did *not* name the car." She turns to Blake and whines, "Blakey, she named the car."

"I heard."

Zoe's attention returns to Dora and a stare-down happens, which Dora loses when her lips begin to twitch into a smile.

"Get in the car, Zoe," Blake orders, putting an end to all the shenanigans.

We stuff Zoe in the back seat and laugh our asses off when her knees touch her forehead.

* * *

"Judging by your sad coma, I take it he hasn't apologized?" As usual, the Slow Drip is packed—a minor miracle we managed to snag the corner table by the window. Zoe's voice still manages to rise above the din of the crowd.

My gaze climbs up and runs into Zoe's hard, unblinking hazel stare. One perfectly groomed brow hitches up.

"Well?"

I take a sip of my steaming hot mocha and my tongue smarts. Okay, fine, I'm stalling, deciding how much to spill and not because I don't trust them. I absolutely do. It's because Zoe's basically a loaded handgun. You have to be extremely careful where you aim her or you could unleash havoc.

I was so worked up over Reagan's failed attempt to patch the rift between us that I told the girls everything. And they couldn't have been any more awesome—ordered pizza, listened to me bitch about it for hours. All the earmarks of true friendship. I've never been a sharer before. Hence, I'm only beginning to understand how effortless it can be with the right people. How it all boils down to trust.

Something I assumed I shared with Reagan.

"Nope," I take no pleasure in admitting. The p pops out of my mouth hard.

Am I still mad? You betcha. I'm more than mad—I'm done. I deserve someone who doesn't belittle and embarrass me in public. But most of all, I deserve someone who wants me.

"Did he crawl on his cowardly belly till it bled?"

"That's gross," Blake comments. She's only voicing what we're all thinking.

"Nope."

"Men are swamp garbage." Zoe sits back, arms crossed, offended on my behalf. Go, girl power.

"Not all of them—" Dora quietly argues.

Tea cradled in her hands, Blake pulls her lips away from the edge of the cup to speak. "I'm with Dora on this one."

"My dads aren't," Dora blurts out. The words peter out, as if she immediately regrets the admission. Doesn't matter. She might as well have dropped a very loud mic.

Zoe blinks, her face morphing from one expression to the next. You can literally see it on her face, her brain working to accept this information. "Wait...wait...wait," she mutters each time her confusion-filled gaze circles around the table. "Did you say...dads?"

"Don't say anything mean," Dora warns her. No pause, no stutter. It infuses my chest with secondhand pride.

Zoe's face finally settles on surprise. "Ramos, you were marginally cool before. Now you're on a pedestal. You were here"—she motions with her hand somewhere around the middle of her chest—"now you're here." The hand shoots above her head.

"Thanks for the visual. We wouldn't have understood otherwise." Blake smiles wryly.

Planting both palms on the table, Zoe leans in. "I need to know everything. Do they make out in front of you, and can I come over and watch?"

"Awww, Zoe," spills out of me.

"C'mon, Zo," Blake adds.

Dora rolls her eyes. "I'd rather not contemplate my parents' sex life—and, no, you can't."

A loud rap at the window startles us. Outside, on the sidewalk, Reagan and Dallas wave. Dallas's expression is all happy, sly mischief. Reagan's on the other hand is straight-up determination.

All I need is another public scene.

"Speaking of assholes and idiots," Zoe absently mutters.

I snort. "That's not what we were discussing."

"We are now. Game face on. Do *not* be nice to him."

"Zoe…"

As soon as they step inside, Reagan heads for our table while Dallas makes for the register. I'm getting the full treatment, the unblinking stare, all of his undivided attention. Try as they may, not even the whistles and shouts of his loyal fandom can distract him.

Resentment and longing flood my veins, every fiber in my body feeling the effects of it. And by effects I don't mean good ones. My pulse races while my stomach twists into knots and bows.

"Hey," he says when he reaches our table.

I finally allow myself a good, hard look. His white t-shirt offsets his tan. His silky black track pants...well, frankly, they outline things I shouldn't be looking at. He seems to have grown even more tempting in the separation. Wonderful.

Dora and Blake return a tight, "Hi." Zoe opts to go with a disgruntled face.

"Hello," I add a long moment later because I won't allow him to turn me into a rude person.

He aims a smiling glance at the girl sitting on the bench at the next table and she immediately perks up. "Do you mind," he says to her. "I need to sit with my friend."

In that case, he needs a dictionary app so he can look up the definition of friendship. "Yes, she does mind," I snap.

"No, I don't," girl-at-next-table insists and sends me an admonishing glare.

He's all yours, sweetie, hangs from the tip of my tongue. Just dangles there. On the ready to be dropped.

She scoots over to make room for him and he squeezes in, despite my lack of invitation. Then he angles his body, giving her his back. Can't say I didn't warn her.

Sitting beside me, he takes up all the space like he's entitled to it. Which, being six-foot two inches of solid muscle, means he's everywhere at once. His leg, from hip to knee, touches mine. His scent, soap and laundry detergent and a hint of chlorine, is in the air. He's too close. He's much too close. By design, I'm sure.

"No, really, make yourself at home, Reynolds. We're so psyched that you would bestow upon us the gift of your illustrious company," drawls Zoe. Watching him closely, she raps four short, midnight blue nails on the wooden table. I shoot her a thin-lipped glare that screams *cut it out* and she rolls her eyes at me.

Reagan extends his arm on the back of the bench, shifts closer to me. To my great annoyance. "My pleasure," he chirps with a wry smile.

His head dips, his mouth almost touching my ear. "I need to speak to you," he whispers. The vibration resonates against the sensitive skin on the side of my neck. The warmth of his breath teases a full-body shiver out of me. My temperature shoots up. Apparently feverish isn't just a turn of phrase.

"Can we have dinner? Like tonight? I need to explain and I really don't want to do it with an audience."

Before I have a chance to speak, Dallas returns with two large take-out cups and hands one to Reagan. Thanking him, he places it on the table next to mine.

"Fancy seeing you here, Bailey. We were just talking about you," Dallas takes pleasure in telling me.

Reagan's head rolls back. He palms his face. "Dall..." There's an edge to his voice. This obviously leads me to wonder what they were discussing.

"What?" Dallas says, wearing the most suspiciously innocent look I've ever seen.

"Don't," Reagan warns him.

Dallas shrugs. His blue eyes take a lap around the table and come to rest on Dora. They sharpen. Curiosity blankets his face. "Do I know you?"

Dora squirms under his intense examination, doing everything in her power to avoid eye contact.

"Weren't you at that Theta UCLA mixer? You're Cat

Woman, right? With the vinyl getup and the red lips?"

Cat Woman? He's such an ass. A harmless one, I should clarify. Since I began filming the team I've learned two things about Dallas and both are one hundred percent accurate. The first, he has one of the most photogenic faces I've ever captured on film. And the second, he's never been anything other than nice and helpful to me. That doesn't negate the fact that Dallas is a major player—something he does not dispute. Problem is, I can't figure out if he's teasing her, or he's actually serious.

The thought of Dora in a vinyl jumpsuit has me grinning despite the *circumstance* sitting next to me.

"W-we have class together," she answers about a full minute later.

Without invitation, he sits on the bench, crams himself between her and another dude, his muscular arm stretching out over the back of the bench. "Russian lit."

"English lit," Dora is quick to correct.

"Right, that's what I said." He searches Dora's face with a pointed look. His cornflower blue eyes narrow. "I know your name...I know it." He taps his lips with his fingers. "Just keep swimming. Just keep swimming."

"That's D-Dory. My name is Dora."

"Huh. I guess that makes you an explorer."

"And I guess that m-makes you unoriginal."

Guffaws and snorts all around. Dallas grins and it's not one I want to see directed at sweet Dora. I'm all for growth and experimentation. Hell, I'm sure that's half the actual benefit of college. But this dude would not be good for her burgeoning self-esteem.

With his hand braced against the back of the bench, Dallas leans in, hovering over her, and she reacts by subtly shrinking away.

"Van Zant, step off my girl. You're making her uncomfortable." Zoe's voice is a sharp knife cutting through all the chatter in the room, the threat clear.

"It's fine," Dora mutters.

"No. It's not," Zoe counters, staring a third-degree burn onto Dallas's already tanned face. When he doesn't move fast enough for her liking, her stare sharpens. "Now."

Dallas leans back, takes Zoe's measure, and grins. "Chill, mama cat. Kitten here has claws. She can speak for herself."

"Kitten?" both Dora and Zoe say at once, their expressions on opposite ends of the spectrum. Dora's surprised and Zoe's disgusted.

Meanwhile Dallas is looking real proud of himself. "Isn't that right, Kitten?"

"I just threw up in my mouth," Zoe declares.

"S-stop calling me that."

Dallas's attention reverts to Zoe. "See?"

"I missed you," the man on my right whispers in my ear. Exhaling a tired sigh, I meet him eye to eye. One way or another this is getting resolved today.

"Yeah, what did you miss? Using me as an emotional punching bag? Or someone to eat with because you don't like to eat alone?" In his defense, he looks hurt.

"It's not like that. You know it's not."

He leans closer. So close that I can count the faint freckles hidden under his deep tan. That I can pick out the sharp needles of dark blue in the rims of his green eyes. That I can see the regret etched in the grooves of his forehead.

"I was wrong." He breathes deeply, pausing to gather his control. Then he lowers his voice. "I should never have treated you that way. I just...I..."

"What?"

"Would you two just fuck already," comes from across the table. "The sexual tension is killing us!"

If anyone's going to die it'll be Zoe and it'll be by my bare hands.

The entire coffee shop erupts...erupts. People cheering, clapping, whistling loudly. And I mean the entire place. She didn't even speak that loudly—not for Zoe.

I erupt too. My face, that is. To the brightest shade of red on the Pantone color scale. This is my basic nightmare. Being the object of everyone's attention. I can't even look at Reagan. If I find indifference or worse, an awkward refusal on his face I will die. So I do the only thing I can do; I get up slowly and walk out.

"Alice," Rea calls out.

"Alice, don't leave," Blake pleads.

Their voices trail after me as I pick my way between crowded tables.

"Zoe, that really crossed the line," Blake scolds her in a hushed tone.

"You were all thinking it. Don't pretend you weren't. I just did them a favor," Zoe argues in a *much* louder one.

"She's right," Dallas mutters.

I push through the glass door and take a deep breath. The crisp October air stings my lungs.

"Alice, wait." Reagan's hand wraps around my bicep,

gently stopping me.

I turn around to face him. "You were rude and insensitive and you embarrassed me in public," I begin without preamble. "You know how much I hate being put on the spot. What kind of friend does that?"

His face pinches. He crosses his arms. Looking off, he rocks back on his sneakers. "A bad one," he quietly admits. "I don't know what came over me…I mean, I *know* what came over me I just don't know why I embarrassed you on purpose."

In the pocket of his track pants, his phone rings. He takes it out and hits the red **Decline** button without even taking a moment to see who may be calling.

"What I was going to say before everyone stuck their noses in our business is that I'm sorry. I am so fucking sorry and—"

His phone rings again. Frustrated, he looks at the screen and pauses, eyes widening in surprise, when he sees the name. "I've gotta take this. Don't go anywhere," he orders. Then he hits **Accept.** "Hello? Hi, Foz…what…where is he?"

He rubs his brow, tips his head back. I watch his throat work as he swallows. Something's very wrong. It's in his body language, his voice.

His attention returns to me, expression troubled. "I'll be there in thirty minutes," he says, watching me as he speaks. "Don't let him leave, Foz…okay…yeah. Thanks for calling. See you soon, man."

Ending the call, he stuffs his phone back in the pocket of his track pants. "I gotta go. I'm sorry. It's my brother. Can I call you later?" His voice is quiet, subdued.

"What's wrong with Brian?"

"He's at the hospital. Someone cut him. One hundred and twenty stitches…I gotta go."

"I'll come with you."

"No. This hospital is in a bad part of town."

"I'm coming with you."

He shakes his head, jangles his car keys nervously. "It's not safe for you."

"We're wasting time."

He exhales, looking momentarily lost. Then he nods.

NINETEEN

REAGAN

One hundred and twenty stitches *to his face*. I'm so tired of worrying. It's hard to explain how exhausting loving someone with an addiction is. There are times when you just want to let go, cut ties. But that kernel of hope is always there, reminding you that maybe this is it, the time he finally hits bottom and turns it around. And there's always someone to feed your false hope. That person that knows someone who knows someone that beat it. So you keep going, keep praying. But that day never comes. Only more disappointment.

I drive to USC medical center on autopilot. I've been there so many times I could find it blindfolded by now. Alice doesn't say much and I say less. She seems to have called an intermission on our spat so I guess that's good.

By the time I park the Jeep in the lot, it's dusk. The top is down. This is the kind of neighborhood that if it weren't for the guys guarding the lot, it wouldn't be here later. We enter the emergency room and I immediately regret my decision to bring her. It's packed. Children crying. One old woman sitting alone in a wheelchair wails. Huddled in their plastic chairs, everybody else pretends they don't hear her.

And the odors...Jesus. A putrid mix of ammonia and vomit.

"I'm sorry I brought you here," I say to her.

She looks up at me with concern. I know I'm being selfish. That I only agreed to let her come because I feel better when she's around. Seeing her here now, though, among all this misery, I don't feel any better. It makes me want to put her back in the Jeep and drive her to safety. Where none of this can touch her.

"Don't worry about me. I'm tougher than you seem to think. Let's find your brother." She walks away, headed to the nurses' station.

"Foz Whitaker called me," I tell the nurse behind the counter, a middle-aged black woman.

Foz is my brother's long-time substance abuse counselor. Over the years, I've met more addiction counselors and therapists than I care to remember, and he's one of a few that truly wants to help. Foz is also the one who picks me up every time I'm close to throwing in the towel.

"He said my brother was brought in. Brian Reynolds."

She purses her lips and gives me a sharp look. "He's here. Punched an orderly in the face and broke his nose. It took three of us to restrain him."

Shame washes over me. She's not happy. I get it. Her job is already difficult, and Brian made it dangerous. I wouldn't want to work an ER in this neighborhood, either. As I say this, EMTs rush in with a gunshot victim. While I'm watching hell break loose, a hand sneaks into mine. Alice squeezes and lets go.

"Third bay on the right," the nurse informs us.

We find it at the end of a long hall. "I'll wait out here," Alice murmurs and I nod.

Behind the curtain, I find Brian strapped to the gurney, bound by his arms and legs. The gash runs in a semicircle from his temple over his eyebrow down his chin and ends at his jaw. It's a miracle he didn't lose his eye.

He picks his head up. "Rea?" Eyes wild, voice stressed.

They already stitched him up, shaved his face to do it. Which is startling because the top half is a deep brown color and the bottom is white. He looks younger with his face clean-shaven but not by much. His eyes are empty. Dull. The rest of him is still filthy. At least he still has the sneakers I gave him.

"Yeah. Bri, it's me."

He struggles against the restraints. "You gotta get me out of here, man. Fuck! Look at what they did to me!"

They did to him? The people that put his face back together? I shake my head. "You punched an orderly in the face. Broke his nose. What did you expect?"

"Get me out of here! I'm going crazy."

Because he's coming down from meth. I rake my hands through my hair, lace my fingers on top of my head. "Who did this to you?"

"No one."

"I'm not helping you until you tell me."

"Arghhh," he screams, jerks on the restraints some more, his body bowing off the gurney, the veins on his skinny arms popping in stark relief.

"Who cut you?"

"I was helping a friend and I got into it with someone."

Last I heard he was sleeping in a tent somewhere downtown, in one of the tent villages that are popping up all over the city. The homeless population in the state of California has blown up in recent years, along with property taxes and the cost of housing. People can't afford the rent anymore. The elderly and those on pensions and disability are most at risk, but substance abuse and mental illness are also part of the problem. And no one has a solution.

"Helping a friend score drugs?"

"No, man. They were gonna rape her and I had to stop them."

This is how it all started. And it's happening again. Brian's savior complex getting him into trouble. If there's a woman in distress in a twenty-mile radius, he'll find a way to get involved. "I gotta get back to her. Get me out of here, Rea. Please!"

Tears appear in his eyes and my stomach twists. As much as I want to help, my gut tells me he's a habitual and crafty liar, willing to do and say anything to score his next fix.

"She's in danger, Rea. I can't let her get hurt."

It's Jessie all over again.

He starts to cry outright, his face crumpling in pain. Fuck. Fuck. Fuck. My throat feels sore and my eyes damp. This is my brother. This is all that's left of him.

"Foz said he'll have a bed for you at the end of the week." I don't even recognize my own voice. It's strained and broken. "I'll sign you out if you promise to try rehab one last time. Do it for…what's her name?"

His head falls back down on the gurney and tears streak down his temples. "Lisa," he murmurs.

"You can get Lisa out of danger, really help her, if you get clean."

He nods. "Okay," he quietly concedes. "Okay. Let me get her somewhere safe and I'll go."

I sign him out a short while later. The hospital doesn't want him any more than he wants to be there. The only reason they patch him up from time to time is in deference to my parents. Although they've never asked that he get special treatment. They'd rather he "learn his lesson the hard way." As if addiction is a lesson to be learned.

They give me a packet with antibiotics and ointment. I hand him the ointment and he stuffs it in his pocket. He won't take the pills. He'll sell them for drug money, which is why I hold on to them.

I introduce Brian to Alice and he immediately gets quiet, avoiding eye contact with her. Part of him is still there, hidden behind the junkie he's become. He's aware of what he looks like to her and it embarrasses him.

Twenty minutes after that, we're driving down S. Central Ave. Late at night, this part of the city is an eerie ghost town. A deserted movie set. We spot a few people sleeping on the sidewalks, covered by cardboard. Other than that it's an occasional car and a lone man pushing a shopping cart full of junk. It's unseasonably warm tonight. I'm in a t-shirt and yet this guy is wearing at least four winter coats and a hood.

Being here makes me uneasy. This neighborhood is absolutely dangerous and having Alice in the car scares the shit out of me. If anything were to happen to her because of me...I can't even go there. It would absolutely destroy me. Despite the urge to hold her hand, I remind myself that I don't have the right.

"Here! Stop here," Brian orders from the back seat. The Jeep hasn't made a complete stop and Brian is already jumping out. "You got any money for me?" He has the balls to hold out his hand while he scans the area nervously.

"No," I immediately fire back. "And if you don't show up on Thursday at the clinic there won't be any more money from me. You hear me?" Brian's eyes get shifty, avoiding mine. "I mean it this time. I'm not going to be responsible for you ODing."

"I gotta go."

"I'll see you Thursday," I hammer again.

"Thursday," he quietly repeats.

"It was nice meeting you, Brian," Alice says in the sweetest voice. My gut clenches. This girl is awesome. The fucking best. I don't deserve to be her friend. Not after the way I treated her.

Brian smiles briefly and looks away. "You guys better get outta here. It's not safe for you."

I want to yell *no shit*. I want to yell at him until he listens.

Brian pivots and runs off.

"Thursday!" I shout. But he's already around the building and out of sight.

* * *

ALICE

With the streets mostly empty, it only takes us half an hour to get back to campus. It's 1 a.m. by the time Reagan parks the Jeep in front of my dorm. We haven't exchanged a single word since we dropped off Brian, his very sweet and very troubled brother.

Reagan turns off the engine and plants his forehead on the steering wheel in between his hands, the knuckles pale. "I shouldn't have taken you. It was stupid and selfish of me."

"Stop that. I made the decision to come along and I'm glad I did. Your brother is sweet."

He snorts. "Yeah, real sweet."

"How did it happen? The cut. God, it looked awful and painful."

"They couldn't give him any painkillers while they stitched him up because he's a known substance abusers," he tells me, his voice dull and distant. "A lot of them will injure themselves to get drugs." A shiver runs up my back. "He was trying to stop some guys from raping a girl he knows. That's how he got cut."

The air gets caught in my lungs, pain and sympathy pool in my gut. "Oh my God. Poor Brian. And the girl, is she okay?"

"For now. He was anxious to get back to her. That's why I signed him out."

I nod absently while the question I'm dying to ask hangs on my lips. "Do you think he'll show up at the clinic on Thursday?"

He still won't look at me. His breathing gets harsh. He sucks in deep breaths of air and expels them loudly. It's then I realize he's trying not to cry. With the heel of his palm, he starts pounding on the steering wheel, slams his body against the back of his seat, and tips his chin up to stare blindly into the cloudy night sky.

"I don't know," he croaks. "Honestly? No. I don't think he will." The truth comes out slowly, painfully. His throat works.

The muscle along the sharp cut of his jaw twitches.

I reach over, slide my hand up his shoulder, grip his neck, hot to the touch, alive under my fingertips, and bring him into my arms. He comes easily, hiding his face and sorrow on my shoulder, his arms banding around me in a crushing grip.

I pet his back and let him ride it out on the curve of my neck, all that anguish he's packed down over the years surging up at once. It's not fair. He shouldn't be carrying all the responsibility of his brother's welfare by himself. His parents are assholes. That goes without saying.

The cotton of my long sleeve shirt is damp when he pulls away. Then in one smooth motion, before I can see it coming, he cups my face between his large rough hands, leans down, and his warm lips touch mine. It's soft and gentle, a question instead of a command. And when I don't object, he kisses me again with more conviction. With urgency that speaks of a stolen moment that may never come around again.

I'm in shock. I'm lost in him. I'm thrilled. My joy climbs so high it is destined to end with a brutally hard landing. I know this. I do. But I want it so badly that I willingly ignore the voice in the back of my mind telling me that he's hurting and alone. That it's only natural to want to celebrate life, to feel something good, something tangible that connects us to another living being when we're faced with our own fragility. That voice urges me to pull away, to stop him. But I don't get the chance because he does it for me.

"I'm sorry. Fuck. I'm sorry, Alice." For a moment his lips hover over mine, unsure whether to stay or go.

Stay. Please stay.

How do I tell him that I'm not sorry? That I want his

sweet, soft kisses again and again. That I want kisses that are not so sweet too. All that and so much more from him.

He sits back in his seat and rubs his face. His lashes, still wet, glisten in the flood of light from the overhead streetlamp. "Please tell me we're okay. I can't lose you. Did I fuck this up again?"

"It's okay. You're upset..." I reassure, giving him the cover that his pained expression and voice are asking of me. "It was just..."

For the first time since we left the hospital, he turns to squarely meet my eyes. "A mistake," he finishes for me, consequently driving a blade through my heart.

"Right..." I get out of the Jeep. "I'll talk to you tomorrow."

I'm halfway to the door when I hear, "Alice." I turn and find him chewing on his bottom lip. "Thank you"

"No need for that."

"You are..." He gives me a funny, frustrated look, shakes his head. "Sorry. Thank you."

* * *

ALICE

Big Deal: a nude beach?

By now, these random texts are no longer cryptic.

Me: Do I have to go full-on nude, or can I start topless and ease into it?
Big Deal: ...
Big Deal: ...
Big Deal: you can ease into it.

Me: Then, yeah, why not.
Big Deal: you're full of surprises.
Me: Good ones?
Big Deal: great ones.

In the days that follow, our friendship is back on track. Even though there's a marked carefulness in the way he treats me that did not exist before. We both seemed to have recovered from *the kiss* without injury. Well, at least I pretend to have recovered. In reality, I'm living in a constant state of frustration and longing for more.

I had a friend in high school who liked to enter sweepstake contests. Anything that had a prize attached, she would enter. She won once. An all-expense-paid trip to London which included a first-class plane ticket and a four-night stay at a five-star hotel.

Her mother was a single parent who worked in a department store. Not only was it her first time out of the country, but it was also her first time out of the state. When she returned I asked her how it went. I expected her to be over the moon, regaling me with details sure to turn me gecko green with envy. Instead, she said it was terrible and depressing, that winning the trip was the worst thing that had ever happened to her. Up until that point, she'd been happy with vacations at the Jersey shore. Her life had been complete, fulfilling. The trip showed her what she was missing out on. She said she wished she'd never gone.

That's what kissing Reagan is to me. My imagination didn't even begin to do the reality of it justice. And now I'm stuck knowing two things. The first is that nothing and no one will ever compare, and the second is that he'll never be interested in me as anything other than a friend. I was a mistake, a lapse in judgment because he was feeling vulnerable.

TWENTY

ALICE

"What are you doing for Thanksgiving?" Reagan asks as soon as I answer my phone. It's the third time he's asked me this same question in the last two weeks. I'm seriously tempted to say I'm busy even though I'm lying in bed, staring aimlessly out the window into a cloudless blue sky.

I couldn't afford to go home and Aunt Peg and Wheels hit the road. They're in Vegas. I declined their invitation to go with them. He knows this. He also knows I turned down Dora's invitation to go to San Diego and have Thanksgiving with her family. He knows Zoe's in Cabo with her mother, and Blake went to New York to visit her sister. He knows all those things because we spend way too much time together. Neither of us voices out loud that two people who aren't dating shouldn't be spending every spare minute together but he hasn't brought it up, so why should I.

"Reading."

"Good. You're coming with."

"Where?"

"To my parents' for Thanksgiving dinner."

He said he wasn't sure whether he was going. He didn't

want to deal with his father riding him about bailing Brian out again. Apparently the hospital had contacted his parents that night and they had refused to get involved. Nice, right?

Brian never did show up the following Thursday at the clinic. Even worse, Reagan didn't seem at all surprised or upset by it. He said he's been disappointed so many times it doesn't even smart anymore.

"No—"

"I'm picking you up in twenty minutes," he says, speaking over me.

There is no way I'm going to Dr. and Dr. Reynolds's house of horrors in Beverly Hills. No way. I don't need to be *Sherlock Holmes* to figure out it'll turn into a disaster. "No."

"Yes."

"Reagan—"

"Alice—"

I fight the smile pulling my lips apart. "I'm really into this book."

That's a lie. A stone-cold lie. I'm really not. Not even a little bit. My mind has been wandering for hours. Turning onto my side, I stare at the contents of my open closet with trepidation. There's nothing in there even remotely appropriate. "And I don't feel like getting dressed."

And that's the truth. The God's honest truth. The last thing I want to do is attend a fancy dinner with Reagan's uptight parents. "I was going to order Chinese takeout and watch *Elf*."

"Great fucking movie."

"Twinsies. You can watch it with me." My voice ends on a high note, hoping that he'll drop it. My hope is thin, however. I've learned the hard way that Reagan has the tenacity of my cousin Marie's rescue Chihuahua, Liberace. You can't play fetch with that dog 'cause he—like Reagan—won't let the damn bone go.

"After we get back from my parents'."

Deep, heavy sigh. I can already see the writing on the wall. "I don't have anything to wear and your parents will hate me." Jumping out of bed, I tuck the phone between my shoulder and ear and rifle through all *three* possible options. All of which are black.

"They won't hate you." I don't fail to notice that he says nothing else to assure me of a warm welcome. "I can't deal with them right now. Not alone. I just…" Trailing off, he takes a deep breath. His exhaustion is so palpable it's coming through the phone and it pains me. I can't even fathom dreading spending time with my parents. "…can't. I need you. I'm asking you as my friend."

Straight to the heart. His words hit me straight in the heart muscle. That sweet voice asking me to be there for him spells game over for me. I'm a goner. I can't say no to him. Not now and, I suspect, not ever—a fact he never needs to know.

"Give me thirty minutes." My voice dies on the last vowel. I sound like a total downer. I know I do, and yet it can't be helped. I've heard enough about his parents to be legit terrified of those people.

They gave up on their son, wrote him off like he was a bad investment they needed to dump. Who does that? Who gives up on their son when he's battling an addiction? And two doctors, no less. I think of all the times my parents have bent over backwards to help me when they had nothing to give, and it leaves me cold and so very grateful. If those people have no sympathy for their own son, what could they possibly think of me?

"I'll text when I'm outside," he answers, suddenly perky.

"Yeah. Fine."

* * *

REAGAN

It's not fair to ask Alice to play buffer between me and my parents. I know it's not, but what happened with Brian is still weighing heavily on me and I'm in no shape to fend off my father today. Two, possibly three uninterrupted hours of him trying to bully me into choosing surgery are coming my way and I don't want this to be the day he finally pushes me over the edge. She keeps me centered, makes me feel like everything isn't spinning out of control. Even when it is.

I texted Alice a minute ago and didn't get a reply. I'm about to jump out of the Jeep and knock on her door when she steps out.

Ho-ly-shit.

I push my shades up to the top of my head to get a better look while Alice wraps one arm across her body and grips the opposite elbow—something she does when she's nervous, I've noticed. She rolls her eyes and the pale skin on her cheeks turns pink.

"Looking good, Jersey."

Her dress is not really showing any skin. Sexy isn't the way I'd describe it. It's black and sleeveless and falls right above her knees. But it grips her curves the way I'd like to grip her...

Better not go there. Maybe this was a bad idea. I'm full of

them lately. Like that godforsaken kiss. Probably the stupidest thing I've ever done. It even tops letting Dallas talk me and the rest of the team into posing nude for a calendar that raised funds for an animal shelter he supports. I spent thousands of dollars trying to scrub that picture off the Internet. I'll never forget that phone call from my father.

"Why am I staring at a picture of your hairless balls?"

No greeting. Straight for the throat. He'd caught one of the nurses on his floor looking at it on her phone. It would've gone over real well with medical school admissions officers too. This is much worse than that.

Imagining kissing Alice is one thing. Actually knowing what her soft, pillowy lips feel like is another. Way to torture myself. Every night since then I've fallen asleep with my dick in my hand and thoughts of those lips everywhere else. And that one kiss is going to have to suffice because she didn't seem to be affected at all. Took it all in stride, telling me it only happened because I was upset.

Bullshit.

I knew exactly what I was doing. And screwed everything up in the process. All that one kiss did was whet my appetite. I want more now, so much more, and I don't know how to get out of the box I put myself in.

Pushing her chin-length dark hair behind her ear, she gives me a shy smile that speaks directly to my balls. They draw up tight. Then my dick gets involved, trying to wave back. Thank God these pants have pleats.

After adjusting my khakis, I jump out of the driver's seat and go to open her door. My father might be an asshole, but he's an asshole with manners and he forced those manners on both my brother and me. She gets in and buckles up while I slide behind the wheel without once taking my eyes off of her.

"Is this okay?" she asks as she tugs on the hem of the dress.

It's pretty obvious she's uncomfortable so I make it a point to check out the dress, the hair, the shoes. She's wearing flats. "Perfect."

She smirks and looks ahead.

Alice isn't my usual type. I date girls that like to do what I do. Hang out at the beach, surf, play beach volleyball. I date beach bunnies and athletes. Not girls that prefer to be indoors and hide from the sun.

But damn if she hasn't changed what my type is.

* * *

ALICE

Wearing a crisp white dress shirt, tapered navy slacks, and driving loafers, Reagan looks like he stepped out of an IG male model feed. He's so jaw-dropping handsome I'm trying not to stare. Or drop a jaw. And especially extra mortifying, I'm pretty sure I look concussed.

I take circumspect inventory of what I'm wearing and suddenly determine I look like I'm wearing a Halloween costume. My black sleeveless jersey dress and my black ballerinas have always been my go-to outfit when I'm in New York and need to go somewhere that requires something other than my ripped skinny jeans. I thought I was okay. I thought I looked good...I don't think that any more.

"Are you sure this outfit is okay?" I tug on the high neckline, which is presently feeling like a noose around my neck.

"It's great," he says, smiling.

"Great if I were trying to look like *Wednesday Adams*? That kind of great, or just great in general?"

Am I fishing for a compliment? Maybe. My ego is going to need the boost if I have to stand next to him all day.

Reagan's green smiling eyes meet my worry-filled ones. "Just great." He reaches over and squeezes my thigh. It happens so quickly had anyone else done it I probably wouldn't have noticed.

Except—it's Reagan.

Which means the feeling is exponentially more meaningful. To me, that is. I'll probably spend the next hour dissecting this action ad nauseum whereas he couldn't be more oblivious to it. He must've sensed me stiffen because he side-eyes me briefly. The look on his face tells me he's wondering why I'm acting so strangely.

"Who will be at your parents' house?" I inquire, anything to distract him from this growing awkwardness between us.

"Some family friends. Maybe the Richardsons...I'm not sure—" He glances my way again and a frown forms on his face. "Is that okay?"

Before I can put a stop to it, the truth inadvertently spills out. "I'm always okay when I'm with you." And the second I realize how it sounds, I flush red-hot, embarrassment crawling all over me at the prospect of being found out.

On the edge of my vision, I see Reagan's head come around. Stare locked on to my profile, expression indecipherable. In the meantime, I do everything to avoid eye contact. And being the good guy that he is, he doesn't press me on the matter.

TWENTY-ONE

REAGAN

This was selfish of me. The closer we get to my parents' house on Roxbury Dr. the more I realize it, the sinking feeling in the pit of my stomach growing stronger as the miles shrink.

We pull in the driveway of the restored 1930s Spanish-style house I grew up in and glance over in time to catch Alice's eyes widen and her lips part as she takes it all in.

"Wow," she whispers.

A massive explosion of bougainvillea vines in every shade of pink and coral carpet the front of the house, covering the white stucco all the way to the red tiled roof.

"It took them years to fix it up."

"I wish I'd brought my camera."

Eyeing the Jaguar parked next to the detached six-car garage, I say, "My parents' friends are here. I used to date their daughter in high school."

Alice examines my face. "Oh, okay...right," she begins awkwardly. It's then I realize my mistake. "Are you uncomfortable having me here with them?"

"No!" bursts out of me. "Jesus. No. I don't want *you* to be uncomfortable if they bring Jordan's name up. Both our parents were pushing for more and they have a tendency to harp on about it."

"Rea, the only people that can make me feel uncomfortable or hurt my feelings are the ones I care about." She gives me a pointed look, no doubt referring to my dick move in front of the shady guy. "I'll be fine."

This girl kills me. I get lost staring at the soft pillow of her bottom lip, the way it gets really full in the middle and tapers on the sides. I want to kiss her so badly again it's painful. Physically fucking painful.

"Rea?"

Her voice snaps me out of my staring jag. "Yeah, let's do this."

We make our way up the steps to the carved mahogany front door and Lionel, my parents' estate manager for the past ten years, is already holding it open. He must've seen us on the security cameras. Not a moment after he greets us, my mother is advancing down the hallway, headed straight for us, heels clicking all the way.

"There's my baby. I see you're still not wearing sunscreen."

With her short blonde hair and line-free face, my mom looks half her age. She's about Alice's height, maybe a little thinner. The only feature we share are her eyes. People have even mistaken me for her boyfriend.

She hugs me quickly, cups my face, and let's go even faster. My mother is a nervous person. Brisk movements, quick smiles, fast talking. It's just how she is. Her keen stare shifts to Alice who's been standing quietly to the side watching us.

"And who's this? A friend?"

"Mom, this is Alice."

Alice comes forward with an outstretched hand and a shy smile and an overwhelming amount of pride invades my chest. It catches me off guard. Then again, Alice has been catching me off guard since the moment I met her. And although I'm not sure yet how I feel about it, I do know that I've never felt like this before.

"It's so nice to meet you, Dr. Reynolds. And thank you so much for having me. Your house is amazing."

Dr. Deb, as Brian and I used to call her just to piss her off, offers her a brief smile and her hand a quick squeeze. "Nice to meet you too, Alice. Reagan seldom brings friends home so it's a pleasure to have you."

The subtext—my mother's fishing for clarification. She's hoping Alice is only a friend. I also note she didn't tell Alice to call her Deborah the way she told Jordan.

Mom's gaze focuses intently on Alice's face. "You have beautiful skin."

Alice grins widely. "Thank you. I wear sunscreen."

Mom smiles back. "I know. I'm a dermatologist. Come in. The Richardsons are already here." While Mom walks ahead of us, headed for the den, I take Alice's hand in mine.

Alice's smile turns into surprise and confusion, but I don't have time to explain that the moment we stepped inside my house a sense of protectiveness came over me. That I feel responsible for having dragged her into a den of hungry wolves. Alice only has a vague idea of what my parents are capable of and it better stay that way.

"Your father is boring them to death with stories about

work. Jordan is so excited to seen you, honey."

Shit. My steps slow. Had my mother mentioned Jordan was coming, I would never have come. My mother walks into the den ahead of us, and I pull Alice back.

"What?" she whispers at my expression of pure frustration.

"Whatever I say in there—just go with it."

"Go with what? Reagan?"

I enter the den tugging her along. My father and Steve Richardson are huddled by the television where the Cowboys are up on the Redskins by a field goal. Glancing over his shoulder, he glares at me. "Reagan, I thought I said four?" It's only 4:20 but the old man never misses an opportunity to bust my balls.

"How's the team doing?" Mr. Richardson calls out.

"Opening round of the NCAA tournament next Saturday," I reply and he gives me a thumbs-up. My old man barely musters a smile.

"Rea!" Jordan gets up from the couch and closes the distance between us in seconds. My muscles stiffen automatically. All except for my dick of course. That's a pretty good recap of our relationship. Hidden behind me, Alice tries to extricate her hand from mine and I tighten my hold.

Jordan, easily five-eleven in heels, throws her arms around my neck and pulls my head closer. She attempts to kiss me on the lips and I turn away in time to avoid it.

"Jordan. This is Alice, my girlfriend." If my turning away from her doesn't adjust her expectations, then my tone better.

Jordan's smile disappears and there's an audible gasp in the room. Not sure if it came from Alice, Jordan, or my mother.

It's a poorly designed plan, on the fly, and the best I can do on short notice. I won't be ambushed, and I can see now it was the plan all along. Which is why *my* plan is to dine and ditch as quickly as possible.

One-handed, I pry Jordan's wrist free from around my neck and drop it. Her sharp blue eyes shuttle between me and Alice who's looking less and less comfortable with more and more attention on her.

"Girlfriend? You never mentioned a girlfriend."

"We haven't talked since the summer. Alice and I met at the start of the semester."

Jordan's attention shifts to Alice. "Hi, I'm Jordan. Reagan's ex-girlfriend"—she holds out a hand—"but I'm sure he's told you all about me."

No. Not really. I mentioned having had a girlfriend in high school once, and only in passing after Alice told me she'd had a boyfriend in high school. I never spoke of Jordan by name.

Alice goes to shake it with a soft smile of her face. "Alice and yes, he did." She lied to spare Jordan's feelings. Damn, I am in deep with this girl. And getting a pressing urge to take her away from here and kiss her until she admits that she liked kissing me too. That she wasn't as unaffected as she looked.

Regaining her footing, Jordan pushes her long brown hair off her shoulder and smiles.

"Well…" my mother interrupts. She smiles stiffly. It's so forced it looks painful. I can't decide if she looks disappointed because I blew up her carefully laid trap, or because she disapproves of Alice. "Let's eat, shall we?"

* * *

ALICE

"I'm ready to come home. I can't take another Boston winter," Jordan says as she cuts her asparagus into tiny child-friendly bites. She's pretty. Tall and willowy with straight, brown hair. Seated across from me, next to her mother, her blue eyes have not left Reagan, who's gone completely silent since we sat down an hour ago. They've all been speaking around me like I don't exist. Which, in all fairness, I prefer.

"No Harvard Medical School for you?" Reagan's dad asks, seated at the head of the table opposite his wife.

Talk about intimidating…he's said a total of one sentence to me since I walked in. "Nice to meet you, Alice." That's it. He keeps giving me the suspicious side-eye, though. That's been fun #houseofhorrors.

Reagan looks like his dad—tall, perfect bone structure—with the exception of his eyes. His father has blue eyes like Brian. The resemblance is kind of creeping me out because he's like…*Evil Reagan*. If this were a Marvel movie, that's who Pat Reynolds would be. By the way, the only reason I know his name is because Jordan addressed him as Dr. Reynolds and he insisted she call him Pat.

All this hidden under a carefully orchestrated disguise. His mother, who I know is in her mid fifties, looks not a day older than forty with her cute, punky haircut and her expensive, casual designer clothes. Same goes for his dad. His hair does not have a single gray hair, I suspect courtesy of a very expensive hairdresser. And his clothes—the slim-fitted pink dress shirt and flat-front slacks say, I'm an easygoing, hip guy. Yeah, no. Easygoing and hip are not even in his vocab.

"No," Jordan answers.

"With your grades, you'll have your pick," Reagan's father claims.

"UCLA is my first choice. I'm looking forward to being back home, close to Mom and Dad." Jordan smiles at her father.

"Liz, you must be so proud." Rea's mom beams at her friend.

"Yes. We are." Liz shares a satisfied smile with her husband. Then she aims her pointed interest at Rea. "What about you, Reagan? Made any decisions?"

"No," Reagan answers without hesitation.

"UCLA. Surgery," his father answers for him and I watch his grip on his utensils tighten.

Jordan grins broadly at Reagan. "That would be so much fun to have classes together again. Isn't it strange how things come full circle? Almost like fate is playing a role in it."

"It's not fate. It's my father not understanding what the hell the words *I haven't made a decision yet* mean," Reagan fires back.

All this hostility reminds me of what I'm missing out on. The screaming kids and the three dogs barking. The cat, the hamsters. All the food and laughter. My parents are, as usual, spending Thanksgiving at Uncle Joe's, my stepmom's brother's house.

I feel so bad for Reagan I want to pull him into a hug and take him away from this awful place.

His father shoots him a warning glare, but stops short of arguing. Then, God help me, Dr. Reynolds's pointed stare moves to me. "What about you, Alice? Any career plans or are you just going to wing it like the rest of your generation?"

Beside me, I feel every fiber of Reagan's being drawing tight enough to pluck.

"I have a very clear career plan, actually," I tell him with my chin held high. "I'm a film major with an emphasis on cinematography. I'm going to be a cinematographer."

"Hollywood is a tough place for a woman. What's your plan B?"

"Pat, things are changing," his mom remarks.

"Not enough. For every ten men maybe one woman finds steady work. What kind of life is that?" he argues with his wife. "Unless she plans on living off her parents. I see a lot of that these days." His frosty gaze is back on me. "What about your parents? How do they feel about you chasing this dream on their dime?"

Wow, okay, it's the Spanish Inquisition. If this is what Brian and Reagan have had to fend off their entire lives, it's a miracle they didn't produce two sociopaths.

A tiny smile flirts on Jordan's mouth. She's enjoying this… the bitch.

"Dad, give it a rest," Reagan drawls with a shake of his head. "She doesn't have to justify her choices to you."

"She's not a child, Reagan. If she can't answer a few harmless questions, how will she succeed in the Hollywood cesspool?"

"My parents have always been very supportive of my choices, Dr. Reynolds. And I'm not pursuing it on their dime. I have a scholarship and I've worked very hard to save up enough to finish my BA at Malibu."

I squeeze Rea's thigh under the table, reassuring him that I've got this. At least, I think I've got this. You need a whip and a chair to fend off these people. Reagan places his hand over mine and rubs.

Pat Reynolds nods. "What business are they in? Your parents?"

"My stepmom is an emergency room nurse, and my dad works for the US Postal Service."

"Your parents are divorced?" Deborah Reynolds asks in a brisk tone.

"No, my mother died of cancer when I was five."

"I'm sorry to hear that." No emotional reaction at all. Eyes cast down, she continues cutting her turkey breast as if I'd asked her to pass the salt. Wow, Dr. Deborah Reynolds's bedside manner leaves a lot to be desired.

"What does your father do for the Postal Service?" This is like tag team wrestling, perfectly synchronized to take the opponent out with a power bomb. I glance at the other end of the table to find Pat Reynolds's cold, rapt attention on me.

"Jesus Christ!" Reagan cuts in, tone exasperated. "Can we talk about something else? I saw Brian. Why don't you take some interest in him."

He's close to losing it. I know what his tipping point looks like now. A beat of tension-filled silence ensues in which Reagan's dad does his best to stare him into submission and fails. Also noteworthy, the Richardsons don't seem fazed by any of this.

"We're not discussing your brother today," Dr. Reynolds declares. "I'd like to have a peaceful meal if you don't mind."

That has me biting back the urge to laugh. I guess I'm not entitled to the same courtesy. I sit up straighter and somehow summon the courage to stare Pat Reynolds in the eye. "My father delivers the mail."

You can hear a pin drop. His parents exchange a look. "That's nothing to be ashamed of," his mother has the audacity to say with a stiff smile. With a smile!

"Mom," Reagan growls, a storm brewing on his face.

"No, it isn't," is all I say out of respect for my friend. I'll walk out of here basically unscathed. But he'll never be rid of these people.

* * *

REAGAN

"Hi, Olga." My parents' housekeeper is bent over the kitchen sink, rinsing dishes and loading the dishwasher. After twenty years of handling all the household business like clothing, feeding, and caring for me and Brian, all the stuff my mother never had time for, I guess I should call her part of the family.

She glances over her shoulder and smiles once she realizes it's me. "Reagan!" I don't come around often. Last time might've been three months ago so it's startling to note the changes. The lines along her eyes more pronounced, the hair completely white.

She dries her hands and closes the distance between us. "So handsome," she tells me as she pats my cheek. "You have new girlfriend, I see." I return a smile because I can't very well tell her the truth.

Her smile cuts off and her expression grows troubled. "You see Brian?"

Brian has always been her favorite. When we were kids, during the summer, the two of them would spend hours by the pool. Olga reading and Brian yelling at her to watch him swim laps. She loved indulging him. And maybe because she doesn't have kids of her own, she thrived off his need for her attention. I shake my head and her mood gets darker.

My mother walks into the kitchen with a smile on her face, completely unfazed by the skirmish at dinner. That's her superpower. Her ability to completely block out the fact that my father is an epic asshole and that she sometimes comes in a close second. Ignore the problem and it ceases to exist. The Reynolds family motto. She did the same with Brian.

"Olga, you don't have to do that," she says. "Leave it. Consuelo can do it tomorrow."

"Thank you, Dr. Reynolds. Good night." Olga's worked here for twenty years, lives in this house, and never once has my mother given her permission to address her by her first name. It has pissed me off since I was old enough to understand.

Olga's grin returns when her attention shifts back to me. "It's so good to see you, Reagan. You come home more, okay?"

"See, even Olga thinks you don't come home enough."

Ignoring my mother's constant nagging, I focus on Olga. "Good to see you too, Olga. Happy Thanksgiving." Yeah, some Thanksgiving.

Nodding, Olga smiles one last time before she leaves the kitchen. Mom grabs a bottle of white wine out of the wine cooler and sets it on the kitchen island.

"Where's Alice?"

"Looking at old family photos." She retrieves a bottle opener from a drawer, places it on the marble counter next to the bottle, and stares at it.

"Honey…" She glances up at me and her expression softens. "She's a sweet girl and I'm sure she's got a bright future ahead of her, but she's not for you." She starts picking at the plastic seal with her nails. "Dammit," she whispers less than a moment later and stops what she's doing to inspect the damage done to her pale nail polish.

I take the bottle out of her hands and rip the seal off, set about uncorking it. "Relax, Dr. Reynolds. No need to plan a wedding…it's casual."

A self-satisfied smile replaces her carefully crafted neutral expression, the same one she wears every time she thinks she has the upper hand. "I see the way you look at her, Reagan. Give me a little credit for knowing my own son's mind."

Instinct kicks in, the pressing urge to protect Alice from my parents at all cost. Because I don't trust them not to tear her apart. Quietly, patiently, with a million tiny cuts. That's how they do it. The same way they did it to Brian. The same way they've been trying to do it to me.

"Then I guess you don't know me as well as you think you do because I have no feelings for her and she's got even less for me."

The minute the words are out of my mouth I recognize them for the absolute bullshit lie that they are. Do I have feelings for Alice? I think so. The thought of her being with anybody else makes me break out in a cold sweat and want to kill someone. So, yeah, I'd say I have feelings for her.

But what do I do about them? My life is so complicated right now I can barely keep my head above water. And Alice… she's the only good thing in it. I can't risk losing her by asking for more and then not giving her what she deserves.

And that doesn't even speak to the fact that she's told me repeatedly that I'm not her type—whatever the fuck that means. Essentially, we're both completely unavailable.

"You've got your entire life ahead of you. Medical school is hell on relationships and residency even worse. You'll be in your mid thirties by the time you have a minute to spare. Do you really want to do that to her?"

"You and Dad survived it," I find myself saying, defending a nonexistent relationship that I know for a fact Alice does not want.

"Barely. And only because I was just as busy." My mother walks around the counter and brushes the hair off my forehead. "If you care about her at all you'll put a stop to it now. Don't string her along. It's not fair to her."

TWENTY-TWO

ALICE

That was fun. Heavy sarcasm. Only a few hours in the presence of the esteemed Dr. and Dr. Reynolds and the secondhand pressure nearly suffocated me to death. It's impossible to breathe around those people. And it breaks my heart for Reagan and Brian. I can't even imagine what it was like for them as children, growing up with all those expectations placed on them.

We drive back to Malibu in complete silence, the tension so thick you need garden shears to cut it. I guess it's the observer in me that made me stop and listen when I heard Reagan talking with his mother. I should've kept walking to the bathroom. I should've stayed home and read my shitty book. But I did neither. Instead I came, I saw, I overheard. I have no one other than myself to blame.

After the "I have no feelings for her and she less for me" remark, I walked away. I know conviction when I hear it. There was force behind those words. And I have my pride. I'm not a complete glutton for punishment.

Speaking of Reagan, he has yet to look at me once since

leaving Roxbury Drive. He's definitely not one prone to broody moods. He's naturally chatty and bordering on almost annoyingly upbeat. Our conversations have always had an easy rhythm, a steady flow. Which is why this behavior is throwing me for a loop. I don't know how to handle this version of him. I've never seen him this shut down before with the exception of the night we saw Brian.

I wouldn't blame him if he wanted to ditch me and spend some time alone. Doesn't mean it doesn't sting, though. The last thing I want to be to him is another burden he can't wait to be rid of.

"Want to crash at my place? No one's home," he says, staring out at the empty highway, tight grip on the steering wheel, broad shoulders at a perfect ninety-degree angle he's so tense.

Okay, I was a little bit off the mark. A slow-spreading warmth that started in the cavity of my chest swiftly travels up my neck and over my face. We've never had a sleepover. This is highly irregular for us, but I don't question it. He doesn't want to be alone and I get it. I know how it feels. Sometimes to ride out the storm all you need is someone to hold on to, a fixed point, a steady presence that doesn't tax you emotionally because you're not invested that way. I'm that to him. Someone he's not worried about impressing. Someone he's not invested in.

Reagan's gaze cuts back and forth from the road to me.

"I don't have anything with me," I remind him.

"You can borrow my stuff."

An image of Reagan in nothing other than his underwear immediately crops up and once again I curse my ability to visualize in fine detail.

You can do this, Bailey. Your friend needs you. Buck up, bitch.

Because isn't that what friendship is? Putting your own feelings aside when you're needed. Stepping up to the plate knowing your heart's on the line, the one that will take the hit.

"Okay," I tell him.

An undeniable urge to gauge his reaction makes me glance his way again and I'm just in time to catch it, the subtle softening of his features, the relaxing of his shoulders. That's when I know I made the right choice.

"Patrick," he cryptically announces out of nowhere. "My middle name is Patrick…I'm ashamed of it."

My heart hurts. It literally hurts for him. "You're nothing like him," I assure him. "You have nothing to be ashamed of."

* * *

REAGAN

"I sleep naked."

Maybe this is a mistake. Judging by the way Alice stands stiffly in the threshold of my bedroom, I would say it is. The abject fear on her face knocks a burst of laughter out of me. "Kidding. I keep my skivvies on."

After the disaster at dinner, I need her here. I need her more than her desire to keep me at arm's length and definitely more than my pride. She gets me. It's not often you find someone that you don't need to constantly explain yourself to. It's never happened to me before and I'm not about to miss this opportunity. And maybe I am asking too much of a girl who has been very clear about friend-zoning me from the start, but I'm going to take anything I can get…even if it comes with the nastiest case of blue balls I've ever experienced.

I grab a t-shirt out of the dresser and toss it at her. Catching it, she holds it up to her body and the hem of my shirt hits her knees. Alice isn't tiny, around 5'6", but I've got a good six inches on her. She giggles, and my heart feels it. I swear the sound of her laughter has the power to push into place whatever it is that feels out of sorts inside my chest. She catches me staring at her mouth and her forehead wrinkles. I clear my throat, look away.

"There are clean towels under the sink and new toothbrushes. Take whatever you need."

"Where's Dallas and the Petermans?"

"Dall got in his car and said he'd be back in a few days. And the twins are with their parents until tomorrow." A really awkward moment of silence ensues where I can't help staring at her and she can't seem to meet my eyes. "Al?" She quickly glances up. "If you're uncomfortable…"

"No, I'm good." She smiles and holds up the t-shirt as she crosses the bedroom headed for the bathroom. "Let me get changed."

"Wanna watch something? I have Netflix and Apple TV."

"Of course you do," she teases. "Pick something and I'll be out in a minute."

The door shuts and I strip down to my black boxer briefs and select something to watch. *Dead Pool 2*. Perfect. After what happened at dinner, I'm wrecked and in dire need of a mindless distraction. I grab a couple of bottles of water out of the small refrigerator in my room, set them by the nightstand. I want her to be comfortable. That's all…or maybe I'm somewhat nervous too.

Alice steps out of the bathroom wearing my favorite t-shirt. It hangs loosely to her knees, except for where the tips of her hard nipples tent the fabric. And the minute I get a good look, I lose what's left of my mind and go full-on cro-fucking-magnon.

This was a mistake. Having her here is a mistake. My dick decides this is a great time to introduce himself, and the best I can do is drop my hands in front and pray she doesn't notice.

"Are you okay?"

"I'm fine." I duck out, turn away from her, and walk into the bathroom without meeting her searching gaze. Minutes later, I step out and find Alice tucked in bed. Without any makeup, she looks so much younger than…

"Are you twenty-one yet?"

"February thirteen." She beams up at me, her full pink lips parting to show her bright white teeth. And damn if she isn't the prettiest girl I've ever seen.

"Don't make plans. I'm taking you out."

Her thumb runs back and forth across her bottom lip as she studies me. "The girls may want to do something, bossy pants."

Bossy pants? Whatever. "We'll take them with us." She can call me whatever she wants as long as she keeps smiling at me like that.

"You'd do that?" The pitch of her voice rises, her excitement palpable. I want her to look at me that way forever—like I can do no wrong.

"It's your birthday, Bailey." I shrug. "I'll do whatever makes you happy."

I find myself staring at her mouth again. Swear to God, I'm

under a spell. One more kiss. Just one. Then I'll slide between those shapely white thighs, push myself inside of her, and fuck her into next week the way I've been dreaming about doing for the past two months.

"What are we watching?" She looks so oblivious to the filthy shit that's playing out in my mind that it almost makes me laugh.

When I don't answer right away, she stares at me blankly, puzzled by my behavior. Can't blame her. I'm standing by the side of the bed, looking at her like a twelve-year-old that's gotten his first peek at Internet porn, so a little confusion is justified.

I slide into bed making sure to stay on my side. It's a California king-size bed. This should keep some respectable distance between us. Otherwise it'll be another sleepless night for me.

"*Dead Pool 2.*"

"Oh good. I love *Dead Pool*. Do you mind? My feet are cold."

No sooner has she made this announcement than her feet are on mine. Cold doesn't even begin to describe them. I yelp, jerking them back. "The hell! Are you...what the...I've dissected dead things with more body heat."

Laughter breaks out. Head thrown back, uncontrollable laughter. It's husky and sexy as hell. A familiar sensation stirs in my balls. This was a mistake.

"Gimme those frozen toes."

Still smiling, she narrows her eyes. "What are you going to do?"

"I'm not having those dead things sneak up on me in the

middle of the night. Hand them over."

Chewing on her lip, she considers my command. "You're very bossy tonight."

There's a teasing note in her voice that feeds my lust. I wonder what it would sound like whispered in my ear as I'm driving my dick inside of her. The image has my heart thrashing inside my chest.

"What are you thinking about? You have a weird look on your face."

I can't answer. I'm too busy watching her pull her legs out from beneath the covers and extending them in my direction. I love her legs. Not a single blemish or freckle. Pale and curved in all the right places. I'd love them even more wrapped around my waist.

She places her feet in my lap, and I shift my hips to hide my hard-on. Her delicate toes are painted light purple and so damn cute. I picture them rubbing up and down my shaft.

"Nothing. I'm thinking about your dead toes."

She laughs again. I take her feet between my hands, push my thumbs into the arches. Her eyelids get heavy and her mouth slack. I give her toes a gentle tug and a soft whimper slips out.

"Oh God, that feels so good…" She gasps when I cup them and gently squeeze. "Don't stop."

And as I watch her face glow with pleasure, I say what's been on my mind since we got back. "I'm sorry my parents were rude to you. I shouldn't have forced you to come."

There's only understanding on her face. No pity, no judgment. I can tell her anything and not feel threatened. That's never happened to me before and the feeling is addicting as hell. I am fucking crazy about this girl and every minute I'm with her I fall deeper and deeper.

I play with her toes, slide my index finger along the sensitive skin between each of them. She shivers and inhales sharply. I look up, into her heavy-lidded eyes, and time stands still. I see my life, next year in med school. No sleep. I'm miserable, just going through the motions. Then I see Alice living her life. Laughing with her friends…talking to the douchebag in her film class. And my heart sinks into my gut.

"Stop apologizing," she murmurs, snapping me out of the moment. "I wanted to go with you. You don't need to be responsible for me the way you are for everything and everyone else…I will say this, they're actually worse than you described them. Now I know why Brian is so troubled." She presses her toes into my abs and I swallow down a groan. "I have no idea how you turned out so well."

"They definitely did their best to screw us up, but my brother started using because of a girl."

Her flashing eyes, burning with curiosity, scan my face. She sits up abruptly, takes her feet back, and crosses her legs. I instantly miss them. "How?"

Exhaling tiredly, I decide on the abridged version. "Brian was always the perfect son. Amazing swimmer, nationally ranked. Great water polo player. Academic highest honors— you know, all that. Sophomore year a girl named Jessie Turner transferred in from Santa Cruz. Gorgeous, best-looking girl in school and that's saying a lot. She ran with a really fast crowd—already doing eight balls as a sophomore."

Alice's eyes get even bigger.

"Yeah. Played the broken damsel part like a fucking Oscar

winner. Brian fell hard for her. He started doing coke to party. She was always taunting him into shit. Saying he didn't have the balls for it…anyway, it worked. He started experimenting. Started cutting school. Got kicked off the water polo team for not showing up for a game. Then he won a swim meet and tested positive. My parents sent him straight to rehab…while Brian was in rehab, Jessie overdosed and died."

A gasp has me looking up into Alice's soft brown eyes. I won't lie. In the past, I've used women as a refuge from all the responsibility weighing on me as much as they used me for their own self-interest. It was a perfect arrangement. The problem is the high-flying vibes only lasted until the following morning. Then I'd wake up alone and find myself scraping bottom again. But Alice? It's not her body that gives a man a soft place to land—it's her eyes.

"He went off the rails. Broke out of rehab and went on a three-month bender that had my parents picking him up in a drug den in San Francisco. After that it was just more of the same. He never even got his high school diploma…"

She takes my hands in hers, tugs on my fingers the same way I tugged on her toes, her gaze cast down on where we touch.

"I was thirteen and the first lesson I learned about love was that it could ruin your entire life."

"Do you still believe that?" She looks up then, and it takes everything I've got not to kiss her.

"No."

Not since I met you, the words form in my head. And that's where they stay.

* * *

ALICE

A chill wakes me abruptly out of a deep sleep. Confused, I scan the room until I'm reminded that I'm at Reagan's. In his bedroom. Alone in his bed. Then it all comes back to me. The horrible dinner. The heart-to-heart. After the talk we were both exhausted. He put on *Dead Pool 2*, and we fell into a comfortable silence. The kind you rarely find and often yearn for. I only made it through the opening credits.

I wish I knew how to keep some emotional distance between us. Which is definitely in my best interest because the mixed signals haven't stopped. I can't decide if *he's just not in to me,* or he can't make up his mind. Neither of which do me any good. And between the sweet gestures and the heartfelt talks, he makes it impossible not to fall for him. After last night I am one thoughtful action away from hitting ground zero in L.O.V.E.

The cable box flashes 2:59. It's creeping me out to be in this massive bed alone so I go in search of him. At the end of the empty, dark, never ending hallway, I hear the sound of splashing water and head for the patio. Across the living room, I spot him through the open sliding doors. The water churns and foams as he swims the length of the pool, each stroke faster than the last. It looks like someone is working out some serious aggression.

Barefoot, I shuffle outside onto the patio at the same time he hits the edge. "Reagan." My voice is raspy from lack of use, but he hears me all the same because he comes up sucking in huge gulps of air and looks over his shoulder.

I expect to find frustration on his face. Maybe a teasing smirk? That I would understand—it's practically his signature. Even exhaustion would make sense. What I don't expect to find is lust, unmistakable, undisguised lust on his face. For me.

His hot stare slowly travels from my toes to my face. Almost instantly I'm engulfed in heat. An aching emptiness develops between my thighs. And my nipples perk up. It's been so long I almost forgot I had nipples. I literally go from barely awake to fully turned on in less than a second…from a single glance. God help me. What would happen if he actually touched me?

"Did you…uh, sleep?" I don't know what else to say. Tension is running inexplicably sky high between us and it's making me nervous and curious as to what the heck happened while I was asleep. Did a flip get tripped in his head? And what tripped it because I was firmly in the friend zone a few hours ago.

That's when he jumps out of the pool and faces me.

And he's naked…*naked*. Gloriously naked.

I can't even pretend that I'm not staring at his penis. I am incapable of speech let alone artifice of any kind so I go right on staring.

It's beautiful, perfect. That's not hyperbole. I've seen a couple, mostly on the Internet, and his is the best by far. Not too big. Not too small. Not too thin. I'm suddenly the Goldilocks of dick. It lies long and thick against his smooth, hairless sac. Sweet Jesus, he shaves.

While I'm staring appreciatively, it starts to grow, standing at attention while water slowly streaks down the rest of his tan, finely honed muscles. His body is unbelievable. At the risk of sounding clichéd as eff—a work of art. I want to spend days staring at it through the viewfinder of my camera, get lost between every curve and hard angle and never return.

He starts moving, coming for me like he means business. Meanwhile I'm frozen, incapable of doing anything other than watching him obliterate the distance between us in a few, long strides.

"No, I didn't sleep," he rasps. Eyelids heavy, chest heaving with deep breaths. "You expect me to sleep with your sweet round ass pressed up against my dick?"

Am I supposed to answer that?

Exhaling harshly, he tips his head back and gives the stars a passing glance before his focused attention returns to me. "No. No, I did *not* sleep," he answers for me and he doesn't sound too happy about it, either. His hot green gaze drops to my hard nipples, poking the cotton t-shirt, and his expression grows pained. "I thought I wasn't your type?"

He's serious? He actually believed me? I guess I'm a better actress than I thought I was.

"I-I uh…" stutters out of me.

Inching closer, he takes my face in his hands. The t-shirt I'm wearing, his t-shirt, gets soaked where my breasts touch his chest. His erection presses into my lower belly. And oh my God, if he just bends his knees a little I am going to go off like a rocket.

"You said I wasn't your type. Did you mean it?"

That's when things go from shocking and borderline amusing—to serious. There's uncertainty in his quiet voice. The swagger is nowhere to be found. No arrogance in the way his lashes lower while he waits for me to answer. He's baring himself to me. His beautiful naked body. The tender vulnerability in his open gaze. He's placing himself at my mercy.

No. I don't mean it. I'm sorry I ever said it. And I've never wanted anyone more. The words circle round my head, hang on my lips. And I do. I want him so much. I'll take as much as he can give for as long as he wants me. Because I'd rather have a little bit of him than nothing at all.

"Heeyyy. Am I interrupting something?" a male voice queries from somewhere behind us.

Our heads jerk in unison to find Dallas standing a few feet away in the living room. His eyes—black and blue and swollen. His lip cut. His arm in a sling.

"What the fuck?" Reagan mutters. "Where have you been?"

"Jail."

TWENTY-THREE

ALICE

"That's pretty cool," Simon says as he and Morgan watch the first cut of the video I'm going to submit for the James Cameron internship on my iPad, the deadline only three weeks away.

On screen, we watch the boys moving in slow motion. Dallas coming out of the water vertically to slam the ball into the back of the net, the water spray trailing the ball creating a perfect arc. All that raw emotion and unbridled energy working in synch. Factor in the animated faces of the players around him and it's pretty awesome if I do say so myself.

The transitions between video and still shots aren't as seamless as I want them to be yet. For that, I need to use a professional editing machine like the one Simon said he has access to.

"Three weeks, people. Do not wait till the last minute. I will not be taking any submissions past the stroke of midnight on the twenty-first. So don't come to me with excuses of your grandmother losing a kidney in a freak motorcycle accident and you being the only matching donor in the world. True story—someone tried that one on me once," professor Marshall barks.

The lecture hall breaks out in laughter.

"The transitions are a little choppy," I whisper. "I'd really appreciate it if I could get some time on the Avid machine…if the offer still stands."

Simon's dark eyes slide from my iPad to meet mine, his face a blank canvas. I can't get a read on him which, in and of itself, is a little strange.

"Uh, yeah. Let me check with my buddy, see when he's got time available." There's a hollowness to his voice that engages my suspicion mode. Maybe he doesn't know how to decline?

My attention swings to Morgan. "What do you think?"

"Semi-naked men isn't a subject that interests me, but the camera work is phenomenal."

I can't help but smile at her honesty. "How's yours coming along?" Morgan told me she's submitting a short on the Manga culture in Tokyo. She lived there in high school while her dad was stationed there as a diplomat.

"Great. I'm done and submitting it tomorrow."

"I know you're supposed to be the enemy but I'm wishing you luck anyway. If I don't get it, I hope one of you two will."

"Same," Morgan states and blows a bubble with her gum.

Simon remains oddly silent. I glance up to find him staring back with a peculiar look on his face. He leans across his desk, into Morgan's personal space, and she sits back to avoid him. A chuckle rises up from my chest.

She's disliked him from the get-go and I can't figure out where it stems from.

"Are you busy this Saturday?" he says, expression guarded.

The amusement drops off my face. Even Morgan's eyes widen. That's why I couldn't get a read on him. He was working up to ask me out again. He's nervous and here I am conjuring nefarious motives.

We never did make it to the Scorsese retrospective all those weeks ago. Between midterms and putting together our submissions, we both got busy. I had completely forgotten about it. Apparently, Simon hadn't.

"Uh...no." That should not have sounded like a question. It should've come out as a firm declaration, fired back without hesitation. I might have flubbed this.

After Dallas showed up on Thanksgiving night, all the heat smoldering between me and Reagan turned into a clammy chill. I haven't spoken to him in the three days since. Only a few sporadic texts between practices. The team's been busy preparing for the championship tournament starting next weekend so that's understandable. What isn't, however, is how we left things.

Somewhere between Barstow and Las Vegas, Dallas dislocated his shoulder by driving his Porsche into a ditch. And that was the least of it. He was charged with reckless driving, evading arrest, and his license has been suspended. All in all, he had a slightly more messed up Thanksgiving than me and Rea.

By the time he'd finished filling us in on the details of the arrest, a palpable awkwardness had settled between us. I don't know what I expected but I didn't expect it to get uncomfortable, for him to drive me back to the dorm in complete silence. So am I available? Yeah, I am.

"I mean, I am—available, that is."

Simon smiles. "Do you like Thai? There's a great Thai restaurant in Westwood...maybe we can catch a movie after?"

God, nervous men are so adorable. Looking into Simon's open gaze, I say, "I'd love to."

Because zebras have no business crushing on Thoroughbreds.

* * *

"Bailey, you coming over?" Dallas says, speaking into Reagan's phone.

I can hear the rest of the guys on the team carrying on in the background, everyone celebrating the big win. A lucky goal by Rea in the last minute of the fourth quarter saved their season. Regardless, a win is a win. They beat Long Beach State fourteen to thirteen in the opening round and advance to the semifinals of the NCAA championship tournament next weekend.

Dallas watched from the sideline. Even if he didn't have a dislocated shoulder, Coach would've benched him for the arrest. Jake Chasen, a freshman and an upcoming star on the team, replaced him. He played really well too. Three assists and one goal.

I didn't go tonight. I wanted to—Zoe offered to drive me—but it was too important a game to risk Reagan being distracted. Which is why I watched it streaming live on my computer between the hands that covered my eyes and with my heart in my throat.

"Sorry about that. Dall stole my phone."

"You two are so sweet. My parents do that all the time too."

"You missed a great one, Bailey. I can't believe you didn't come." He sounds happy. I know it's because of the game but the perkiness bugs me. It's the first time we've actually spoken all week and he wants to pretend like nothing's happened? No. He doesn't get to do that.

"Busy editing the video all day. I need to submit it in the next ten days."

"You're going to get it. I know you will."

"I wish I had your level of confidence. The competition is stiff."

Shit, bad choice of word. There's a strange pause, which sends a surge of unease sliding down my back. Rea clears his throat.

"No one's up for a big party. The next game is in three days so it's just the guys and a couple of their girls."

I stop towel drying my hair and take a deep breath. It's time. It's past time actually. "I can't," I find the courage to voice out loud while I absently stare into my closet.

"Yes, you can. Brock went shopping. We have chicken wings, steaks, salmon. I'll be at your place in fifteen minutes to pick you up. The bus is pulling into campus now."

"No, I can't. I have plans, Reagan."

"Plans?" The note of surprise in his voice grates on my nerves.

"Yes, plans."

"What kind of plans?"

"A date." Funny how life works. When I finally stopped getting my hopes up that Reagan would see me as something other that his security blanket, Simon asked me out this week. On a real date. With plans and everything.

"A date? As in a *date*?" he says a good sixty seconds later, sounding genuinely shocked. That really ticks me off.

"Yeah, you know, not the oval fruit of the Medjool variety. Not the one on a calendar, either. The other one. Two people go out, eat food, talk, see if they like each other."

"I do know, Bailey. We do it all the time."

"Except this guy is interested in me romantically. We may even want to see each other naked."

Pause. Long, heavy pause.

"You've seen me naked—"

"And then you got weird on me again," I jump in, talking over him. I can't. I really can't do this, the back and forth, anymore. So here we have it, a test of true friendship. Can it survive us dating other people?

Aside from idle background chatter, another sixty seconds of silence passes. "Shady Sean?"

"Simon. His name is Simon. And he's not shady."

More silence. This time with the addition of an occasionally hollered, "Bailleeeyyyy," in the background.

He exhales loudly. "I guess I'll talk to you tomorrow." His voice is low, laden with disappointment. Join the club. I'm disappointed too.

"Hey, good game," I tell him. He's one step closer to winning his first championship as captain of this team, and he should know someone recognizes how hard he works. And regardless of everything, I'll always root for him.

"You watched?"

"Of course, I did. You were amazing. Played your heart

out." When he doesn't respond, I put us both out of our misery. "Night, Rea. I'll talk to you tomorrow."

* * *

REAGAN

"Knock it off. Not in the communal living area. I mean it, D," I bark.

Across from me, some chick is straddling D's lap and his hand is on her ass, pushing her shorts aside. Even one handed, he's dangerous.

My mood is currently taking a tour of hell and everything is pissing me off. The guys playing video games in the living room inside. The ones smoking at the edge of the beach. The one practically fucking in front of me.

All I wanted to do was come home, hole up in the privacy of my room, and get wasted. But no, the guys wouldn't have it. Now it's almost midnight, half of them are still here along with a bunch of girls I barely recognize, and I'm stuck on the patio watching Dallas get it on. I'm not drunk enough for this shit. Unfortunately, I'm not drunk at all.

He pulls his tongue out of her throat long enough to flip me off. I think she said her name is Karen, or Katherine. Not sure. Don't care. He slaps her ass and she gets off his lap, walks inside with an unsteady swing to her gait.

For the millionth time tonight, I pull my phone out of my pocket and stare at it. No texts from Alice. My finger hovers over the screen. I start typing…erase it. Type…erase. I can't. The phone goes back in my pants. I'm not drunk enough to fire off a text that will probably end our friendship for good.

Across the way, I catch Dallas eyeballing me. He comes over and inserts himself between me and a passed-out Cole whose head is on my shoulder. He had the right idea, went straight for the tequila when we got home and now he's contently snoring like a middle-aged man.

"Where's your girl?"

"Not my girl." The words taste so fucking bitter on my tongue I have to wash them away with a mouthful of warm beer.

Do I want her to be mine? From the day I met her she's made me want things I'd never considered before. Companionship, affection, stability, someone all mine. Yeah, I want her. And I was sure we were finally going to go there on Thanksgiving until Dallas showed up to ruin the moment.

After he finished explaining what happened and we called Coach to let him in on it, Alice was looking so painfully awkward I didn't want to push it. Besides, I'm still not sure I won't screw it up. And then what will I have? No friend, no girlfriend, no Alice. And we've already established I can't be without Alice.

He hums, looks me over. "You look like shit."

I rest my head on the back cushion and palm my forehead. "I feel like shit. I think I'm catching the flu."

"Nah, bro. You're catching feelings. That's love making you feel like shit. Welcome to hell."

Digging my fingers into my hair, I scrub my scalp. It feels like my head is fighting what my gut's trying to tell me. "I'm trying to get drunk in peace if you don't mind."

"At least you didn't deny it. My new shrink would be

proud of you."

With a sideways glance, I check him out. "Why are you still sober?"

"I'm gonna quit booze and pills for a while. See what happens."

This must have something to do with the new therapist he's been seeing. Some of the guys dabble in Molly, better known as ecstasy, and coke. Some weed. I never have. After what drugs have done to my family, I was never tempted. The standing policy among us is don't ask don't tell. Everyone knows what's at stake, what the consequences are if you get piss tested.

"She's on a date." D blinks, staring at me like I'm speaking in Chinese. "Alice. That's why she's not here," I clarify.

The confusion on his face transforms into a loud burst of laughter.

"Great. That's just great." My mood takes another turn for the worse.

"And you let her?" I barely hear D say.

My head is filled with too many images of Alice on a date doing God knows what. And what if she wants to keep dating him? I'll lose her anyway. It feels like my heart just took a running head dive into a cactus. Snatching the phone out of my pocket, I type.

Me: be with me.

With my heart thundering inside my chest, I press **Send** before I have a chance to erase it.

Katherine/Karen stumbles over to us towing her friend along. Long red hair, porn star rack. She giggles. It's obnoxiously high-pitched. I recognize this one. I watch her size up Brock who's been nursing the same beer for the past three hours.

He peels his eyes off the TV where highlights of the football game are playing to kill whatever plan she was concocting with a cold, hard stare and a shake of his head. Brock's not an approachable dude on a good day. And never if you're a semi-sober girl on the prowl.

"Reagan, have you met Tara?" Katherine/Karen says.

"We've met." I tip my chin up, force a smile. I've met her more times than I care to remember, and she still doesn't interest me.

They trip over each other and somehow Tara winds up in my lap with her arm around my neck and her tits in my face. Next to me, Cole's head falls off my shoulder and he jerks awake. Tara giggles.

And that's when Alice walks through the sliding glass doors.

I don't know what comes over me. I honestly don't have a clue except maybe a recessive male gene accidentally trips. Because seeing her standing in the open doorway dressed in a short blue skirt, a tight white shirt, high heels, and wearing makeup—*Makeup*. She never wears makeup—short-circuits my brain.

Instinct takes over, the ugly side of it. The side that makes me want to hurt someone. Unfortunately this usually ends with the wrong person getting hurt. I grab giggling Tara by the back of the neck and smash my mouth to hers. The kiss lasts a good long while because, once given permission, Tara's reluctant to let go of it. When I finally do come up for air, Alice is gone.

Cole is the first to speak up. "That was immensely shitty of you. Like something I would do. I don't know what's changed, but I don't like it. Change it back."

Extricating himself from the couch we're all piled onto, he walks away.

TWENTY-FOUR

ALICE

This was a bad idea. I've had a few lousy ones. This one, however, wins a blue ribbon for sheer stupidity. I can't believe I paid for an Uber to come all the way over here only to get my teeth kicked in!

He saw me. He saw me standing there and he kissed her! Kissed her is an understatement. More like he ate her face. I'm so mad I could bend a crowbar...around his neck.

I'm glad I kissed Simon tonight. I was feeling really bad about it earlier. It sure felt like I was betraying Rea at the time. But now I'm glad I did. Besides, you can't betray someone you are *not* in a relationship with. And in my defense, I only kissed Simon to see if there was any chemistry between us.

Mark that down as a big, fat no.

Unfortunately, zebras shouldn't mate with jack asses, either. The kiss was lackluster at best—a close cousin to what kissing the back of my hand felt like when I was eleven—and the rest of the date was even stranger.

How did I not notice how self-absorbed he was before? If he's not talking about himself, he's discussing pop culture ad infinitum. Not once did he ask me something personal. Not a single question. And when he dropped me off at my dorm and I leaned away when he came in for a second kiss, I got this—

"How about some head, then?"

Which naturally prompted me to request, "How about you leap off a tall building into a concrete pit?"

He didn't even wait for me to get inside before he peeled away. I guess I won't be using the Avid machine. It breaks my heart. The Avid machine, that is.

"Alice!" I hear a familiar voice shout at my back. I'm thinking he needs to go look for a tall building too.

Headed nowhere in particular, I pick up my pace down his street, each house I pass bigger than the last. It empties directly onto the beach so I figure I could work out the major fit of anger I'm having before I order another Uber that I really can't afford.

The electric blue Manolo Blahnik sandals I borrowed from Blake hit a rock and my ankle wobbles. This is why I don't wear heels. Although I catch myself in time, it scares me enough to stop and take a breather. Last thing I need is another sprained ankle.

"Alice! Where are you going?"

"Go back to your party." *Asshole.* I leave that part out. He doesn't need to know that I'm so jealous I'd like to take these sandals off and throw them at his junk. Behind me, I hear running footsteps. A large hand cuffs my bare bicep and I yank on it, breaking his hold on me.

"Don't touch me," I spit out, wheeling around to face him.

He looks crazed. His eyes wild, his hair disheveled, his lips pink and puffy from the *When Animals Attack* episode he was imitating only a moment ago.

"It's midnight. Where are you going?"

"Nowhere. To call an Uber. I shouldn't have come," I huff, exasperated, angry. I feel a thousand mixed emotions right now and most of them are telling me to hurt him. Turning, I continue my march to destination unknown. He catches up, takes my arm again. This time his grip isn't going anywhere.

"What are you doing?" I whisper-hiss as he hauls me off the deserted road and drags me toward the houses on our left. It doesn't escape me that I look ridiculous tiptoeing as fast as I can down a narrow stone walkway.

"This is private property!" I screech very, very quietly when he leads me between two gigantic beach houses with barely a few feet separating them. "They probably have security cameras everywhere!"

He spins me around and backs me up against the house, caging me in with his body, his hands planted on both sides of my head.

"I kissed her on purpose."

Oh, please. Does he think I'm clueless? "I don't care."

"Yes, you do," he insists with careful patience. As if speaking to someone who doesn't have the mental capacity to know her own mind. I am pumped with indignation at this point.

"No, I really don't," I snap. "As a matter of fact, why don't you go back to eating that chick's face off. I think you missed a spot, *Hannibal Lecter.*"

It's dark. The dim light of the streetlamp is all I have to go by. And still, I see him tip his face down to hide the grin. "I'm glad you think this is funny. Now let me go."

When he doesn't respond, I push at his pecs and he leans closer, his chest grazing mine. His head dips and he places a soft kiss on my neck. "I wanted to make you jealous the same way you made me jealous." He kisses the other side of my neck and my chin lifts involuntarily, giving him better access. I'm annoyed at this, my body's inability to resist him. It's not even putting up the slightest fight.

"Going on a date with shady Simon was mean. It hurt my feelings."

"Stop trying to be cute. It's not going to work on me anymore."

I have no strength to push him away. The kisses are diabolical, sapping me of all my anger. And my willingness to say no.

"Not trying to be cute." He kisses the corner of my mouth. "It *did* hurt my feelings." A tiny, little baby pang of guilt hits my heart. He sounds earnest.

"I needed to know if you want me as much as I want you," he murmurs into my skin, the vibration making me shiver.

The declaration does, however, manage to snap me out of the lust-induced daze. Palms to chest, I push him back far enough that I can look into his eyes.

"You're the one that friend-zoned me. *You're* the one always pushing and teasing me, and then pulling away. And now you want to place the blame at my feet?" My voice rises and falls. The anger bleeds away and a stale, hollow feeling remains. "You know what I just realized about you, Rea… you're a fucking coward."

That finally wipes the amusement from his face and a nameless emotion clouds his eyes.

"I have an expiration date hanging over my head. It haunts me every day. I've had it since I was fifteen and Nancy told me that there's a chance, somewhere down the road, I'll get the same thing my mother and grandmother had, and you don't see me scared to give anything a chance...to give us a chance."

He cups my cheek with one hand and I brush it away. I'm on a rant now and I intend to finish it.

"And I'm so sick of your mixed signals. Will he? Won't he? Will he? Won't he? You're worse than a virgin. I'm done." I duck under his arm for a quick exit and he stops me.

"Check you texts."

"What?"

"Check your phone."

Huffing, aggravated. Knowing he won't let me go until I do, I pull my phone out and see the unread text from him.

ig D al: e wit m

I hold up the phone. "I don't know what this means. Are you not even writing in complete words anymore?"

He stares at the screen and scowls, looking more than a little frustrated. "Your phone is trashed. How do you read anything on this thing?" Fishing his phone out of his shorts, he scrolls through it and hands it to me. And while I read, my pulse speeds up as if it intends to win the race.

"Do you mean it?" I look up into his serious expression. "Or is it only because you thought Simon was stealing away your toy?"

He leans into me and I can feel his erection. I could probably feel it if I was standing a foot away frankly. "I've wanted you from the start. I was just…afraid to lose you, afraid to screw everything up between us…and I did anyway." He shakes his head. "This has nothing to do with tonight. I thought I made it clear on Thanksgiving how much I want you," he admits in a low, quiet voice.

He kisses me gently, then, nips my bottom lip, testing how much I'm willing to allow. Breaking news: I'm allowing everything. Because despite the fact that he's been an ass tonight, I still want him more than my next breath of air.

We start kissing in earnest. Our hands get involved. His over my shirt, squeezing my breast. Mine wrap around and palm his butt. His hips drop. He grinds against me and I just about come undone from the friction. It's been a while. And with all the teasing and touching that's going on, I am primed to go off at the slightest provocation.

His hand glides beneath my short skirt and over my underwear. Back and forth, back and forth his knuckles stroke. It's not enough. My hips buck, chasing the pressure he keeps denying me.

"This what you want?" His whisper slips into my ear as smoothly as his fingers slip past my panties to play with me.

I'm close. So, so close. Knees locked. Muscles trembling. God, I'm so close. I'm close to begging him to finish me off. He pinches my nipple over my shirt and I moan. Then he drops to his knees and I'm bracing against the wall for support. His hands work assertively, shoving up my skirt and pushing my underwear aside. Cool air hits me.

"I've dreamed about doing this." The low, gravelly declaration reaches me despite the blood rushing in my ears. Then I feel the warm puffs of his breath on my privates and it pulls me right out of the moment.

"No, Rea. No, that's not my thing." I try to close my legs and he pushes them wider. I look down. The wide breadth of his powerful shoulders are rounded to fit closer, his dark head wedged between my legs—I've never seen anything sexier. Not even in my dreams, and I have a very vivid imagination.

"This is why you think food is better than sex." He chuckles, and sweet baby J, I feel it on my clit. Every muscle in my body tenses and quakes. But that was just the beginning. He puts his mouth on me and tugs, his fingers digging into my hips to keep them in place. And then he lavishes me with his tongue. I almost scream.

"No screaming."

"W-what?" is all I have a chance to say because he sucks on my clit and enters me with three fingers and I am gone, shouting as the orgasm blasts through me. An electric current that leaves nothing but euphoria in its wake.

That's never happened to me before. I'm usually so much in my head that I have to fake it to get them to stop.

My legs are shaking when he comes up and kisses me hard. I can taste myself on him. There's something so primal and sexy and wrong about it. He levels me with a smug, lazy stare.

"Now it's your thing."

Floodlights come on.

The cold hard light hits us in the face and we scramble. I don't get a chance to think. I don't even get a choice. He simply hauls me up and throws me over his shoulder. A moment later he's jogging, actually jogging with me over his shoulder, back to the house. Good thing it's only one block away.

"I'm going to toss my cookies!"

"You better not."

A bunch of the guys are on the couch, playing video games, when Reagan walks through the door carrying me.

"Welcome back, Bailey," one drunk idiot snickers.

"Long time no see," adds another.

As soon as we're in his bedroom, Reagan kicks the door shut and places me back on my feet. I wobble and fall against his chest. He wraps his arms around me and holds me closer.

We're both smiling and breathless. "We're really doing this? You're not going to get weird on me tomorrow?"

He leans down and murmurs in my ear, "Nobody is getting weird. And the only thing I'm doing tomorrow is hiding between your legs."

A shiver runs down my back. Backing away from him, I walk over to the bed and strip my shirt off, sit on the edge in the only cute bra I own.

"I'm not on the pill." Best to get the important stuff out right away. "I can't…" My gaze moves down. His stare is so intense I can't look him in the eye as I bare my soul. And however unsexy this conversation is, we have to have it. "It messes with my hormones and with my family history it's too much of a risk."

"We'll use condoms." His feet walk into my line of sight. He opens the drawer of his nightstand and pulls out a strip. My stomach twists and turns. I won't deny that seeing them ready to go by his bed bothers me.

"When was the last time you got tested?" I muster the courage to say.

"Beginning of the semester. I haven't been with anyone since."

That's when my eyes finally lift to his. And there, in bottle green, is the indisputable truth. His mouth hooks up in a small smile. "You're surprised that there's been no one else?"

I nod, speechless from shock.

He shrugs, trying to seem casual and failing. "You've taken up all the space in my head." His smile melts, his tone serious. "You've owned it since the day I met you."

It downloads all at once, critical information. I'm in love with him. I am madly in love with him.

Oh, shit. This feels scary. As if I'm out on a limb by myself.

"What about you?" he says and swallows. Is he nervous? He can't be. Can he?

I stand and slowly inch forward, closing the gap between us. A few inches away I stop. Reaching out for me, he grips my hips and pulls me closer. My hands slide up his sculpted chest, muscles honed by years and years of grueling workouts, skate up the column of his corded neck, his skin hot and silky. His Adam's apple bobs.

I want to lick him there, taste the heat and the salt, inhale his scent. "You're asking me if there's been anyone else? For real?"

He grins, a face-breaking ear-to-ear one. "My ego needs to hear it."

"Your ego needs no such thing." His smile melts into something more important. His humor turns to reverence. "But if you must know then, no, there hasn't been anyone. Not for a while. Not since you drove into me—I mean into my life."

A slow grin takes over his face. He sighs and leans in, closes his eyes, and places his lips on mine. Sweet, searching, testing. The kiss deepens and a minute later he's moaning into my mouth. His arms wrap around my waist. His hands palm my ass and squeeze, pressing me against his erection.

"Why did we wait so long to do this?" he says against my lips. Truer words were never spoken. He's right. It feels so good I want to cry.

Gripping my ass, he lifts me up. I wrap my legs around his waist, and his erection, hard and thick and perfect, nestles between us.

"Bailey, swear to God, I'm going to blow a load in my pants if you keep doing that."

"The bed. The bed," is all I can manage in between the thrill of having his hands on me and the kiss to end all kisses.

He drops me on the bed and takes my foot in his hands, slowly and deftly unbuckling the delicate straps of the sandals. He chucks the shoe over his shoulder and starts tugging on my toes. Holy triple gasp. I moan, my head falling back in utter erotic ecstasy. "Those aren't mine. Don't ruin them."

He does the same to the other sandal, the other toes. Then he steps away, grabs a handful of his gray t-shirt, and pulls it off. This view never ever gets tired, or stale. His body is a masterpiece, a perfect example of the sheer beauty of the human form. The result of unrelenting hard work and dedication.

"Can I ask you something and you can say no."

"Yes. My answer is yes to any question you have while you look at me that way."

A grin explodes on my face. He hooks his thumbs on the

edge of his silky shorts and pushes them down, taking his underwear with them. And holy quadruple sigh, the man is beautiful.

"Can I photograph you naked?" I chew on the tip of my thumb as I wait for his reaction.

His eyebrows go up. "Nudy pictures? Didn't see that as your kink."

"Stop it. I just think your body is beautiful...it's art."

The smirk drops, replaced by a tender vulnerability that makes me want to hug him. "Okay. Anything for you."

His erection slaps him in the belly as he reaches for the strip of condoms. As soon as he rips one off, the mood shifts. He crawls onto the bed and comes after me. His fingers hook over the edge of my skirt. I barely have enough time to unbutton it before he tugs it down, taking my underwear with it, and pulls it off.

"The things I'm going to do to you, Bailey—you're going to pay for every time I had to shoot a load in the shower just to get some relief. Every time I chaffed my dick at night thinking about you."

He sounds so genuinely irritated about it that it makes me laugh. "That's the nicest thing you've ever said to me."

He retaliates with a nip to my hip bone and a dip of his tongue into my bellybutton. Then he kisses me between my thighs and I become a throbbing, aching, empty ball of need. *The* Reagan Reynolds is a shameless tease.

He pushes the cups of my bra down and under my breasts. They feel heavy and neglected. Propped up and on display for him, he spends time worshipping them, sucking on each nipple until they're hard and sensitive and I'm incoherently begging him for more.

Up on his knees, he looks down on me with undisguised triumph on his face while he rolls the condom on. My gaze travels to his big hand, gripping his cock.

Hello, new friend.

"Alice…"

It's the tenderness in his voice that gets my attention. It's all there, in his naked eyes. Everything I need to know about this moment. His feelings, the friendship, the affection, the sense of relief. All the same reasons I'm here right now, in this bed with him. I open my arms and he comes willingly into them, leveraging his considerable body weight on an elbow.

"I…" He pauses. His lips part again. As if he's trying to force the words out.

"I need you," I whisper, saving us both from embarrassment, from something neither of us can handle right now.

Taking his shaft in hand, he rubs the fat head of it against my swollen lips and slowly sinks in, filling up the empty space the same way he already has in my heart. He's right. It *is* space, a quantifiable amount of real estate, and there is only so much any one of us can give. And I give it all to him.

"How's this?" he says after a deep, lazy thrust.

"It'll be great when I'm able to breathe again." My toes curl and my back arches as I reach for it. The slow friction is making me crazy. My eyes roll into the back of my skull. "Rea—stop torturing us!"

His forehead hits the bed next to my head and I feel his body shake in laughter. "Then stop squirming, or I'm going to go off before you can finish."

He starts moving again. Brows slanted inward, beads of sweat accumulating at his temples, he bites his bottom lip. I laugh at the effort he's making to go slow. Then I grab his ass and squeeze, and a mask of defeat falls over his face. His rhythm changes, each jack of his hips harder and faster than the last, and my body demands I meet him stroke for stroke. For a moment we are rhythm and breath and scent and touch in perfect harmony, everything else bleeding away. Until I come, bursting into a million pieces.

The bed starts to move across the wood floor just as I'm hitting another orgasm for the record books, the charge set off as his pubic bone kisses mine over and over again. I tip over the edge laughing, all my muscles contracting and bearing down on him, and the surprised look on his face makes me laugh even harder.

His eyes squeeze shut, his back arches, and his abs draw so tight I can see each and every delineated band of muscle in contrast to the other. Rocking into me one last time, he bottoms out and stills. A groan so loud and guttural spills out of him, Cole bangs on the adjoining wall. Serves him right after what I had to witness.

Reagan's eyes are already beginning to fall shut when he collapses next to me in a sweaty heap. I turn my head and catch him watching me through his dark lashes, expression unreadable. "What are you thinking?"

He smiles tiredly. "Shoulda done this the first time I wanted to," he rasps.

"When was that?" I ask as I push the wet hair off his forehead.

"The day you ran me over," he mumbles. His eyes fall

shut, and the smile I was holding down gets loose. I don't think he realizes what he said.

We get only a few restless hours of sleep that night. The rest of the time we spend lips to lips, pelvis to pelvis. One body worshipping the other. Making up for lost time.

TWENTY-FIVE

ALICE

"Hey, Bailey?" Dallas calls out. I glance up to find him sprawled out on the outdoor bleachers next to some of the other guys who are still hanging around.

The team just finished their last practice before the semifinal round of the championship tournament this weekend and Coach asked me to meet with him after I finished shooting some extra stills. There's a lot riding on this meeting and to say I'm more than a little nervous is an understatement.

"Yes, Dallas?" I intone while I break down the tripod and put it away in my equipment bag.

"I'm still the most photogenic guy on the team, right? You're not going to play favorites now, are you? Because that would be unethical."

Chuckling, I ask, "What exactly do you mean?"

He sits up and rips his sunglasses off, his expression one of great resolve. The blond curls falling carelessly around his face kind of kills the fierce blue stare, though. "What I'm getting at here is—am I still the star of your movie?"

I bite back the urge to laugh at the pout. If he wasn't such a wild one, Dallas Van Zant would be a total catch. "It's not a movie, Dall. There are no stars. But you do have a star-making moment in it."

"That's all you had to say." He slams his sunglasses over his eyes again and gives me a big toothy grin. "Do you need any more shots of me? 'Cause I have some time now."

"I think I've got enough." I wink as I head to Becker's office.

Ten minutes later, sitting on the other side of his enormous desk, I'm sweating bullets.

"This is excellent work," he says as he watches the video with undivided attention. I finally exhale the breath I've been holding since he pressed play. Fingers crossed he likes it enough to buy it.

"This is what a fully produced product should look like," I explain. "As you can see it's really fast-paced and colorful. Lots of action. Geared to appeal to my generation." The video makes the guys look like action stars. Dallas included. It's also sexy as all get-out, but I can't very well tell Coach that.

"Frankly, I only agreed to this arrangement because Reynolds said he'd assume the cost if I didn't care for it. I'm glad he talked me into it. This is exactly what I need to get an upper hand on UCLA and Stanford. Everything is about optics these days. And as you said, this speaks to a younger generation in their language."

Coach Becker's face breaks into a small smile that I would be able to appreciate if I wasn't currently in shock over the bomb he just dropped in my lap.

Reagan agreed to pay for the film if Becker didn't like it...

He would've forked over two grand and I would've been none the wiser...

Even more vexing—I'm so confused. I don't know whether to be upset or grateful. But business is business, and boyfriend problems are something else. So casting aside by mixed emotions, I start my pitch.

"This is a mockup. I have all the raw material ready for you on a flash drive. You can either hire another production company to put something together. In which case, it will not resemble this one whatsoever. Or you can buy this one and I'll finish mixing the sound on it. It still needs to be cleaned up a bit."

Coach shakes his head. "No question, I want to buy it. Send me a bill and I'll submit it to the head of the athletics department." Turning off the film, Becker sits back in his chair and examines me closely with what I would describe as a fatherly expression. Under his scrutiny, I start to fidget.

"I'm not guaranteeing anything, mind you, *but*...If he likes it, he may even hire you to produce one for the other teams."

At what is undoubtedly a look of barely contained exuberant gratitude on my face, Coach says, "You alright?"

"I'm fine," I croak. "Better than fine."

Now all I have to do is figure out how I feel about what Reagan did.

* * *

REAGAN

The locker room is as quiet as a graveyard, everyone zoned in on what we need to accomplish. There's no question Stanford is going to be hard to beat. Especially with Dallas and his dislocated shoulder on the bench.

We barely scraped by USC yesterday in the semifinals. My goal put us into overtime and Warner's won us the match but nobody celebrated. It could've gone either way and we got lucky. Luck isn't going to cut it today.

I glance over and find D smiling at his phone. Something is up with him. He's been in a strangely good mood considering he's got no car, no license, and the accident pretty much spelled the end of his water polo career.

This game marks the end of the line for most of us. Even if we manage to win today, no city will be hosting a parade. No rings will be issued. Our water polo careers end here unless we're lucky enough to be selected for a national team and play in the Olympics. I've been doing this most of my life. Countless hours dedicated to it. And the odd thing is, I'm not as upset about it as I imagined I would be.

Maybe I have Alice to thank for that.

"What are you smiling at?"

His blond head snaps up. He shuts off his phone and pockets it. "Nothing."

Coach walks in. Standing in the middle, he glances around, meeting each and every gaze that stares back at him in eager anticipation of his motivational speech.

"I'm all outta magic, so if you're waiting for me to turn a turd into a pot of gold, you'll be waiting a long time." In the pause, Coach's chin tips down and his hands get shoved into his pockets. All around me, pensive glances change into frowns. There's a palpable sense of confusion in the room.

"Our journey here hasn't been pretty. We've dropped a couple of stinkers."

A bunch of us nod in agreement.

"There have been times I didn't think we'd even get this far, but I'll tell you something else…That's how I judge the cut of a man's character. Not when the stars align and everything is going right. Not when we get lucky and draw a shit team to play. But when we face adversity—"

"Yeah," the chorus chants.

"And when we fight like hell to earn the win."

"Damn straight." The cheering and clapping starts.

"This year is special because you men earned this one, fought tooth and nail to get it done. Pulled out your best play when this team most needed it. That's what separates the winners from the losers.

"You don't have to be the most talented, the fastest, the strongest. What you must do is recognize you can't do it alone. That when you come up against a brick wall, you're smart enough to climb over it with the help of the man next to you. That's what Sharks water polo is."

Westbrook whistles. Peterman shouts, "Yeah!"

"I'm asking you to do it one last time. To dig deep and give this team all you got. And don't do it for me. I'll be here next year and the year after that. Do it because it's a chance to make history, to be part of something bigger than yourself. Do it for each other."

The locker room explodes, everyone already riding high on a cresting wave of adrenaline.

"Let's go kick some Cardinal ass!" Cole shouts.

Grabbing our gear, we head out of the locker room to the indoor arena. My phone chines. I glance at the screen and smile before shoving it back in my bag.

Jersey: Go get them, Flipper. Three kiss emojis.

I'm pumped, and for the first time all season, feeling good about this game. Knowing the girl I'm crazy about is in the stands makes it even better. I'm not saying it's going to be easy, but I think we have an honest shot at winning this thing.

* * *

By halftime we're down four goals. I'm not feeling good about this game at all, and I'd never say this to the guys, but we have no shot at winning this thing.

"The fucking Hungarian almost broke my nose." Warner pushes the tampon up his left nostril.

"That was a love tap," Quinn says to Warren. "Stop your bitching. Your supermodel nose will survive." He looks at me. "And you—play faster."

I flip him off. Warner goes with a death stare.

"I don't give a shit if you have to foul him," I tell Brock. "Take Papp out. He's blown up every one of our power plays."

The Hungarian is ranked the best player in the league with good reason. He's big, fast, strong—and has no scruples.

Brock glares at me. "You don't think I'm trying?"

"Try harder," I urge. "Because if something doesn't give, it's going to get embarrassing."

"I don't play dirty, dude. Don't ask me to."

Brock and his squeaky-clean morals. "That's going to be cold comfort when those assholes are hoisting the trophy."

"Leave it to me. I got this." Those are Quinn's words every time someone's about to get thrown out of the game.

"That's exactly what I'm worried about."

And then it dawns on me. Stanford is well coached and well prepared. They've studied all the tape there is on us, know each of our individual strengths and weaknesses. They assume we wouldn't swap the starting lineup in a crucial game. "They haven't seen Finley play yet, right?" The guys exchange curious glances. "We have to mix it up, throw them off, somehow."

Finley, a freshman with no actual playing time in a live game—let alone a playoff final—is the fastest swimmer on the team.

"What if Coach swaps me out? Warner, you take lead two-meter specialist. Let the kid take the ball down, but you have to keep up with him. Speed alone won't win this."

The gloom on their faces turns into a spark of hope.

"Can't hurt," says Cole.

Quinn nods. "Let's shake it up."

* * *

The noise level in the house is sure to have the neighbors calling the cops. The guys deserve to celebrate, however. It wasn't pretty, but a W is a W and that makes us NCAA Champions.

Lil Wayne's *Right Above It* comes on and I groan. Not again.

No hard liquor tonight for me. When you're this tired, one beer will knock out a full-grown man and I want to enjoy this moment since there won't be another.

After Brock and I talked to Coach, he got on board with our plan fast. Down four goals, we had to at least try. And it worked for a while, an entire quarter. Then they got wise that the kid was easily rattled by size and they double-teamed him. By then, we'd blitzed them for five goals in the third quarter and added four more in the last. Quinn started shit-talking one of their defensive players. The guy threw a punch, which got him ejected, and a man down, we kept scoring. Three of which were mine.

"Hey, Smith," I call out. He tears his mouth away from some dude's neck to glance up at me. "What'd you say to Stenovitch to piss him off like that?"

Not for nothing the guy's nick name is Steely Sten.

"Only the truth. That his brother's a lousy fucking lay."

The room reacts accordingly, roaring in laughter and cheering him on. Next to me, leaning against the wall, Brock shakes his head but he can't keep the smile off his face.

I tap my beer bottle with his. "You still mad at me?"

"I wasn't mad at you. I just don't like to do anything for the wrong reason."

"I saw the Hungarian take a knee to the thigh. He stopped destroying our power plays, which means you fouled him more than once."

"Yeah, well, winning this game was the right reason."

He turns and looks me over. "Everything good with your girl?"

I look across the room, and feeling my eyes on her, Alice stops talking to her friend and looks up. Damn. Someone must've hit me with a mallet over the head because I'm seeing stars and hearing trumpets.

An automatic smile takes over my face. "Everything's great."

Brock nods. "Did you tell her you love her?"

My smile drops. "Way to kill a good mood. For a guy that never dates, you sure as hell have all the answers."

"I'll take that as a no."

His assumption feels like sandpaper on an open wound. An accusation. In other words, not good. Telling Alice that I love her is a big step I don't think either of us is ready for. We're just hitting our stride now.

Things are great as they are. I get to have my best friend and the best sex of my life. Complicating the situation with promises and declarations of love can only put unwarranted pressure on it. It could screw things up big-time and I've been trying to avoid screwing things up with her since the day we met.

Besides, she knows how I feel about her.

* * *

ALICE

"Has he told you he loves you yet?" Zoe queries absently. Her attention has pretty much been glued to Brock Peterman since we got here.

"You're not at all nosy," I deadpan with a smirk. I catch Reagan watching me and take out my phone to text him. A couple of kiss emojis. I almost hit the purple heart emoji, but pull back at the last minute and hit **Send**. Hearts would've gone too far.

The team toughed it out, beating Stanford sixteen to thirteen. Rea was magnificent in the fourth quarter, racking up three goals in the last two minutes alone.

"Jesus, Zoe, maybe she doesn't want to talk about it," Blake chides.

"Have *you* told him?" Dora jumps in. I roll my eyes and she smiles back wickedly.

"Proud of you, Red," Zoe remarks, taking her eyes off Brock for a fleeting moment to wink at Dora.

"No, I haven't and neither has he," I finally answer because I know the questions will not stop until Zoe gets what she wants. "I'm not in a rush. Besides, I prefer action over words. I'm good with where we are right now."

And that's absolutely true. Reagan does show me every day that he cares about me.

"That's all good and fine, but I've been reading this book—" Zoe starts again.

"No," I cut her off before she goes any further. "Nuh huh. No, thank you."

"Just sayin'. I've got it. I'm happy to lend it to you. It's chock-full of great advice. Like don't become his hump toy."

"Truth," Blake chimes in. "I've read it. The author makes a lot of good points."

"Like don't ever say *I love you* first."

"I don't believe in any of that," I tell them. "This isn't a power struggle."

Zoe tilts her head and smirks. "Isn't it, though?"

* * *

Two days later I'm in the library, studying for finals, when I receive an inauspicious email from Professor Marshall asking me to meet with her. A knot immediately forms in my stomach. Naturally, I answer that I'm available right away. Whatever this is, best to deal with it immediately rather than to have to endure days of anxiety.

Marshall responds that she can see me now in her office located in the film and television building. Fifteen minutes later I find her at her desk, chair tipped back, watching my reel when I walk in. Her gray eyes lift to mine.

"Alice, come in," she tells me in her usual brisk voice. Marshall has a face that even at rest looks like she's in a bad mood, but who's actually funny and sarcastic. She's not at all as severe as she looks. It's her accomplishments that intimidated the crap out of me.

I take the chair opposite her desk with more than a little trepidation. She leans forward in her desk and laces her fingers together and I know it's going to be bad.

"I'll get right to it. I'm not going to be able to submit your reel for the James Cameron internship. It's come to my attention that this was produced with outside funds, and as you know, that's one of the stipulations. We insist it be funded entirely by the students. If we allowed outside funding, it would get out of hand quickly. People would raise money with GoFundMe accounts, private investments, etc. The budgets would skyrocket. It wouldn't be an even playing field. Frankly, I don't think it's one now, but it's the best we can do."

I'm stunned. "I...uh, Professor Marshall. This was funded entirely by me. The camera equipment I own outright."

"This is shot with a Blackmagic. You want me to believe you own this equipment?"

"I've spent *years* saving up to buy this equipment." An angry, startled burst of laughter escapes me. "I can show you the receipts. And as for the reel, yes, the athletics department is paying for it now. Coach Becker liked it so much he only decided to purchase it *after* I shot and produced it. So it was all shot on my time, with my equipment. None of it was funded by *outside money*."

Marshall's wide mouth purses. "I'm sorry Alice. One whiff that I accepted work that was purchased by the school, whether they supplied the funds or not," she adds quickly as I'm about to argue. "will reflect badly on me and the program."

"So that's it? I'm being punished because someone decided to purchase my work?"

"You're not being punished. I need to maintain the integrity of the program...for what it's worth this is very good work."

Very good work? That's cold comfort. My shoulders fall in defeat. I don't remember being this disappointment in a long time.

"Let me talk to Becker...I'm not promising anything, but I'll look into it before I make a final decision."

"Okay," I mutter as I get to my feet, gather my book bag, and sling it over my shoulder. I make it to the threshold of her door when she says, "There's always next year."

Yes, there is. But right now, I'm devastated.

TWENTY-SIX

ALICE

Ever try to buy a plane ticket right before Christmas? Yeah, super expensive.

"I'll pay for the ticket," my mother insists. The time on my laptop reads 11 p.m.

"Are you home yet?" My dad always stays up waiting for her when she works a night shift. We live in a pretty safe neighborhood, but my mother works in Newark so the commute takes her through a rough area. We worry.

"No. I just punched out."

I close my laptop and place it on my nightstand. I'm taking two finals tomorrow, and if I'd stayed at Rea's, no studying was happening, which is why I'm sleeping in my dorm tonight.

"You always say that and you know how guilty it makes me feel. We knew the next two years were going to be hard when I left. We talked about me not being able to come home."

"I know, but Thanksgiving was so lousy without you."

"Trust me, mine was lousier. Those people...*brrrr*. Scary."

"That bad?"

"They're like…" I search for the right description. "The rich villains in a 1950s movie, trying to keep their son away from the girl from the wrong side of the tracks. Except with hip haircuts."

My mother chuckles.

"I have no idea how Reagan turned out so well-adjusted. If he didn't look exactly like his father, I would question whether they stole him as a baby. Or bought him from some destitute, single teenage mother whose parents were ultra religious."

"You *do* have a vivid imagination."

"You haven't met them."

"Do you think I will? Is this serious?" Mom's voice gets a little shrilly. Like she can't decide if she should be excited or alarmed.

"I don't know…" I feign. "I mean, he's amazing and sweet and funny and generous and…he's my best friend."

"Ohhhhhh. Alice, you're in love with him."

"I don't know. Maybe? Probably? I think I might be. Don't tell Dad yet."

When she doesn't say anything I get a little worried. "Ma?"

"Promise me something?"

"Yeah…" I reply, already wary of what's coming.

"Love with everything you've got, but never forget yourself."

"Why would you say that?" I'm almost a little offended. Does she not trust me to take care of myself?

"Because I know you. Because when you're in, you're in a thousand percent. And you've never spoken of a boy this way before."

* * *

It's seventy-five degrees and sunny on Christmas Day, the sky completely cloudless. And surreal—Christmas lights and palm trees should not go together.

Reagan has been summoned to his parents' house. He begged me to go with him, but I've had enough of the Reynolds's house of horrors to last me a lifetime. I'm sure they were ecstatic when he told them I was having Christmas at Aunt Peg's.

"The turkey is almost ready." Aunt Peg leans further out of the kitchen window. "Wheels! Did you hear me? The turkey is almost ready. Time to get cleaned up."

The macaw squawks.

"I'm comin'!" he bellows back.

"Men," she says, her matte peach-colored lips pursing. Her perfectly blown-out hair swings as she crosses the room to place a breadbasket full of assorted rolls on the table, which is all set up for the meal with Christmas-themed plates and linens. The entire trailer is decorated.

I smile. "What does he do out there?"

"He loves his plants. He just loves 'em. Growing some fancy hybrids, says they could be medicinal."

Through the glass sliding door, I watch Wheels bending over a bench to sink his hands into a terra-cotta pot.

"So—tell me *all* about him," she intones, her excitement palpable.

The idiotic grin I can't seem to shake should be a good indication. "He's...nice."

Aunt Peg frowns. "Nice? You can do better than that." Joining me at the table, she sits and arranges her red silk caftan while she waits for me to elaborate with a dimpled smile.

I grab a piece of bread out of the basket and munch on it. "He's amazing. He's kind and funny and...he's the best."

She smiles encouragingly.

"And...and he's going to medical school next year. And I'll be here, focusing on getting my degree..." The thought of not seeing him every day makes my stomach hurt. And then there's Jordan. She'll be taking classes with him. Best not think about it now, or it'll ruin my appetite.

"His parents are wealthy and not very nice." I smooth my napkin. "Not that those two things go hand in hand. I'm just saying that I'm pretty sure they don't approve of me."

The back door slides open and Wheels comes up the ramp. "I'm getting cleaned up. Gimme fifteen minutes." He disappears into the bedroom and Aunt Peg levels me with an intent stare.

"I'm going to say something to you that my mother, your grandmother, God rest her soul, should've said to me if she'd ever imparted a kind word, which she never did because she was a religious zealot and an all-around mean person—" Peg leans in, expression solemn. "Fuck more, worry less."

A burst of choking laughter hurls out of me. "Aunt Peg!"

"It's the secret to a happy life." She grins brightly. "And good skin."

Peg's skin *is* flawless porcelain perfection.

A knock at the front door gets the macaw squawking. We both lean to the left so we can see out the glass picture window. Sunglasses on, hands shoved in the pockets of his gray trousers, Reagan stands patiently.

The sight of him makes my hopelessly devoted heart skip

a beat.

Aunt Peg's ginger eyebrows nearly reach her hairline. She stands. "Oh, yes. He looks like a real *nice* guy."

I bite down on my cheek to stave off a grin while she goes to answer the door.

Two hours later, we're all sporting food babies made of turkey, stuffing, and candied yams, and surfing a tryptophan high. My aunt loves to cook as much as she loves to eat and it shows.

The sun has set and the tiny white Christmas tree lights Aunt Peg has strung around her trailer cast a romantic glow. Under the table, Reagan held my hand throughout dinner. When I asked him about his unexpected arrival, he only said, "I couldn't take anymore."

"Coffee, anyone?" I can hear Peg call out from the kitchen, where she's arranging coffee cups on a tray.

"None for us, thank you," I answer.

"Decaf for me, doll," Wheels adds.

When she returns with the tray, she says, "If Jennifer could see you now. She'd be so proud of you, Alice."

The mention of my mother stiffens my posture. "Alice looks just like her mother, Reagan. Her birth mother," she corrects herself. "She was such a beauty. Billy and I grew up next door to her so I knew her all my life."

"Billy is my dad," I whisper and Rea squeezes my hand, sensing my discomfort.

"If I recall correctly, they were maybe ten and twelve when they became inseparable. Then of course in high school they became sweethearts. But when your grandmother died, well…after that, Billy was always over there, helping out."

My palms are getting clammy. I can feel Rea's attention on me, and the last thing I want is his pity, one of the many reasons why I never discuss this with him.

"...but he seems happy now with Nancy," I hear Peg say, having tuned her out for a moment.

"Yes, they're very happy." In the silent pause, I glance at the cable box. "It's getting late. We should get going."

After a lengthy goodbye, and many promises made to visit soon, we thank my aunt for the fantastic meal and head back to Reagan's place. Dallas is in Houston visiting his mother— no, I'm not kidding. And the Petermans are home with their parents.

"I have something for you," he says as I'm pushing my skirt off my hips. It stops me short, takes me by surprise. We had agreed no presents because I couldn't afford anything.

"We agreed no presents," I remind him.

He throws his dress shirt in the hamper and the sight of his bare chest and the V descending into his unbuttoned and unzipped pants almost has me forgetting why we agreed.

"You agreed," the sneak claims. "I just stayed silent." Naked, he closes the distance between us and wraps me in his arms. If the goal was to distract me, then he succeeded brilliantly. The sight of his beautiful body never gets old.

He pulls a small gift wrapped box out of the dresser drawer and hands it to me.

"That's not fair," I murmur while I unwrap it slowly to reveal a brand new iPhone X.

"Merry Xmas, babe."

"I didn't get you anything. I feel terrible."

He kisses me, relentlessly hard, until I'm forced to look up into his face. I watch his throat work, his lashes lower, and his forehead pucker in deep thought.

"I've got everything I need right here."

* * *

New semester, new class with Marshall. This one called Documentary Film and Video Production. Same group of students. I take my usual seat, and smile when I spot Morgan coming up the aisle to take the one next to me.

Who's conspicuously sitting three rows down and over and flirting with a new girl? That's right, Shady Simon. He notices me watching him and his fake smile drops faster than an R. Kelly album off the Billboard charts.

Marshall e-mailed me to meet her in her office after class. The email was vague and frankly does not bode well for my reel getting submitted for the internship. As bummed as I am about it, I've had time to prepare for the worst. And between finals, the holidays, and basking in the afterglow of epic sex, I can't seem to muster the energy to be upset about it.

"What happened with you guys?" Morgan whispers as Marshall begins her lecture.

"He turned out to be a major douche is what happened. All he talked about was himself and then he asked for head at the end of the date."

Morgan makes a gagging gesture and I snicker.

"I always thought he was a little shady," she says out of the side of her mouth.

Eye roll. Am I the only one that didn't see this? "I wish you would have told me and saved me the trouble."

"You wouldn't have listened."

And then I realize…she's right.

* * *

As soon as class ends I head to Marshall's office. A few feet away, I hear the indisputable sound of two people arguing, the voices escaping through her cracked open door.

"It's unethical. She's banging one of the guys. That's how she got access to them. It's not fair to the rest of the people submitting…" Simon's voice is sharp and combative.

I'm actually surprised he would speak that aggressively to Marshall.

"—and who knows what other special favors she's gleaned from her relationships," he continues.

Who the heck is he talking about?

"I've researched the matter personally, Mr. Lewis. Whatever your beef is, I assure you Miss Bailey was given permission by Coach Becker through merit. Furthermore, she owns the equipment with which it was shot and she incurred all the expenditures…I see no reason not to let her reel be included."

*That mutherf…*I push the door open with fire shooting out of my eyes and ears.

Marshall is sitting behind her desk, leaning back in her chair, with her hands casually laced on her lap. As casual as her posture is, her expression is entirely different. On the opposite side of her desk, standing, Simon levels me with a look of pure contempt.

"So this is where the complaint came from?" I exclaim, completely flabbergasted. "He's using his friend's access to a professional editing machine, and he has the gall to accuse me of having an unfair advantage?"

Marshall's irritation turns on Simon who suddenly looks sheepish. She lets him sweat it out with a full minute of uninterrupted silence.

"Your reel will be included, Alice. Now can you please shut the door. I need to explain the definition of unfair advantage and ethical practices to Mr. Lewis."

* * *

"I can't belieeeeve I didn't see what a miserable piece of shit he is. I should have known. I really should have. That date was a major sign."

I pace in circles in my tiny dorm room. No space to do much else.

"The date?" the beautiful man lying on my twin bed with his skilled hands tucked under his head says.

"Yeah, *that* date. The one I will forever regret."

I stop pacing and look him over. He dangles his feet off the side as he stares up at me with his eyes blazing and a tiny smirk lifting one side of his mouth.

"What are you thinking right now?" I ask. "You have a weird look on your face and I'd like to know what this means."

"Honestly?"

"Yes, honestly. I just found out I was almost gaslighted out of a chance to work with James Cameron. I would like to know what my boyfriend thinks."

Ooooh, shit. Did I say boyfriend? Out loud? I halt, wide-eyed, waiting for him to either get weird, or give me a thumbs-up.

"You just handed me the perfect excuse to beat the shit out

of him. I've been looking for one and you just dropped it right in my lap—say that again."

"That I was nearly robbed by Shady Simon?"

"No, the boyfriend part."

"Oh." I crawl on top of him, straddling his lap, and in zero to sixty, his dick gets hard under his sweatpants. I lift the elastic waistband and stick my hand under, palm his shaft. "Is that okay? That I call you my boyfriend?"

His eyelids get heavy and his nostrils flare. He wraps a hand around my neck and pulls me down for a kiss. A face-holding, to-die-for, we're-officially-a-couple kiss for the ages.

"You better. Otherwise we're going to have a problem. Now, be a good girlfriend and take off your panties."

"Aye aye, captain."

TWENTY-SEVEN

REAGAN

The distant sound of a phone ringing wakes me up. It takes me a while to realize that it's mine. Alice is already sitting up in bed, rubbing the sleep out of her eyes when I fumble around and somehow manage to turn the lamp on. As soon as I glance at the screen of my iPhone and see the name, my stomach drops and blood rushes in my ears.

It's Foz calling. Which can only mean this is about Brian. "Hey, Foz," I say, my voice cracking from disuse.

"Reagan…" My name hangs in the air, suspended for what feels like an eternity, implying everything and saying nothing. A sharp pain spears my chest.

"What is it, Foz?" I say louder this time, force out the words. It's impossible to take a full breath. I know what's coming. I've prepared myself for years, rehearsed it in my head a thousand different ways. At least, I thought I did. Because it doesn't feel any easier right now.

"It's Brian," he finally offers up, confirming what my gut was already telling me. "I'm sorry, man. I'm…I'm really sorry."

The pressure gets to be too much. The dam breaks. My

body goes limp, my head falls into my hands, and tears fall down my face.

* * *

ALICE

It takes me forever to get Reagan dressed and into the Jeep. It's like he checked out. He cried in my arms for ten minutes and then he just checked out.

Located downtown, I drive to the police station very slowly. Not only do I not know where I'm going, but I'm worried about Reagan. All he's done is stare blindly out the passenger side window for the past twenty minutes.

At the station, we check in and the officer manning the desk tells us the detective handling the case will be out shortly. Reagan's face pinches in confusion. Otherwise he remains silent.

Detective Mahomes, an attractive black man probably in his late forties, inspects the both of us closely as he greets us. Then he escorts us down the hall to his desk and gestures to two empty chairs next to it.

"Have a seat," Detective Mahomes invites, and we fall into the chairs opposite him.

"I don't understand why I'm even here," Reagan remarks. He still sounds out of it, not like himself. "Foz Whitaker identified the body, right?"

Mahomes nods. "He did. He was at the scene shortly after I arrived."

"Then why is this a case? He overdosed. End of story. My brother has…" Catching the error, Reagan pauses. "Had a long history of drug use."

The detective places his forearms on his cluttered desk, his face set in a pensive frown. "Mr. Reynolds, this is a homicide. Your brother was murdered. He didn't overdose."

Reagan jerks back, his face a mix of shock, anger, and confusion. "Murdered?"

I do my best to hide the same emotions that come over me. He's not a faceless victim. This was Reagan's brother and someone I've met. Someone I wanted to know better. Whatever I'm feeling, however, needs to take a back seat to whatever Reagan needs. And right now, it's my support he needs most. Reaching out, I take his hand and lace our fingers together on my lap.

"Yeah." Mahomes exhales deeply. He looks genuinely troubled by what happened; a person who still cares about helping people. "Stabbed eighteen times. His girlfriend found him in an alley a block away from tent city...We caught the guy. Another tweaker. He confessed to everything."

"Why? I-I don't understand. Was he trying to protect his girlfriend? He got cut a few months ago trying to protect her." The words tumble out of Reagan's mouth barely audible.

"He wanted your brother's sneakers and your brother wouldn't give 'em up." Mahomes stares back flatly. Like he's seen too much stuff he'd like to unsee. "The perp was wearing them when we caught him."

Other than a blink, Reagan's expression is completely blank. "Can I see him?"

Mahomes makes a face. "You sure about that? He got kicked in the face pretty badly."

"Yeah, I'm sure," Reagan answers.

* * *

REAGAN

Staring in the bathroom mirror, I retie my tie for the third time. Then I determine it's too wrinkled to wear, take it off, and chuck it in the garbage pail. It lies next to a used condom coiled like a snake. It was a shitty tie anyway.

I hate green. I've told her I hate green a thousand times, and she continues to buy me green clothing.

It was in my stocking this Christmas. The one that should've been hanging next to Brian's but wasn't because my parents cut him out of the family. I'm glad I walked out. I wish I'd cut them off. Or threatened something, anything, to make them think twice. I wish I'd been stronger then, but it wasn't so easy without my trust fund to fall back on. Not as easy as it will be after this funeral today.

"Almost ready?" Alice's sweet voice cools my anger. Leaning against the doorframe, she pushes her sleek, dark hair behind her ear and inspects me in the reflection of the mirror.

I don't know where I'd be right now without her, without her steadfastness holding me up. I've never had that before— someone keeping me together. I wish I didn't need it but I do and it scares me that she may find out. I'm not strong the way she seems to think I am. If I was, I wouldn't have been doing the shit my parents have dictated all my life.

"Yeah."

"No tie?"

Turning to face her, I place a kiss on her soft lips because I need it. I need to touch her. "I don't have a good one to wear."

She blinks in confusion. "You have like...thirty ties in your closet. I've never seen so many outside of a department store."

"My mother bought me those."

"Oh." She looks away for a moment. When her attention returns, she tilts her head and looks me over. "No tie works for you." She gives me a soft smile, her big eyes fixed on me. "We should go. We don't want to be late."

I kiss her again, harder this time. Slip my tongue in her mouth and taste the orange she ate an hour ago. With my hands on her waist, I place her on the granite bathroom counter. Her legs dangle and widen to welcome me, her dress rides up.

In the mirror, I watch myself slide the zipper of the same black sleeveless dress she wore on Thanksgiving down slowly and push it off her shoulders. I watch myself kiss a path from the curve of her neck up her throat, her pale skin glowing in the shaft of sunlight from the skylight.

I need her. I can't tell her, though. The words won't come out. No matter how much I want them to.

"We're going to be late," she whispers in my ear and a shiver races over my skin, which is hot and tight and uncomfortable. She shoves the jacket off my shoulders and my hands slide up her bare thighs. We're so good together. Like I knew we would be.

"Then we'll be late." One finger hooks around her underwear and pulls down. Rocking her hips, she lets me take them off.

Her slender fingers squeeze my shaft over my pants and a low groan slips out. I'm hard as fuck. A few strokes over our clothes isn't going to cut it. I need to come. I need relief. I need her.

The pants get unbuttoned. The zipper comes down. Her cool hands slide beneath my boxer briefs to grip my ass. My dick gets free, standing erect between us.

Out of the drawer, I grab a condom and rip it open with my teeth, roll it on in a hurry because I can't wait another minute to be part of her, to lose myself in her body, to forget everything and everyone outside of the two of us and this bathroom.

She's all that matters, all that exists to me anymore. Let the world catch fire. Let it all fuck off.

Her head tips back and her dark hair sways. She sucks in a breath as I thrust inside of her. And them I'm gone, so gone, far away. With my mouth attached to her neck, I fuck her hard while she holds on to me tightly. I come as soon as she does, with the full weight of my body collapsing against her. And this small girl, a third my size, holds me up, holds me together.

I hug her tightly. She doesn't say anything, just lets me hold her. I love her. I think I've loved her for a long time and didn't know it.

* * *

ALICE

Dallas and Brock follow in Cole's car. The rest of the guys on the team meet us at the Episcopalian church in Beverly Hills. Inside, it's wall-to-wall flower arrangements. The expensive kind. Not a single carnation to be found anywhere in the entire church. A closed, lacquered maple casket sits in the middle. A glamorous picture of a young and very handsome Brian Reynolds sits up on an easel next to it. I can see the strong resemblance now. Not so much when I met him in person.

By the time we arrive, late, it's already standing room only. Judging by the ages, most of the people here must be friends of *the* Dr. and Dr. Reynolds.

As we walk up the aisle, Reagan stops to hug and backslap a small black man with silver hair. His dark eyes move to me, and when I hold out my hand, he hugs me.

"Foz Whitaker. You must be Alice." I hug him back and pull away far enough to speak but he beats me to it. "Brian told me all about you."

Inexplicably, tears burst from my eyes. Embarrassed, I hurriedly wipe them away while Foz pats my shoulder.

"You better get on up there," Foz tells Reagan and he nods in agreement.

As we continue up the aisle, I spot his parents for the first time since we got the call. Sitting in the first row, Deborah Reynolds's expression is stoic. Her makeup flawless. Her hair a hip, carefully styled mess. The dress she's wearing—tailored, black, and sleeveless—contours every inch of her slender body. It actually looks a lot like my dress with the exception of the price tag. I'm fairly certain hers had a few more zeros attached at the end.

Pat Reynolds is wearing a navy suit and his usual expression of boredom. As if he has somewhere better to be.

Can I say that I hate them? Is that allowed?

Noting our arrival, they move down the pew to make room for us. "You're late," I hear Pat Reynolds tell his son.

"Where's your tie?" his mother adds.

Garbed in an ivory robe with gold trim, Pastor Peterman,

who looks exactly like an older Brock Peterman, walks to the podium—or whatever you call those things. Clearly church is not a thing in my family.

The service is a short one. No mention of all the years of struggle, or the demons that haunted Brian. Only a passing mention of the pitfalls of human desire and how we should do our best to curb them. Along with a short list of his accomplishments in high school.

Reagan keeps hold of my hand on his lap throughout the service.

Once it's over, we all file out slowly. The sun shines brightly in a cloudless sky, the air crisp and cool. I wonder if Brian is at peace now. I wonder if he can see us. I wonder about my mother. I wonder.

We all get in our cars and a long, fancy procession follows the hearse to the graveyard. At the grave site, we crowd around the casket. His parents take a seat while Reagan remains standing among his friends, with me by his side. Pastor Peterman begins to speak.

That's the first time I see her, a lone tall figure in the distance smoking a cigarette and shifting nervously on her feet. She's painfully thin with stringy red hair and dressed in tattered jeans and a dirty, oversized L.A. Lakers t-shirt. It's kind of hard to miss her.

When she catches me looking her way, she moves behind a giant oak. I squeeze Reagan's hand. He looks down at me and I motion with my chin in her direction.

Once Reagan's intense green stare locks on to her, everything happens quickly. He immediately drops my hand and strides in her direction. Everyone turns to stare. Even

Pastor Peterman pauses the service.

"Reagan? Where are you going?" His mother makes a feeble attempt to stop him, outrage in her voice. She has no clue who her son is.

We all watch as Reagan approaches her with his hands raised. She looks ready to run so I understand the gesture. Her gaze flies between the casket and Rea while he talks. Then slowly, together, they begin walking back to us. Halfway, she gets antsy, her steps sticky, and he reaches out and takes her hand.

I love him. I love him like I never knew I could love someone.

The crowd parts to make room for her, this tall skinny stranger with hollow eyes and weathered skin, and her face cast down—too scared to make eye contact with anyone. With her comes an undeniable smell, and still, Reagan holds her hand.

I love him. I love him for everything he is and even more for everything he's not.

The skinny stranger gets major credit for bravery. This is an intimidating crowd but she came anyway. I give her credit because she did it for Brian.

TWENTY-EIGHT

REAGAN

"The G wagon is, at best, a second car. Too uncomfortable for everyday use. I always end up driving my S-class," says one of my father's asshole friends to the other.

The idle chatter is like battery acid on my nerves. I finish off my whiskey, my third, and glance around from my chair in the corner of the room. Leave it to my mother to have the service at the Beverly Hills Hotel because she "didn't want people traipsing all over her rugs."

Priceless.

The only kernel of anything good to come out of this shitshow was Lisa. She refused to come along, but at least she took my number and promised to call if she needed anything. I have to help her. I *want* to help her. I'm going to get her into rehab. Brian would want me to.

"How are you holding up?" Brock asks. Grabbing a chair along the way, he plants it beside mine and drops in.

I shrug and shake the leftover ice in my tumbler. "I could use another drink." Alice is at a small table with her friends. She catches me watching her and frowns at my glass.

Brock side-eyes me. "I know you're in a shit place right

now, but getting drunk is not the answer."

"Do you ever get tired of being perfect?" I can't help it. The last thing I need right now is anyone giving me advice.

"Good whiskey is always the answer. As a matter of fact, I'll join you." Dallas walks over and does the same, grabs a chair, drags it close to ours. He turns his around and straddles it. "Let's get trashed. I can make a couple of calls and get some Molly."

I can't be responsible for that. I'm responsible for too much already and I'd rather not load more guilt on my plate. "I'm not helping you off the wagon. If you wanna get wasted, find your own excuse."

"Dude—" His brows pull down. "You're a mean drunk." There's no heat to his words. Just Dallas being Dallas.

"I'm not drunk," I grumble. And convince no one.

"You're definitely on your way," Brock argues.

"I know you're going to law school next year, but could we shelve the debates for today?"

"Reagan," my father calls from a few feet away. He's standing next to someone I've never seen before. Tall, tight expression, expensive suit. Basically looks like all of my father's acquaintances. What the hell is he doing inviting strangers to my brother's wake?

"Care to tear yourself away from your buddies for a minute to be with your family. Dean Sullivan would like to have a word with you."

Fucking hell. "No, I don't care to," I shout back. The entire room goes silent. All hundred or more people turning to watch us. None of which are here for Brian. At the edge of my vision, I see Alice stand.

My father's blue eyes narrow. "I'm only going to ask you one more time—come here." His jaw twitches. "And out of respect for your brother, keep your voice down."

A molten-hot wave of rage breaks over me, turning me blind and deaf and unable to keep it all down anymore.

"Me?" I shout. "All I've ever had was love and respect for him. Can you say the same, Dad?" I stand, the rage demands it. "Do your friends know that you cut him out of your life, out of the family, years ago? That you haven't seen or talked to him in three years?"

"Reagan," my mother hisses, leaving her friends a few tables away to get in the middle of this.

"That you had him arrested for trespassing when he showed up at the house, and that you and Mom threatened to have him arrested for breaking and entering if he ever set foot on the property again?! Do they know that you don't give a fuck that he's dead?!"

My mother grabs my arm and I shake her off. "Outside, right now!" she orders between clenched teeth.

"Why? Am I embarrassing you?" I'm still shouting. Now that I've started I can't seem to stop, years of repressed thoughts and feelings coming out at once.

"Yes."

"Well—here's the good news." I raise my hands and make sure everyone is watching the show. "The junkie son is dead. Murdered for his sneakers. Sneakers *I* gave him"—I pound on my chest, tears burning my eyes—"and insisted he wear because I was worried about his feet. He was stabbed eighteen times for them!"

"Shit," comes from my friends. A gasp from Alice.

"He won't be embarrassing you anymore," I continue. "And the one that's still alive never wants to see either of you again."

With that, I turn and make for the door. Ten minutes later, as I'm walking up Sunset Blvd., I hear a familiar voice call out, "Need a ride?"

I stop and take a long look at Alice in the driver's seat of the Jeep. She's wearing black Ray-Ban Wayfarer today. I just noticed that. The dark bangs, the sunglasses. They look cool on her. Like a girl out of the fifties. My cool girl is the only thing that looks right in my world anymore.

Taking my hands out of my pockets, I grab the roll bar of the Jeep and jump into the passenger side.

"Where to?"

My eyes drink in the sight of her. Damn, she's beautiful. "You feel like fish tacos?"

"I could eat." She gives me a small smile and I lean over the partition, cup her face, her skin soft and cool in my hands, and kiss her.

Words are limited. There are only so many ways you can put them together. And when it comes to Alice, I love you doesn't seem enough.

* * *

ALICE

There are times in life when silence speaks louder than words. I'm not purposely trying to avoid talking about the bombshell he dropped at the wake, but the look on Reagan's face when he kissed me a few minutes ago said to give it time.

We drive up Pacific Coast Highway with the sun

beginning its journey down, the sky turning every shade of red and orange edged in purple. By the time we pass campus and head north for Neptune's, it's close to sunset.

Reagan tells me to wait in the Jeep while he picks up our food. When he returns, he gets in the driver's seat.

"Where are we going?" I ask as he pulls back onto the highway.

"You'll see," he tells me.

A few minutes later we're driving down a dirt road that leads to a small alcove, and further down below, a deserted beach. He parks the car and gets out.

I can see why he wanted to show me this place. The view is breathtaking. A kaleidoscope of colors paints the horizon. The small cliffs that drop down to the beach are a cool gray. It makes for an interesting contrast. There's not a soul in sight. The only sound is that of the gently crashing waves.

He takes off his suit jacket and throws it in the back, rolls up his shirtsleeves. Then he sits on the hood and pats the spot next to him. Reaching down, he holds out a hand and pulls me up. In silence we sit side by side and eat our fish tacos watching the sun dip into the water.

I finish before he does and lean against his warm hard body. He puts his arm around me and when he's done eating, throws the bag with our trash into the car and pulls me onto his lap. He buries his face in the curve of my neck.

"You always smell so good...Alice..."

"Yeah." The silent pause goes on for so long I start to wonder if he's okay.

"I love you."

My entire body braces. As if I needed to ready myself to

absorb the words. Little by little my muscles relax, mold themselves to his, and a slow-spreading heat starts in my chest.

There's absolutely no doubt about how I feel about him. My fingers trace the hard bar of his collarbone, move over his Adam's apple, travel up the closely shaved skin of his throat and jaw, and brush over his lips. "I love you too."

He places a kiss on my fingers and I slide off his lap, stroke his thighs as he watches me with heavy-lidded eyes. I unbuckle his pants and he slides off the hood of the Jeep.

Looking into his eyes, I slip my hand inside his underwear, palm his erection, fully hard already, and cup his balls. He grunts, gripping my shoulder for support as his chin falls forward. I push his pants down his hips, far enough that I can wrap my fingers around the base of his shaft. Bending, my mouth covers the head and he gasps. His grip on my hair tightens.

"Is this okay?" I hear him ask in a husky, broken voice.

I run my tongue up and down his perfect penis, suck on the tip. "It's okay," I tell him. I play with his smooth balls and he widens his stance. "Is this okay?"

"Fuck yes," stammers out.

I swallow down the urge to laugh. Those are the last words we exchange for a while.

* * *

Two nights later, I wake up to find his side of the bed looking mauled. The sheets twisted and sliding off. A cold, empty dent in the mattress. It looks like the pillow suffered the worst of the unprovoked attack.

No need to guess where he is—I can hear the water splashing as soon as I step into the hallway. From the edge of the patio, I watch him swimming slow laps. He doesn't notice me watching. That's not unusual. Lately, he's often lost in his head, far away from me. I'm trying not to push him to talk. I'm trying to give him the time he needs to process his emotions, but it's starting to worry me.

He comes to a full stop in the middle of the pool, sucks in a deep breath, and goes under.

I'm lost in this love for him. His pain is my pain. I feel it acutely, a weight sitting on my chest growing heavier every day as I watch him slip further and further into depression. I don't know how to make him believe that it wasn't his fault. That his brother's blood is not on his hands.

Jumping in the water, I sink to the bottom and open my eyes to see the blurry outline of him illuminated by the pool floodlights. He's sitting cross-legged at the bottom. I take his face in my hands and he opens his eyes. Together we kick to the surface and come out of the water sputtering.

"You're scaring me," I whisper.

The stricken look on his face makes me feel even worse. "I'm not trying to hurt myself if that's what you're thinking…" He takes my silence as a sign that I don't believe him. "When I was younger and the trouble with Brian started, I used to do that a lot…it helps to block everything out."

"It's dangerous," I point out. "People have blacked out that way and drowned."

"I know," he murmurs quietly and brushes the water sliding down his face off. With his arms around my waist, he pulls me closer and in turn I wrap myself around him.

"Your mother keeps blowing up your phone. I don't know how in the world she got my number, but she even texted me to have you call her."

"I'm going to block them. I don't want to see or hear from them again."

I understand where all the animosity is coming from. His parents sunk to a new low at the funeral. I also know that carrying a grudge isn't going to do him any good. I save that discussion for another day, however. All that toxic emotion won't allow him to hear what I have to say.

"I don't think my father ever wanted me and Brian," he murmurs absently. "He loves my mom, worships the ground she walks on. He'd do anything for her...I think he had us because she wanted kids."

He sounds heartbreakingly certain of it.

"He's always treated my brother and me as a burden, a chore...I can't remember a single moment that he looked happy to see us." A bark of dry, humorless laughter comes out of him.

"I guess he just got what he wanted." His gaze returns to me, taking in every detail of my face. "You're the best thing that's ever happened to me. You know that, right?"

I fall deeper, faster, harder.

"I have to say this..." I suck in a deep breath, summon all the strength I can scrape together. "I know you feel responsible. But Brian was in danger every day he lived on the streets. Every day he used."

His face morphs into intractable determination. "I insisted he wear those sneakers. I was actually worried he would sell them for smack," he says with force and shakes his head. So

295

much self-inflicted blame. "They killed him. He kept his promise to me and he died because of it."

"Reagan...it's not your fault." He looks away. "Why didn't you tell me?"

His eyes lock back onto mine. There's a sharpness in them I don't like. "The same reason you never talk about your mother and grandmother dying. The reason you don't discuss that you think you'll get it too."

His words hit like a hammer. "That's really mean of you."

Remorse and shame blanket his face. "Let's get out." He jumps out of the pool and offers me his hand. The conversation is as good as over.

TWENTY-NINE

ALICE

February comes quickly. My birthday rolls around but I don't mention it to Reagan. In light of what's happened it seems stupid and selfish. What's to celebrate when Brian will never have another?

"We're going to the Avalon tonight. Marcus Schulz is DJing," Zoe tells me in no uncertain terms and by the look on her face it's going to be a hard-fought argument.

I pause the *Game of Thrones* rerun I was absently watching and turn in my seat on the couch to take in Blake's sympathetic expression and Zoe's determined one. "I don't think I'm feeling like celebrating."

Zoe sits on the couch next to me. "Look, I get it. It's fucking sad as shit what happened. But this is your day. It's not often you turn twenty-one, and damnit, you, *we* need to celebrate that."

One night of respite from the sadness does sound tempting.

"What about Reagan? What do I say to him? Sorry you're in a deep state of depression, but I'm going to a club with my friends."

"Basically," Zoe answers without an ounce of remorse.

"Just tell him that your friends insist on taking you out for your birthday," Blake cuts in after scowling at Zoe. "Which is the truth."

I chew on the inside of my cheek, deliberating what to do. One night out does sound fun. "Okay," I murmur.

An hour later, I call Reagan and detect the raspy note of the sleep in his voice. "Hello?"

"Rea?"

"Yeah."

"Did you make it to class today?"

I await his answer with a knot in my gut, already anticipating what the answer will be. He's barely been out of the house all month. And if he keeps that up, he'll fail every one of his classes.

"Uhh, nah. I'm just so tired."

"I know, babe," I sympathize, my voice breaking. I don't know how to help him and it's killing me. "I wanted to tell you that the girls are taking me out tonight and I won't be able to come over."

"Out? Why?" He sounds genuinely confused.

"It's my birthday," I gently remind him. "The thirteenth of February."

"Is it?"

"Yeah."

"Shit. I'm sorry, babe. Happy birthday."

"It's okay. I know you have a lot on your mind."

"Where are you guys going?"

"The Avalon. Zoe made plans."

There's a long pause, after which, he says, "You guys have

fun. Happy birthday."

"I'll see you tomorrow," I croak, tears burning my eyes.

"Alice…"

"Yeah."

"I love you."

"I love you too."

* * *

"This club is dope as fuck!" Zoe walks inside shouting, arms raised, her ass swaying in the short white dress she's wearing.

Dora, Blake, and I nod and smile at the doorman, trailing after her as if she were the Pied Piper of fun. The first floor is the lounge area. It's decorated beautifully in lush velvet, rich dark wood, and crystal chandeliers.

At one of the VIP booths we spot a major movie star and his model girlfriend. At another are two actors I recognize from television. On the far end of the bar sits a rock legend talking to a girl a third his age.

The place is packed with beautiful people. Most of the women and some of the men could grace the covers of fashion magazines. All of them seeking attention.

"What are you guys drinking?" Zoe shouts over the din of the packed bar.

"How are you buying? You're not twenty-one yet," I remind her when she starts waving her black Amex.

She smirks. "Oh, Alice. You're funny. Not intentionally of course. I've had a fake ID since I was sixteen."

Dora's eyes bug out. "I'll have a Diet Coke, please."

Zoe rolls her eyes. "Why am I not surprised."

"Z, c'mon, cut them some slack tonight," Blake chides.

"One shot and then we dance. But you all are having one shot tonight. You too, Red. No excuses. I don't want to hear about your perfect parents disapproving."

"Fine," Dora mutters, Zoe squeals, and we all cover our ears.

Like a pro, Zoe flirts shamelessly with the ridiculously good-looking bartender while she orders. "Four Red-Headed Sluts, please." She hands one to each one of us and raises her glass. "To Alice. Happy twenty-first birthday and to many more."

We bring our glasses together and toast. "And to friendship," I add. Everything that's happened only reminds me how precious each minute is, each person that's in my life. "I don't know how I would've survived this year without you guys. I just want you to know how much I love you."

Zoe's eyes run over with tears. Blake smiles through hers. And Dora wipes her damp cheeks. We all down our shots and Dora comes up sputtering and choking.

"What the heck was in that?" she rasps.

"A good time," is Zoe's quick response. "Let's dance!"

We make our way to the top floor where the EDM music pumps loudly and the bodies are all smashed up against each other on the dance floor. Marc Schulz comes on to DJ and the crowd goes wild. A few hour later we're all soaked in sweat and laughing and having a good time. It feels so good just to lose myself in the moment, the music, the good company of my friends. I'd forgotten how gratifying it can be. A couple of guys have already tried to join our little party of four and have been sent packing.

I feel a hand grip my hip from behind and react without

thought, elbowing the stranger in the gut before he can press his body against mine.

"Easy. It's me," Rea murmurs in my ear, gripping my arm to shield himself.

He came. He's miraculously here. He made the effort to get out of bed. This is the sign I've been waiting for, that he's on his way up from bottom. An overwhelming sense of relief washes over me. Like being out in the cold for so long that a small blanket feels like salvation.

Wrapping both arms around me, he places his face in the curve of my neck and his mouth on the damp skin of my throat. His groin presses into my butt and the unmistakable feel of an erection growing under the zipper makes me lean back in to him. He's lost weight. I can feel it in his thighs and biceps. In the way my fingers fall into the grooves between his ribs. I'd guess around a good fifteen pounds and he didn't have any to spare. We haven't had any sex lately either. Depression is an equal-opportunity thief that steals all your desires: to move, to eat, to talk, to have sex…to live.

Anchoring me to his body, he moves his hips slowly in tandem with mine like he means to tonight. I feel the rasp of his tongue as he licks me, the gentle nip of my earlobe. His hands on me possessive and teasing at the same time. I never thought sex could be this…sensual. I thought it only existed in the minds of women, in the fantasy of the romance novels I occasionally read. Not in real life. Not in my life.

In his arms, I turn to face him and stare up into his beautiful face, illuminated by the blue and purple florescent strobe lights, his expression serious as he studies me.

"I love you…do I tell you enough?"

I'm nodding as tears well in my eyes. "Yeah, you do."

"Good." He exhales. I can feel his chest expanding against mine. "I…" His face breaks wide open, pain written in the grooves of his pinched-together eyebrows. "I don't ever want you to doubt it."

He brushes the wet strands of hair away from my lips and kisses me. The kind of kiss that demands sex, not the kind that's meant to comfort. Fueled by a million volatile emotions, it gets out of hand fast.

His hips, anchored to mine, sway to a stop. He pulls back and looks beyond me. "I'm taking the birthday girl home, ladies."

Although Zoe eyeballs him with naked disapproval, she manages to stay quiet on the matter. I breathe out a sigh of relief. That could've gone either way. "Can you do me a favor and drive Dallas home?" Reagan asks.

"He's here!" Dora exclaims out of nowhere. I'm not sure if she sounds excited or worried. Judging by her expression, I settle on worried.

All heads turn to find Dallas at the bar, waiting to be served. Smiling at us, he runs a hand through his blond curls and waves with four fingers, which makes me laugh.

"That's asking a lot," Zoe remarks with a pout.

"I'll owe you," Reagan tells her with a smile.

"Yes. You will."

A few minutes later, we're driving out of the parking lot and headed back to Malibu. As soon as Reagan parks the Jeep in the driveway, he makes good on his silent promise, takes my face in his capable hands, and kisses me like he's out to prove something. I jump him, wrapping my legs around his waist, and let him carry me inside to his bedroom where he undresses me slowly. And once he's done and I'm lying back naked on his bed, he stands before me and undresses himself slowly, watching me with undivided attention, like he's committing this moment to eternal memory. He pushes inside of me looking into my eyes. I don't know what spurred this change in him tonight and I'm not about to question it. He's present, here with me, for the first time since Brian died. I'm just grateful to have him back. Changing the angle, he drives his hips harder against mine. Two thrusts and I'm coming. A few more and he shouts his release.

Shortly after, he falls asleep holding me tightly. In the meantime, I send up a prayer of gratitude. I've never really prayed before, but I figure it's never too late to start.

* * *

The next morning, I wake up with a renewed sense of hope nipping at my heels. It follows me around everywhere. In the shower where I wash my hair with Reagan's department-store-brand shampoo while whistling a happy tune. Into the kitchen where I make us two omelets.

"I'm starving. What smells so good?" he asks in a husky voice.

"You're always starving," I remark from the doorway, holding his dish.

Not lately, crosses my mind. I take it as another indication that his mood is improving.

Lifting his head off the pillow, he aims a sleepy smile at me that I'm sure the fertility god invented because that smile makes me want to get undressed and ride him for the rest of the morning.

But I can't, I remind myself. I have an eight thirty class, and later in the afternoon, the interview for the James Cameron internship. Besides, we have all weekend to make up for lost time.

Walking into the room, I hand him a plate and fork. "What time is your first class today?" I ask him while he digs into the omelet.

Glancing up with the fork halfway to his mouth, he says, "Not till later. Take the Jeep to school."

Thank God. He's let me drive before—that's not why I'm grateful. It's because frankly I'm a little sore from all the action last night. Reagan woke me at dawn for a very vigorous round two and walking all those hills does not sound appealing at the moment.

"Good plan." Leaning down, I take his face in my hands, and tip it up to plant a kiss on his lips. "Love you."

"Love you too." I'm practically out the door when I hear, "Thanks for feeding me, Jersey."

* * *

My morning classes go by quickly. By the time I glance at my shiny new iPhone again, it's already one o'clock and I haven't heard from Reagan. Maybe he slept through his class again? Maybe Brock or Cole gave him a ride? Either way, it doesn't sit right that he hasn't texted me. At the very least, to inquire when I can meet him to return the Jeep. Dora promised to drive me to the interview in Santa Monica at four so it's important I return the car before then. I get back to the dorm and change into my black knee length-sleeveless dress and flats, watching the phone with a growing sense of dread. It's three by the time I'm done putting on mascara and blush. Bile swirls nervously in my gut and it has nothing to do with the upcoming interview.

I call him and it goes straight to voicemail. Which means he turned off his phone. For a fleeting moment, the thought that he would harm himself does cross my mind. After last night, however, I quickly cast the thought aside. Reagan has never been able to hide his emotions from me and I would've noticed something as critical as him sinking even lower. Still, I'm not an expert and the thought circulates some more.

I call four more times and leave increasingly angry and worried voicemails. By three thirty, I'm worked up in a frenzy and text Dora that she doesn't have to drive me to the interview. I'll go to Reagan's, and after making sure he's alive and in one piece, I'll make him drive me as punishment.

As I'm pulling out of campus, the thought strikes me to call Dallas. He may be home and can check on him.

"Hey, Alice," Dallas answers on the first ring. He sounds subdued and Dallas is not often, if ever, subdued. Another bad sign. At this point my heart is practically jumping out of my chest and my hands tremble on the steering wheel.

"Is he there? Is he okay?" Anxiety makes me forsake manners and everything else.

A scary long pause happens before Dallas speaks again. "He's gone."

Gone? "What the fuck does that mean! Is he alive?" I scream into the phone. Somehow the car takes me on autopilot down Reagan's street.

"Yeah, sorry. I mean he left. He texted me an hour ago that

he was leaving and not coming back…to get rid of his stuff."

I pull into the driveway and jump out. Brock is already there, holding the front door open. "Alice," he says in a sober tone. "Alice, wait."

I run past him without a word and march down the hallway to Reagan's bedroom.

Dallas is inside, staring into the walk-in closet. He turns when he hears me, his expression the epitome of discomfort with a side of sympathy. I step inside the empty closet with my heart galloping inside my chest, the simple act of breathing nearly impossible.

"I'm sorry, Jersey." Dallas's voice reaches me from the doorway. The nick name is salt on an open wound. It stings like a bitch.

"Do you have any idea where he could have gone?" My voice sounds disembodied. I barely recognize it.

He shakes his head and tips his chin at the envelope on the nightstand. Rushing over, I tear it open and pull the yellow legal paper out.

alice.

i'm sorry. i just can't do this anymore. the jeep is yours. i bought it myself so don't worry about my parents.

don't wait for me.

love, r

That's it? That's how he leaves it? I don't even warrant an explanation other than *don't wait for me*?

A bout of rage surfaces with enough force to shove all the hurt I'm feeling out of the way. Then I recall the look on his face while we were on the dance floor, the utter anguish in his eyes that he couldn't keep hidden from me as hard as he tried, and the anger quells instantly. Behind, it leaves a sickly, weak-kneed tremble.

I pull my iPhone out of my back pocket and type.

> **Me**: Wherever you go. Whatever you're feeling. Whenever you're lost. Know this. Feel this. My arms are around you, holding you. I love you.

The text goes unanswered. The kernel of hope I'm hanging on to vanishes. My heart gets shattered.

THIRTY

ALICE

What is he doing? Oh dear God. Dallas is on the dance floor and I'm pretty sure he's attempting to recreate the Jennifer Grey/Patrick Swayze lift from *Dirty Dancing* with Brock—and Brock is not having it. A burst of laughter crawls up my throat when Brock stops him with a straight-arm block.

The music turned nerve-shredding half an hour ago. It's 11 p.m. already, the graduation party well underway. I don't even mind being the only person still at our table. I prefer it actually, less chance for small talk and forced smiles.

Crossing my legs, I adjust the short flared skirt of the white Herve Leger dress Zoe forced me to wear. Its square neckline and cap sleeves flatters my less than generous breasts and skinny arms. I'm pretty sure it was wishful thinking on Zoe's part that Reagan would show up and we'd have some ridiculous OTT Hollywood ending. Which is not happening.

I haven't seen or heard from him in four months, since he left, and that is not changing tonight.

On the dance floor, the guys are making asses of themselves. They are so wasted. They look like they're having a blast, though. The shenanigans draw a reluctant smile out of me. Some of them will be leaving in the next few weeks for a new start. Might as well enjoy it while it lasts.

As for me, I have another internship lined up for the summer. No, it's not with James Cameron's production company. I never did make it to the interview all those months ago. And in the end, it all worked out for the best.

Morgan got James Cameron, and I got a small production company run by a couple of scrappy female filmmakers. Unbeknownst to me, Marshall recommended me. Apparently she liked my reel more than she let on.

They just won the option for a huge YA bestseller. And I've been told there will be plenty for me to do that actually involves the process of making films. No fetching dry cleaning and picking up dog food for me.

My dream turned out to *not* look anything like I wanted it to look. It's even better than I could've imagined.

Blake walks over and plops down into the seat Dora vacated only a few minutes ago. "Hey. You haven't moved from this table once."

She's wearing a hot pink silk dress. Off the shoulder and short. Minimalist cool. The color complements her brown skin beautifully. "Love this dress on you."

She gives me a look. "Calvin Klein and don't try to change the subject."

"I'm leaving. I'm being a total downer and I hate that."

I don't think I can bear to be here for another minute. Among all the joy. All the love. My friends are happy and I'm happy for them. I just don't know how to stop feeling like a walking gunshot victim, with a smoking hole where my heart used to be.

"Give it a little more time. What if he shows up?"

Head shaking, I repeat myself for the umpteenth time this evening. "He's not coming. Everyone needs to get over it."

Grabbing my purse, I stand and Blake follows suit. We hug tightly. "Say goodbye to the other two bitches for me, okay? I don't feel like making the rounds."

Blake knows how much I hate being under the microscope. Almost as much as she does.

"Zoe and I each got rooms here. Why don't you stay here the night? Order room service, watch porn."

I chuckle. "That sounds like a single girl's dream, but I'm heading back to the dorm. I just…need to be alone."

She nods in understanding, and I slink away.

Outside, I watch cars zip up and down Ocean Blvd. Santa Monica is still teeming with activity at midnight. A gust of wind blows my hair back, not quite standing on end since it's longer but it reminds me of the time in the Jeep. The Santa Anas. Reagan. His smiling face assails me.

What nobody tells you is that heartbreak is not a one-and-done deal. It happens in small, slow increments every day. A hairline fracture that compounds, branches until it becomes a map of all the pain you've endured. Until there's nothing left of your heart other than a few sharp pieces you can't keep together.

I hand the valet the ticket to the Jeep and wrap my arms around myself. He smiles before running off. I'm chilled, goose bumps breaking out on my arms even though it's in the eighties. I'm always chilled these days.

A cab pulls up to the hotel entrance and the doorman

quickens his pace to open the door for whomever's in the back.

A large male hand curls around the roof of the taxi. One long leg ease out. A sharp, midnight blue suit emerges. Standing a solid six feet plus, he straightens, squares his broad shoulders, and tips his chin at the doorman.

That's when I'm certain I still have a heart because if I didn't, I wouldn't be experiencing an explosion of pain in the middle of my chest.

Hair longer, messy, streaked in gold. Scruff covering the bottom of his face. Eyes glowing in contrast to his tan. He really needs to learn how to use sunscreen.

"Reagan." My voice is a broken whisper, my chest burning with all the unspoken sentiments I've kept to myself in his absence.

His head snaps up and his gaze finds me standing a few feet away. Shock registers on his face as obviously as it's on mine.

The Jeep pulls up. The valet jumps out, walks over, and hands me the keys. Absently, I take them. I can't even acknowledge him because I'm lost in bottomless green eyes, no less stunning than the first time I saw them.

"Yo, sir?" the cab driver calls out.

Snapping out of his trance, Reagan grabs his duffel bag and shuts the door. The cab takes off, and its just the two of us and the ghost of our past.

His face softens as his gaze traces each and every one of my features. He runs a hand though his hair and exhales loudly, nostrils flaring, jaw clenched tightly.

"I was hoping you were still here." His voice falters. When I don't respond, concern fills his eyes. "Alice?"

I nod. It's all I can do. With so much emotion clogging my throat it feels like I'm going into anaphylactic shock, everything closing up.

"Can we talk?" he asks softly, taking two very tentative steps closer. "I know I'm asking a lot but I…I have a lot I need to tell you, to explain."

As tempted as I am to put him out of his misery, I can't. I've spent months in hell, wondering where he was, if he was happy and healthy. Who he was with. As much as I love him, I need to start thinking of myself.

"Can we?" he repeats.

I nod. "Zoe…" I start, motioning to the door. "She has a room here. We can use it." It feels like I'm having an out-of-body experience. I've wanted this for so long and now that he's here I feel unprepared to handle it.

He takes another step closer and I turn for the front door of the hotel. I'm not strong enough to fend him off. If he touches me, I'll surrender faster than you can spell no self-respect. On the way, I hand the valet the keys again.

Back inside the party room, I push through the drunken masses and find Zoe who's jumping up and down on the dance floor and bumping hips with Blake and Dora.

Her eyes widen when she sees me. "You're baaaack. Al!! Don't leave us. C'mon dance."

I pull her face closer, bring her ear to my mouth. "Don't repeat it out loud, but Reagan's here. Can I use your room?"

Her mood sobers at once. She stops dancing. Her eyes narrow into two vicious slits. Leaning in, she says, "You better make that motherfucker pay."

"First, I'd like to hear what he has to say."

"Okay. I'll make that motherfucker pay."

I send her a warning glare. "Zoe…"

"Fine, ugh, you're no fun. Room 1814." She hands me the key card out of the micro Celine purse and when I turn to leave she stops me. Her usually jaded eyes soften and her flawless features pinch in concern.

"I know," I tell her before she can get a word out. She's a good one. As loyal as they come. All that ferocious confidence put to good use in our defense. "I'll be fine."

I find Reagan hovering by the elevators, one hand gripping the back of his neck, head tipped forward, nervous energy all about him. He doesn't see me approach. I take notice of the fine cut of his suit, the crispness of his stark white shirt. He's so handsome it hurts to look at him. His fine features—so familiar. And yet simultaneously, distance and time have made him unapproachable.

His head comes up when he hears me. His face relaxes. "I thought you were going to bail on me," he murmurs while I walk up and press the elevator call button.

"I don't bail. I thought you knew that about me."

His shoulders slump, his expression distressed. "I know. I know. You're right. You never have."

I'm not trying to hurt him, just stating a fact. "Your friends are in there." I hook a thumb at the room I came out of. "I didn't tell them you're here, but I know they're dying to see you."

"I'm not here for them—" When he goes to speak again, the elevator door opens and people pour out. We step inside and three others join us.

"Eighteen, please," I instruct the guy standing closest to

the panel. Reagan slides next to me. The wool of his suit brushes my bare arm, sending shivers up my back and my stomach somersaulting.

I've been anticipating this moment for four months, imagining the things I'd say, dreaming about touching him. And now that he's here, I'm speechless, at a total loss as to how to begin articulating what I'm feeling.

At floor eighteen, we silently file out. I open the door and walk to the wall of windows that overlooks the shoreline from the Santa Monica Pier to Malibu, a Christmas tree of lights snaking up the coast.

"I missed you," he says.

"You have a funny way of showing it."

The AC clicks on and a cold blast of air hits me. I'm shaking and I'm not sure it's because of the chill. Sliding off his suit jacket, he goes to the thermostat and turns the AC off, then he meets me at the wall of windows and slips his jacket over my shoulders.

His body heat clings to it. So does his scent. It takes me right back, wipes away months of anguish and puts tears in my eyes. Why does love have to be so hard?

He leans a shoulder against the glass and stares down at me, expression walking a fine line between frustration and longing.

"You're so beautiful...I'm sorry if I can't stop staring." He licks his lips nervously. His gaze slides out the window for a moment, as if searching for courage out there into the dark unknown.

"You left without even a goodbye, or see ya later—maybe. I didn't know if you were starting over somewhere else, *with* someone else. Or destroying yourself over what happened...I lived in a constant state of anxiety for four months, Rea. Four!"

He nods, gaze cast on the beige carpet.

"I don't even know how to begin. "

"Start anywhere. Just start. Because it's getting hard not to walk out that door."

He clears his throat. "I made it to Patagonia. It was beautiful, everything I thought it would be." He frowns. "I missed you there." His throat works, Adam's apple rising as he swallows.

"Kenya was next. I got mugged. Don't walk around at night in Mombasa. I thought about you that night. You're all I thought about—what it would be like to never see you again, and it scared me more than the gun that was pointed at my face." He jams his hands in his pockets and leans a shoulder against the glass. "I saw more amazing sunsets than I've ever seen, even better than the ones here. I missed you there too." There's an edge to his voice. As if he's admitting something he wishes weren't true.

"Reagan—"

"I didn't want to miss you but I did."

And there you have it. "Stop. I don't want to hear anymore."

"I worked my way through Europe," he continues, talking right over me. "France, Italy, Spain. I thought I saw you there—in Spain, chased a girl for two city blocks down La Rambla before I caught up to her and realized it was only my mind playing tricks on me."

"Reagan..."

"I made it to China—" He exhales harshly. "Missed you

there too."

"Reagan—"

Facing me now, I can see his eyes are glassy, his cheek twitching, mouth drawn tight. He's barely hanging on.

"I'm sorry I left. I didn't know what else to do. It just got to be too much. The guilt. The pressure. I was starting to resent you."

"Me?" My voice is pitchy, sharp. Nothing could've surprised me more. Not even if he had slapped me. "Why would you resent me?"

"Because you're so fucking strong." The words come ripping out and peter to a whisper. His head shakes, his voice flattened by something that worries me. Something that sounds a lot like hopelessness and resignation. "And I'm not... I'm not."

"Stop saying that. You *are* strong. That's the problem. You take on too much. You assume you can carry the weight for everyone, but here's the news flash, Reagan, you're not superhuman. What you went through would've destroyed anyone."

Staring out the window, he looks...lost.

"I couldn't take it anymore and you...you don't let anything knock you down..."

"Stop trying to be everything that's expected of you," I murmur quietly and yet desperate to make him understand. "The good son, brother, boyfriend. The difference between you and me is that no one expects anything of me so I'm free to be anything I want to be. Who would you be given the same chance?"

He watches me intently, lashes lowered. The silence as

meaningful as a million words.

Reaching out, he slowly slides his warm fingers up the side of my neck and cups my neck, guiding me closer. And I let him. I let him put his arms around me and hold me tight because I love him. Despite the pain he caused me. Despite the fact that nothing is settled.

"Take me back," he says quietly. His face crowds my neck and his shoulders curve around me, the muscles hard and taut with tension.

"Take me back, Alice." It's muffled, soundproofed by the fabric of his suit jacket. He lifts his head and bloodshot eyes meet mine. "You said you'd try anything. Give me a chance to make it up to you. I'll beg if you want. I'll do anything."

Always stoic in the face of adversity. The slight tremble of his chin gives him away. It doesn't seem right to keep him in suspense and I've never believed in delayed gratification.

A smile sneaks up on me, sends even more tears running down my cheeks. "I never gave you up, dummy."

His eyes spark, flying all over my face. "Really?"

Love doesn't exist in a vacuum. It's inextricably intertwined with self-sacrifice, vulnerability, risk...and yes, pain. Maybe that's why we're so often disillusioned by it. We demand it to be perfect when in essence love can't exist without the risk of pain and the cost of safety.

His head lowers and his lips touch mine carefully, with all the apprehension in the world while a soft tremble ripples down his back.

"I missed, missed, missed you so fucking much." The words trip from his tongue in a convoluted mess, in between soft, fast kisses. His arms hold me tighter, his hands climb higher. They curl around the back of my head as his kisses turn feral, hungry, starved by all those months of absence.

Clothes get shed on our way to the bed. My dress, or rather Zoe's dress, may no longer be wearable with the way Reagan rips it off of me. His shirt suffers a similar demise. "Worst case of blue balls I've ever had in my life. I'm warning you now, don't plan on leaving this bed for days."

"It's Zoe's bed." I squeak when he nips my ear. "I don't think you want to get her any more mad at you than she already is."

"Thanks for the heads-up. I'll barricade the door," he says, smiling against the skin of my neck.

We fall onto the bed together. He braces himself before landing on me with his full weight. Then he gets up on an elbow and stares down. "I didn't, you know. I would never…" His fixed stare won't let mine go.

"It's been four months. You didn't sleep with anyone?"

Now he looks offended, maybe even a little mad. "No. You don't think I can keep my dick in my pants for a few months?" For a moment I lose him to his thoughts. "Did you?" comes out very carefully.

"What if I said yes? What if I said I didn't hear a peep out of you and came to the very painful conclusion that I probably never would have? Would it be wrong of me to have seen someone else?"

His body relaxed into mine, his erection pressing between my legs. "No," he murmurs.

"I didn't leave you. You left me."

His mouth lowers, searches the corners of my lips, travels along my jaw. "I know," he whispers and kisses me there.

"Never again. Never, ever again. I'm going to prove it to you."

After that, he turns his words into action and makes love to me like he never has before, his thrusts slow and deep, drawing out the pleasure until we're both sweaty and exhausted. I push him onto his back and he lets me. Riding him, I go off like a Fourth of July fireworks extravaganza while Reagan watches me closely.

"I love you," he says, voice husky, the undeniable evidence of his feelings reflected in his eyes. "I am crazy in love with you." And then he follows, jacking his hips up, holding on to mine in a painful grip. Together, we tumble headfirst back into it. This thing that exists between us, that won't let go.

"I wasn't," I say to him later, when we've both caught our breath and we're staring at each other, making up for lost time. His head comes up and his expression sparks.

"I wasn't with anyone else," I confess. "I love you. I couldn't be with anyone else."

He falls onto his back, arms spread wide, and exhales harshly. "Hate to sound like an asshole but is it okay to say I'm relieved?" He chuckles.

Not really when I think about it. I'm definitely relieved that he hasn't been with anyone else.

I straddle his lap and his hands skate up my thighs. Then he pushes my hair aside, watching me like it's the first time he's ever seen me. "Move in with me."

It takes me a minute to shake off the surprise. "You want us to live together?"

He sits up and hugs me. "I'll be here another semester, and then there's medical school." I'm about to speak when he explains. "Not for surgery, for psychiatry. I want to specialize in addictions."

The smile is involuntary. I brush my fingers up the side of his arm, remembering every dip and curve. Slide them into his hair. "I think that's amazing." Tears of joy sneak down my face.

He wipes them away. "I can't see anything, feel anything without thinking of you. I love you. I love you beyond reason. I want a lot more—but we have to start somewhere."

I don't have to think twice. "Okay."

"Yeah?" His lips part into a breathtaking grin.

"Yeah."

Reagan seals it with a kiss. One that speaks of hope, of second chances, and new beginnings. I don't know what the future holds and neither one of us harbor any illusions that it will be easy. But I know I don't want to face it without him. Because, although he started as nothing but trouble, he's become everything and more. And, God, do I want a new beginning with him.

I want it all.

Stay tuned for more of the **Malibu University Series** with…
Nothing But Wild.
Nothing But Good
Nothing But Heart

ABOUT THE AUTHOR

P. Dangelico loves romance in all forms, pulp, the NY Jets, and to while away the day at the barn (apparently she does her best thinking shoveling horse poop). What she's not enamored with is referring to herself in the third person and social media but she'll give you the links anyway.

Facebook Reading Group (P. Dangelico's Mod Squad)
Facebook Page
BookBub
Pinterest PDangelicoAuthor
Instagram PDangelicoAuthor
Twitter- @PDanAuthor

Or find me here

www.pdangelico.com